THE
KILLING
FOREST

ALSO BY SARA BLAEDEL

The Forgotten Girls

THE KILLING FOREST

SARA BLAEDEL

TRANSLATED BY

MARK KLINE

GRAND CENTRAL
PUBLISHING

New York   Boston

Copyright © 2016 by Sara Blaedel
Translated by Mark Kline; translation copyright © 2016 by Sara Blaedel
All rights reserved. In accordance with the U.S. Copyright Act of 1976, the scanning, uploading, and electronic sharing of any part of this book without the permission of the publisher is unlawful piracy and theft of the author's intellectual property. If you would like to use material from the book (other than for review purposes), prior written permission must be obtained by contacting the publisher at permissions@hbgusa.com. Thank you for your support of the author's rights.

Grand Central Publishing
Hachette Book Group
1290 Avenue of the Americas
New York, NY 10019
Hachettebookgroup.com

Printed in the United States of America

RRD-C

First edition: February 2016
10 9 8 7 6 5 4 3 2 1

Grand Central Publishing is a division of Hachette Book Group, Inc.
The Grand Central Publishing name and logo is a trademark of Hachette Book Group, Inc.

The Hachette Speakers Bureau provides a wide range of authors for speaking events. To find out more, go to www.hachettespeakersbureau.com or call (866) 376-6591.

The publisher is not responsible for websites (or their content) that are not owned by the publisher.

Library of Congress Cataloging-in-Publication Data has been applied for.
ISBN 978-1-4555-8154-2 (hardcover edition)
ISBN 978-1-4555-6395-1 (international edition)

THE
KILLING
FOREST

1

He hesitated before grabbing the dead chicken his father held out to him, its white feathers peppered with blood close to where its head had been chopped off. Sune had always hated blood, the smell of it and the intense, dark color when it flows and forms a pool.

He couldn't let his father see his disgust. Not today. It would have been easier if his mother had come, he thought. He blinked a few times. She was dying. He had sat beside her bed almost all day. The worst was the IV; he couldn't stand to look where the needle entered her hand, even though a Band-Aid covered it. She had been asleep when his father said it was time to go.

For several months he had been looking forward to the initiation; to the ritual and party. Many times he had tried to imagine what it would be like to leave the house as a child and return that same night as a grown man.

1

At least he would be considered a man, with the responsibilities and rights of one. Everyone else in his class had already gone through confirmation. But as an Asatro, a believer in the old Nordic religion, Sune had to wait until he turned fifteen to confirm his belief. Today was the day.

He dropped the chicken into the bucket his father had found in the laundry room, then set it on the floor mat on the vehicle's passenger side. Getting in, he sat scrunched up with his feet on the seat. His father had packed the white van with all the necessities for the midnight sacrifice; Sune had brought along two small gifts to the gods. One symbolized his childhood, the other his future. For the former, he'd decided on a book he'd grown up with, but he found it incredibly hard to part with the worn-out edition of *Winnie-the-Pooh*, its spine held together by tape. His mother had read it so many times that the pages had begun falling out. The choice of the book had irritated his father, who'd suggested a soccer ball. But his mother sided with Sune.

He would also be parting with the big pocketknife his father had given him. Sune hoped the gods would reward him with courage and strength in his adult life, even though he had no plans to become a butcher like his father and grandfather before him. He just hadn't been able to think of anything better. And his father had been pleased.

Sune would also receive a gift, one that would nudge him in the right direction. His father, Lars, had gotten a butcher knife. Lars hadn't been particularly adept at reading or writing, so after his initiation he had left school to enter an apprenticeship under his own father. Sune had

2

heard about a boy who received an airline ticket, with orders not to return until he stopped being a mama's boy. He never came back.

Sune hoped for a silver chain with Thor's hammer, which symbolized their Nordic belief. Wishing for the chain was actually his father's idea. As the van turned onto a narrow forest road, his father asked him if he was ready. To which Sune smiled and nodded.

He spotted the torches and bonfire in the distance. Twilight was falling, and the night sky threw dark shadows down between the trees, highlighting the fire, which was golden and inviting. Flames from the torches danced in the dark. His chest tingled when he saw that the others had arrived early to prepare everything for him.

Tonight the sacrifice would be in *his* honor. For the first time, he would join the men's circle. As far back as he could remember, Sune and his parents had met in the forest with the other Asatro. He loved the atmosphere, the great feasts held after the adults prayed to the gods, but had never been part of the circle. Until now he'd been under no obligation. After tonight, though, he would be forever bound by his vow. The circle could only be broken by animals and those too young to understand it was holy. Usually he was sent with the other children to play behind the enormous bonfire site, with strict orders not to interrupt unless one of them was seriously hurt.

From now on he would be a part of the circle that called on the gods. He would participate when the drinking horn made its rounds, and as thanks for his initiation he would offer up the chicken to the gods, confirming his Nordic belief. During the past few months they had been going through all the rituals. His father had told him about the oath ring and impressed upon him that when you swear on the ring, you make a promise to the gods that cannot be broken.

He thought about the pig lying in the back of the van. At the end of the ceremony, it would be killed, its blood given as a sacrifice: the family's thanks to the gods for accepting him.

His father led the way to the bonfire, around which torches formed a ring a few meters out from the flames. It resembled a fortress. The silence suddenly felt awkward to Sune; it didn't help that the men solemnly lined up and hugged him. He wasn't sure what to say. He didn't dare smile, didn't want to look childish. The gothi slipped his robe on, and silently the men gathered around the fire. The gleam of the torches screened off the forest.

Now, Sune thought. *It's happening. In just a few moments, I'll be a man.*

He'd thought that the gothi would take charge, as he normally did when the adults formed the circle. But his father stepped forward instead, his head slightly tilted, and smiled as he looked at his son.

"Sune, my son," he began, sounding a bit self-conscious. "Tonight you'll begin your life as a man. You're no longer a child, and there's a lot you have to learn."

A few of the men cleared their throats; a few coughed.

Sune recalled the saga of Signe, King Vølsung's daughter, who sent her sons out into the forest when the oldest was only ten. Neither of them had been found brave enough to survive. The dark forest frightened even Sune, and he was fifteen. He'd never been particularly

4

brave—he knew that. For a moment he thought about his mother again.

"Happy birthday, son," she'd said when he'd brought breakfast to her bed that morning. She didn't eat much anymore; most of her nourishment came through a tube. But she had smiled and taken his hand. "Are you looking forward to what's going to happen tonight?"

Now his father pushed Sune into the center, and the gothi began to sing as he slowly walked around the circle. He stopped at every point of the compass to call on a god. At north, Odin, the greatest of the gods. At south, Thor, the protector of mankind. At east, Frey, the god of fertility. And at west, Frigg, Odin's wife, who symbolized stability in couples and marriage.

"The circle is closed," the gothi declared when he returned to his place.

Should anyone later have asked, Sune doubted he could have repeated what he'd been told during the ritual. The drinking horn was passed around several times; he'd remembered to turn its tip toward his stomach and lift it carefully to his mouth, to avoid creating a vacuum and splattering the mead all over his face. His father had taught him that this was the sign of a newcomer to the circle. His cheeks reddened from the bonfire and the strong fermented honey. He felt groggy as the men stepped into the circle, one by one, to recite a verse for him. Several had chosen lines from the Hávámal, and he also recognized a few passages from Vølven's Prophecy, but soon the words were jumbled up in his head.

Once all the men had spoken, they sang for him. Sune lay his gifts to the gods on the ground. The drinking horn made the rounds again, then the circle opened. Several of the men yelled and lifted him up, and again they all hugged him.

Unlike the ritual, he later remembered every second of the magical time when he was sworn into the brotherhood. He stood at the bonfire as the other men gathered a few meters away under the enormous sacrificial oak, which was over a thousand years old. As a child, Sune had loved hopping into and out of the hollow part of the broad trunk while waiting for the ceremony to end. This evening, the hole looked like a black eye staring at him in the near-darkness. Chills ran down his spine, though not in a bad way. On the contrary. He didn't feel the least bit afraid.

The gothi dug up a section of peat and stuck it onto two flexible limbs, which were raised and bowed to form a narrow entryway. Sune had always been fascinated by the saga of Odin and Loke, the pact that made them blood brothers. Now he was a part of the same ritual; walking under the peat with the others symbolized their shared rebirth.

Everything happened in slow motion once his father took his hand. The gothi walked right behind, and when Sune came out on the other side, the moon seemed to shine directly on him. He knew it was his imagination, but the feeling was powerful. And even though he feared the moment when they took turns cutting themselves to spill a few drops of blood where the peat had been dug up, it wasn't terrible.

He was then given a bronze spoon with a long, broad handle that looked like a ladle, only heavier. Sune felt a surge of courage and pride as he was told to mix the blood on the ground. Then the gothi freed the peat from the limbs and covered the blood with it to seal the pact. They stomped the peat into place as Sune was pulled back into the circle. He felt like a man when the gothi declared that he was now bound by the vow to honor and safeguard the others.

"We look after each other," his father had explained when Sune asked him what it meant.

Sune stayed behind when his father walked to the van. He wanted to sneak away, to get out of watching them slaughter the pig.

"Won't you help unload everything?" the gothi asked.

He'd taken his robe off. He pointed at the bonfire, where several white coolers from the butcher shop, containing the food for the celebration, had already been hauled in. Luckily they wouldn't be eating the pig, Sune reminded himself. It would only be butchered and hung up so its blood ran down on the ground, a pool of liquid for the gods. The carcass would be brought home and cut up the next day, which was against the food administration's regulations. But what they didn't know wouldn't hurt them, as his father always said.

"Raise the hook!" his father yelled from the van, and two men trotted up with three heavy iron rods, sticking them into the ground by the sacrificial oak, forming a tripod held together at the top by a large iron ring. They fastened a butcher's hook onto it, and his father backed the white van all the way up to the tripod, shut the engine off, hopped up into the back of the van, and began pushing the pig out. He'd already anesthetized the animal before loading it; it weighed a goddamn ton, his father had said on the way there.

Sune still didn't understand why his father hadn't just shot it in the head with the bolt gun. Then he wouldn't have had to go through all this. He hated the thought that they hung it on the hook alive, and cut its throat.

He turned his back and continued unpacking the food. The mead was gone, though there were several cases of beer. The men were already soused from the ceremonial drinking. Sune looked around for a cola but found none. Apparently no one had been thinking along those lines.

"Ain't it about time for the kid to get his present?" someone yelled from the other side of the grounds.

It was too dark for Sune to see who had yelled. He glanced around, searching for his father.

"Damn right it is," another voice answered.

Suddenly everyone disappeared and he was alone at the bonfire, wondering what he should do. A car door slammed somewhere in the forest. The men appeared as a group now.

At first Sune thought they'd brought his mother as a surprise, mostly because of the long, loose hair he saw. He couldn't make her out until they were close to the bonfire. It was a young woman, much younger than his mother, but older than him. His father stood at the back, his hands in his pockets. Sune felt uneasy, and he began walking toward him.

"Stay right there," the gothi said.

The men stopped between the bonfire and the old oak, where the white van was still parked with the back door open.

"We've brought you a present."

Sune had never seen the woman before. He looked down at the ground. He didn't understand; he didn't know what to do.

"Your father says you spend all your time reading books," the gothi said. "We intend to change that."

A raw laughter rose up from the men.

Earlier that evening he'd felt butterflies in his stomach, but now they were slowly turning into a knot.

"Tonight you will honor Freya and perform the fertility ritual."

The gothi nodded tersely at the woman. She walked toward Sune, the men gathering in a half circle behind them.

"This will strengthen your manhood," the gothi continued. "And manhood is our gift to you."

Sune looked up and shook his head. He tried to catch his father's eye as the woman began unbuttoning her black blouse. She smiled at him as she tossed it on the ground, signaling to him to come closer. But he couldn't move.

Her hair spilled down over her shoulders, radiant in the darkness with the bonfire's flames glowing behind her. He tried to look away, but he couldn't tear his eyes from her naked breasts. It was the first time he'd ever seen a woman's body in the flesh, the first time he'd trembled this way. She unzipped her black skirt and took another step toward him before letting it fall to the ground.

Sune continued staring at her breasts. He couldn't look her in the eyes now that she was standing naked in front of him. He sensed that a few of the men were growing restless. The woman ran her hands over her naked body and stepped in closer to him, so much so that her fragrance sent a jolt into his groin. She spread her legs slightly; her hips began to sway as if they were dancing. He felt her unbutton his pants and heard her pull his zipper down. Bewildered now, he tore loose and stumbled a few steps back. Before he got any farther, a hand gripped his arm.

"You're staying right here, boy!"

Sune looked at the men closing in around them.

"Get down to business now," the gothi snarled.

The forest darkness seemed to descend and cover him. For a moment all was quiet in his head, as if sound had ceased to exist. He swiveled around, desperately seeking a way past the naked woman and the wall of men looming over him.

He caught sight of his father. Sune wanted to run to him, but his body felt like a lead weight. Before he could move, someone from behind pushed him so hard that he almost fell. The men's voices returned as he tried to wrestle free, but whoever held his arm wouldn't let go.

"Fuck her!" someone yelled.

"No! I don't want to!" Sune screamed.

The young woman stepped back and leaned over to pick up her clothes.

Immediately one of the men was at her side. "You're not going anywhere," he said, ordering her to get back over to Sune.

"No one should force the boy if he doesn't want to," she said. When she made a move to put her skirt back on, she was punched in the face.

"You'll do what we paid you to do." He punched her again, and a thin stream of blood ran out of her nose.

Before Sune could react, two strong hands pulled his pants down and dragged him over to the woman.

"You get that dick of yours up and get to work!"

"No, I don't want to," he whined, shaking his head. His lips were quivering, his cheeks stretched out; he lost all control and began to cry. He bit his lip in a desperate attempt to stop the tears while his father, right beside him now, spoke into his ear.

"Do it, boy. Don't make a goddamn fool out of me."

The young woman rushed over and shoved his father. "Leave him alone!" she screamed. "You can't force him to do this if he doesn't want to!"

The arms holding Sune relaxed for a second, just long enough for him to pull his pants up and sprint into the forest, away from the bonfire's flames, the torches, and the men. He didn't stop until he was dizzy from the blood pounding in his temples. He leaned over with his hands on his knees and spit on the ground. He gasped for breath as sweat ran cold under his shirt.

The image of the woman's naked body returned to him. Again, he felt an unaccustomed stir down below. He squeezed his eyes shut, but it didn't erase the image of the thin red line of blood. He jerked up at the sound of her screams splitting the darkness.

Reluctantly he stopped, turned around, and began walking back.

By the time he was close enough to see the bonfire's flames through the trees, the woman had stopped screaming. Sune leaned against a tree in shock when he saw why. Her mouth was bound with something white. He couldn't see her face, but she was struggling, desperately.

He tried to force himself to look away, but his eyes locked on to the men holding her. He noticed his father hunched over behind her. Then he zipped up his pants and stepped aside for the next in line.

The young woman kept struggling as the line continued, every man having at her. Each time she pushed or kicked, they punched her, and only when the last man had finished did the two who had held her arms during the gang rape let go. She sank to the ground and lay motionless.

Sune's scream stopped at his throat. Suddenly he was freezing. He ached for the warmth of the fire but couldn't move. He watched the men pull at the woman's arms, shaking her shoulders. Finally the gothi leaned over and felt for her pulse. He let go of her arm and shook his head.

The men gathered at the bonfire. Sune heard them speaking but couldn't make out what they were saying. Then several of them walked behind the van and disappeared into the forest while the rest began to pick up in the clearing.

Sune had no idea how long he'd stood there motionless, staring. All he knew was that the young woman, the same one who only a brief time ago had stood smiling in front of him, was no longer moving.

"We're ready!" someone yelled from behind the van. The gothi walked over to the woman and lifted her. Her arms and legs dangled limply as he carried her into the forest.

Sune trembled. His right foot was asleep, and his leg

gave way when he tried to back into the woods. It was as if his brain refused to accept what his eyes had just seen. His body felt leaden, his heart pounded in terror. He knew the young woman was dead; he'd known it the moment she fell to the ground motionlessly.

He crawled a few meters away. Finally he got the circulation going in his foot. It stung. He should run and hide, he thought, but where to? He peered into the coal-black darkness of the forest. A few limbs cracked as he struggled to get to his feet and grope his way through the trees.

Suddenly he heard voices calling his name. He knew they were coming for him. He held his breath and hunched up, then crawled in under some branches on the forest floor.

The voices called again. They were closer now.

"Sune, come on out here!"

It was his father.

"Come out, now, you're a part of this. You can't just run and hide!"

Twigs broke as someone strode by him. He held his breath; then they were gone.

He didn't dare move. Soon he heard limbs crunching, leaves rustling—they were back. He hugged the ground and held his breath again, the forest floor moist against his cheek.

They crisscrossed the area where he lay until he heard a sudden loud whistle. Then another. Like a siren voice in the oppressive quiet of the forest night. The men returned to the clearing around the bonfire as if the search had been called off.

Finally, when the footsteps had disappeared, Sune relaxed. He breathed deeply and turned, glimpsing the moon shining clearly through the treetops. His heart pounded as he prayed to the gods that the men wouldn't find him.

Down by the sacrificial oak, the gothi put his robe back on. The men gathered again. The bonfire was dying out, its flames flickering as darkness overtook the clearing. The men formed a circle, and the gothi closed it. Sune stared at what was being passed around from hand to hand. The oath ring.

The chill of the night spread into his chest as he realized that this was the reason they had been looking for him. He was a grown man now, a part of all this. He had sworn with his blood that he was one of them. They expected him to stand together with his brothers as they took an oath of silence, one they could never break.

2

Louise Rick glanced around the allotment cottage. She had gotten up early to pack and load the car. While on sick leave, she'd been staying in this small, black wooden house in Dragør that she and her neighbor Melvin Pehrson had bought.

She was returning to her apartment in Frederiksberg and her job at National Police Headquarters. Not that the easygoing routine out here she and her foster son, Jonas, had slipped into hadn't been pleasant. In fact, it had fit her frame of mind perfectly. It was exactly what she needed.

Every morning after sending Jonas off to school on the bus, she'd made a pot of tea, packed it in her bike basket, and ridden to the beach with their dog, Dina, running beside her. Dina also went along on her morning swims. Dina had a puzzled look when Louise swam back to land, as if the dog were trying to convince her to stay in the water longer. And once in a while, Louise had the urge to do just that. To swim all the way out and be swallowed by the waves; to disappear. But each time she had signaled to her deaf pet to follow her in.

She'd kept Dina at a distance until she shook off. If the morning was gray and rainy, she would wrap herself up in a thick towel and crawl in under the Scotch roses, gazing out over the sea while drinking her tea. Dina loved to run back and forth across the sand and eat mussels that washed up on the beach.

She'd been on a leave of absence since the shooting at the gamekeeper's house, where a man had been killed while attempting to rape her. But it wasn't the images of her own naked body and the man behind her that haunted her. Nor was it the bullet wound in his head or the blood that had spurted all over her body.

René Gamst, the man who had saved her. The lust in his eyes as he waited to fire the fatal shot, the scorn in his voice when he said it was clear she liked it. That's what she couldn't shake.

But worst of all was what Gamst said about Klaus, Louise's first love, who had hanged himself the day after they moved in together:

"Your boyfriend was a pussy. He didn't have the fucking guts to put the noose around his own neck."

The words had been echoing in her head since the ambulance drove off with her that day.

The hospital examination had revealed three broken ribs on her left side, but otherwise only scratches and bruises. She was released that evening. Her boss, Rønholt, suggested she take sick leave, and she had agreed, but only because Gamst's words had reached that private place inside her she'd hidden away for many years. Not only from the outside world, but from herself.

She and Klaus had been together since Louise was in ninth grade in Hvalsø School; on her eighteenth birthday he had given her an engagement ring. A year later, after he finished his apprenticeship as a butcher, they had moved into an old farmhouse in Kisserup. Two nights later he was dead.

In all the years since stepping into the low-ceilinged hallway to find him hanging from the stairway, a rope taut around his neck, she had been plagued by guilt. For going to a concert in Roskilde the previous evening and staying over with her friend Camilla. For apparently not being good enough. Because if she had been worth loving, he wouldn't have taken his life.

She'd never understood what had happened that night, all those years ago. Not until Gamst spoke up.

If he were telling the truth, Klaus hadn't slipped the noose around his own neck.

René Gamst was being held in Holbæk Jail. Shortly after his arrest, he had admitted to firing the two shots, and everyone knew he had shot to kill. The rapist had first broken into his home and assaulted his wife, but Gamst claimed he meant to save Louise. He stuck to that story, and it was difficult to prove otherwise—that he had killed to take revenge.

The day before she prepared to move out of the cottage, she had gone through every detail in the case again with Detective Lieutenant Mik Rasmussen in his office at Holbæk Police Station. She wasn't proud of what had happened. Especially when she had to explain how René Gamst ended up with a broken arm. He hadn't said anything about it, and up until then her explanation had been vague. Yesterday, however, Mik had put her through the wringer when she finally admitted that she'd been rough with him after the shooting.

Many years earlier, Louise had been stationed in Holbæk for a short time, and afterward she and Mik had been lovers. He ended it after a big scene, but even though several years and some distance had passed between them, he knew her well enough to know when she was hiding something.

And it came out. The entire story about Klaus and all the years she'd been saddled with guilt. About the reason she had treated Mik badly, and her anxiety about committing: Since Klaus's death, she had entered relationships only halfheartedly.

Louise knew this last confession hurt him, even though he tried to hide it. But she also sensed that he understood her better now.

She described what happened after René's revelation about Klaus: She had kicked the rifle out of his hands, twisted his arm around his back so violently that he had screamed, and thrown him on the ground and handcuffed him.

"But I didn't hear his arm break," she'd said, trying to forget how it had sounded as she tightened the narrow plasticuffs. "I just wanted him to tell me what he knew."

Louise hauled the last things out to the car, then went back to see if she'd forgotten anything. Melvin had complained a few times about how high the weeds had grown, but she *had* cut the grass. Actually Jonas had, because he thought the old push lawn mower was fun, and because the whole lawn could be trimmed in ten minutes.

A message came in from Jonas when she pulled out of her parking spot. He had stayed overnight with a friend; they were probably on the way to school, she thought. She missed him. This evening she would hang out with him, lie around on the sofa and order takeaway.

Going home to Nico's and out to see a movie, okay?

Louise didn't see much of her fifteen-year-old foster son these days, and even though she would never say it out loud, once in a while she felt rejected when he wanted to be with his friends instead of her. But before that feeling hardened, she scolded herself, so harshly that any hint of jealousy disappeared.

She was happy that he was doing well; very well, in fact. Recently he'd had a difficult period at school, and she had been seriously worried about him. He'd had enough sorrow in his life. Both his parents were dead, and not long ago he had lost a very close friend. She needed to get a handle on her own loneliness. Which was her fault, she reminded herself, before writing *OK*, followed by a smiley face, a heart, and a thumbs-up.

On her way into town, she thought about what it was going to be like back at the office. The work didn't worry her; questioning looks and, especially, pity from her colleagues did. They all knew what had happened, of course. She just really didn't want to talk about it.

And then there was Eik.

"You go out together, you go back in together," her partner had said when he wanted to ride with her in the ambulance. But she had said no. She'd crawled into her shell, huddled up with René's words.

Eik had called several times since then, but she hadn't gotten back to him. One day a letter lined with bubble wrap arrived; inside was a Nick Cave CD. She hadn't even thanked him for that.

Louise knew that Eik meant well, but she just couldn't see him. All this about Klaus had simply been too much. So much so that the night she and Eik spent together, right before everything fell apart for her, seemed more like a distant dream than a fresh memory about great sex and the surprising feeling of falling in love.

After parking and turning in the key, she sat for a moment and gazed at the tall windows of her department. Suddenly she felt his presence again, in a way that made her skin tingle.

3

"Remember to check your mail," Hanne called out when Louise walked past the secretary's office. She stopped, turned on her heel, and walked back with a smile plastered on her face, only to discover that her mail slot was empty.

She'd known Hanne Munk since the secretary was in Homicide, Louise's former department. At the time she had thought that Hanne was a breath of fresh air, with her mountain of red hair, loud clothes, and exaggerated gestures, but after Louise transferred to the Search Department her relationship with Rønholt's secretary had been strained, to put it mildly.

"Thanks for reminding me," she said on her way out of the office. Even though she knew Hanne's style, it annoyed her that the secretary hadn't even in the tiniest way welcomed her back.

Menopause, lack of sleep, too little sex, Louise thought as she answered another message from Jonas, who asked if it was okay for him to stay over with Nico after the movie.

Does that boy ever change his clothes? Louise rushed down the hall to the Rathole, the double office she had been given earlier that year after being chosen to head up the newly formed Special Search Agency in the Search Department. They were responsible for cases of missing persons when criminal activity was suspected.

There was more than enough space for the new unit, which up to then consisted of her and Eik Nordstrøm. Yet it irritated her that Rønholt couldn't find a different locale for them; they were right above the kitchen, and they were privy to the menu every day. The shabby office had even been invaded by rats, though Pest Control had finally taken care of that.

She opened the door and immediately froze: A large German shepherd growled viciously at her, its shackles up and teeth bared, its eyes fixed on her. She leaped back and slammed the door shut. Hearing Eik's voice farther down the hall, she turned to see him walking out of the copy room, stuffing a flattened pack of cigarettes into his pocket.

Earlier, while driving in, she'd thought about seeing him again after all this time; about what to say. And now he was standing in front of her. Her whole body felt warm, all the way to her fingertips, and when he spread his arms to greet her, she completely forgot why she hadn't felt up to seeing him out at the cottage.

"How are you, beautiful?"

He pulled her close, but then he apparently remembered her broken ribs and let go.

"Sorry I didn't call you back," she mumbled awkwardly, and immediately changed the subject to the dog in their office.

"Let me go in first," he said. "It's Charlie, and I probably ought to introduce you two."

"I've already met the beast," she said. "It nearly went for my throat."

"Don't be silly, he wouldn't hurt you. He just has to get to know you. You're an intruder to him; he's been with me in the office while you've been gone."

Eik opened the door to the Rathole and sat down in the doorway as the big dog ran toward him. Louise noticed that the dog limped and that his right rear leg hung in the air. He landed in Eik's lap and began licking his face so eagerly that he almost knocked Eik over.

"What happened to him?" Louise asked. She stayed out in the hall while her partner got to his feet and grabbed the dog's collar.

"Charlie boy here caught a bullet while he was chasing a bank robber in Hvidovre. It tore his thigh up. Luckily the vet thinks he'll be able to use his leg again, though he'll never go back to the dog patrol."

"So he's a police dog," she said.

Eik nodded while scratching the dog's snout.

"And his trainer?" Louise asked.

Eik nodded again, looking sad now. "He's the one who shot and killed the bank robber."

Every police officer knew about the Hvidovre case, an armed robbery. A few months ago two masked men had entered the bank with sawed-off shotguns, forced a few customers down on the floor, and confronted the bank's employees. Louise couldn't remember how much they got away with, but it didn't matter. The police had arrived quickly, and in the nearby parking lot they surrounded the two robbers, who were carrying a bag stuffed with money.

One of the robbers began shooting at the police and hit the dog. Not long after, the man also lay on the ground. Dead. Nineteen years old. The other robber was his father. Two men with no criminal record, who chose the worst possible solution to their desperate economic situation.

The tabloids screamed the story of the father whose painting business had gone bankrupt. Two years earlier, he'd had twelve employees and a large residence in Greve. The son had been a trainee in the business. Then it all fell apart, leaving the father hopelessly in debt and the son adrift in life.

"No one robs banks anymore," Eik said. "Everyone knows they'll get caught. He's a ruined man."

"The father?" Louise asked. She hadn't followed the trial. Armed robbery meant a lengthy sentence, and the fact that the other robber, his son, had been killed wasn't going to shorten it.

"Him too," Eik said, nodding again. "But I'm talking about Charlie's father. He's sitting at home now, staring at four walls. I don't think he'll be back. We were at the police academy together. We haven't seen all that much of each other since then, but he and Charlie did drop by occasionally. So I told Finn I'd take care of the dog until he got back on his feet."

And that was that, Louise realized. She couldn't come up with anything to object to, either. She nodded and took a few tentative steps toward the office.

Charlie sat up beside Eik's leg.

"Come on over and say hi to him."

Louise grabbed the dog biscuit he pushed over to her. But before she could offer it to the dog, he was on his feet, teeth bared again. She hopped back into the hall.

"Okay, we'll save the introductions until later," Eik said. He pulled the big German shepherd over to his desk while scolding him as if they were an old married couple.

"Stop!" Louise said. "I want him out of here!"

"Wait a second," he said. He grabbed a leash and wrapped it around a leg on his desk a few times, then attached it to the dog's collar. He ordered the dog to lie down.

Louise finally walked to her desk, accompanied by a low snarl.

"Honestly," she said. "Can't you take him home? It's ridiculous, him lying there growling at me."

"He's used to coming along. Otherwise he'd have to be fenced up, and I don't have a fence."

"That's too bad, because he can't stay here!" she said.

"Come on, Louise. Charlie's a good boy. You just have to get to know each other."

Now she was getting mad. In the first place, she was the boss of this two-person unit. In the second place, she would never dream of bringing Dina along with her to work if the dog bothered anyone. But before she could say anything more, her telephone rang.

"Special Search Agency, Louise Rick." She turned her

back to Eik, who was still talking to the dog, trying to get it to shut up.

Her stomach knotted the second she heard Mik's voice. She knew he was about to inform her that disciplinary proceedings would be brought against her concerning her treatment of Gamst during the arrest at the gamekeeper's house. She also realized in that split second that she didn't regret a thing, even though it could affect her career.

"Hi, Mik," she said, her voice calm. She sat down.

"We have a case here that I'm passing on to you," he began. Nothing in his voice hinted that she'd poured out the tale of her shattered life to him the day before.

Louise immediately pulled herself together; after all, she headed up the Special Search Agency of the Search Department.

"Why, what is it?" she asked.

"It's a missing person report from a few weeks ago, but there's something suspicious about it. Rønholt asked me to give it to you," Mik hastened to add, as if he was apologizing. "A boy from Hvalsø disappeared."

She groaned inside. She didn't need more ghosts from her past creeping into her life, and certainly no more cases involving people she'd known while growing up.

"The boy's name is Sune Frandsen," Mik continued. "He's the son of Frandsen the butcher. The one with the white van."

Louise stiffened. The butcher. She had reported him for illegal sale of meat and dealing on the black market. Actually, all she had done was tell Mik about it, because she never could catch the men who once had been part of

Klaus's circle. He'd probably escaped with a warning, she thought.

"Okay," she managed to say. "I didn't even know he had a son."

"Sune disappeared on his fifteenth birthday, which was about three weeks ago," Mik said. "And we haven't found a trace of him. He left his wallet and phone in his room. The family is already in a bad situation—his mother is dying from cancer. That's had a big impact on the boy."

Louise jotted notes down on a pad.

"He was in the eighth grade at Hvalsø," Mik continued. "The principal of the school and the boy's parents are afraid that he ran away from home to take his own life. His father describes him as unusually quiet before he disappeared. As I've said, he was very unhappy about his mother's illness; he was having trouble dealing with it. The school reports that Sune had skipped a lot of classes the past few months, and that his classwork generally wasn't going well. Apparently that wasn't like him."

Louise nodded. She was well aware that boys committed suicide more often than girls. Especially when carrying around this type of emotional burden.

"I still don't see why you and Rønholt decided to give us the case."

"Sune's class teacher has just been in to see me," Mik said. "He brought along a newspaper, *Midtsjællands Folkeblad*. It's a local rag. Delivered door-to-door," he added, as if the explanation was needed.

Louise knew the paper, which her parents got.

"He showed me a photo of a few fox cubs from an ar-

27

ticle in the paper's nature section. They were taken from one of those photo hides that nature photographers use, so they don't scare the animals away. The cameras take pictures automatically; they have a motion sensor or an invisible infrared ray. In other words, the photographer wasn't there when the picture was taken."

"Okay," Louise mumbled, nudging him on.

"The fox cubs were, of course, in the foreground, but far back to the right there's a boy sitting on the ground beside a small campfire. The teacher is absolutely certain it's Sune."

"Okay then, so all you have to do is find out where the photo was taken. Then drive out and bring him home," Louise said. She still didn't understand how this involved her unit.

"It's not that simple," Mik said. "Yesterday, when the paper came out, the teacher drove to the parents' home to show them the photo, and it ended up with him being thrown out of the house, literally. Sune's father ordered him to keep out of the family's business. He refused to look at the photo, and he didn't want to hear that his son could be hiding, in need of help."

"How much does the boy in the photo resemble the butcher's son?" Louise asked. She looked over at Eik, whose desk was pushed up against hers. Obviously he hadn't been following the conversation; his eyes were glued to his computer screen. Louise realized she didn't even know if any new cases had come in while she'd been gone, or if he was looking at some of the old cases they had been given. Somehow she had managed to push work completely out of her head.

"It looks a lot like him," Mik said. "This seems to be a clear missing person case to me, and we've had it for two weeks now without making any real progress. That's why I'm sending it to you."

He was following procedure. When a missing person hasn't been found within two weeks, local police stations shuttle the case on to the Search Department, which then picks up the investigation, tracking the movements of the person and collecting identification information.

It was almost too strange that the butcher from Hvalsø ended up on her desk, Louise thought. True, her unit—she and Eik—primarily investigated and did fieldwork, while their colleagues in the department for the most part worked in the office, coordinating registers and searching international data banks for personal information pertaining to searches. But she had been back for all of ten minutes and there he was. The butcher. If Mik had called Friday, it would have been Eik or one of the others who would been sent to the small mid-Zealand town.

"I don't think I've ever heard of parents accepting the disappearance of their child," she said. She glanced over again at Eik, who was still staring at the monitor. "In fact, they usually have a horrible time dealing with the situation, even when there's a corpse involved."

"Exactly," Mik said. "Something's wrong here, and that's why I think you should look at it, too."

4

Camilla Lind picked up the pace. What had looked like a small shower when she left home was now a downpour. Maybe she should turn around, she thought. But she loved the smell of the wet forest floor, the raindrops plunking her sweaty forehead.

She had begun running after moving into her in-laws' large manor house, Ingersminde, in Boserup, not far from Roskilde. She never went very far, but at least she ran, which gave her the opportunity to explore the large section of private forest on the property.

The path narrowed and curved to the right, passing through a small thicket that quickly gave way to the more open space of forest. As she ran, she tried to come up with a good title for the interview she'd been working on all day. She was a freelance journalist, currently taking assignments for the paper in Roskilde, and once in a while they gave her some doozies. But it had been a pleasure to interview Svend-Ole at his little workshop out in Svogerslev. For the past thirty-five years he had emptied the slot machines in Tivoli, and he had a large collection of one-armed bandits in his garage that he and his wife enjoyed playing.

Suddenly Camilla caught sight of something between the trees. She slowed down. Everything looked blurry through the rain, but she could make out a boy crouching under a big tree, eating something he picked up off the ground. Even at this distance, she could see he was soaked to the skin, his wet hair plastered to his head.

She started walking over toward the clearing. As she drew closer, she smelled wood burning, a sour odor, and she noticed a large area where there had been bonfires, which made her wonder. She'd definitely never been here before.

"Hi!" she called out. "Aren't you cold?"

The boy started when he heard her voice, then immediately jumped up and ran.

Which surprised Camilla, who called out, "Hey, wait!"

But the boy sprinted off. Strange, she thought. She decided to run after him.

Just before reaching the tree, her legs slipped out from under her. She swore loudly as she fell, landing on her stomach in a mud puddle.

Slowly she stood up. Besides being shaken by the fall, she was covered with mud. She walked over and sat down with her back against the tree. A wet pile of picked-over food lay where the boy had been sitting. She thought it looked like leftovers from a grill party. It troubled her that the boy had been eating it. Some animals in the forest seemed to have been feasting, too, from the looks of the several gnawed bones scattered around. But they'd left some of the food. They must have been interrupted. Maybe by the boy, she thought, shuddering.

She was getting cold, sitting there in her wet jogging clothes, but she couldn't stop thinking about the boy. Though the forest was private property, everyone had the right to walk through it, meaning that he had no reason to run. Some people did drive in, which was forbidden, but Frederik or the manager gave them hell when they caught them.

Camilla winced from the pain in her knee. After standing up and carefully shaking her leg, she leaned over to wipe the mud off. Strangely enough, the mud was more red than brown. Suddenly she realized it was blood, not mud.

Desperately, she wiped her hands on the tree trunk, then she jogged through the trees toward a small stream she'd discovered earlier. She felt foul, unclean. Along the way she tore off leaves from saplings and bushes, and tried to wipe the blood off.

She was freezing by the time she found a path down to the stream. Cautiously, she stepped onto the stones sticking up out of the water and squatted to wash her face. She cleaned her arms with leaves and let the icy water run onto her legs. Muddy blood streamed down her thighs and calves. She scooped up more water; the thought of being covered in blood nauseated her.

She heard a sudden noise in the forest behind her,

twigs being stepped on, something being dragged along the forest floor. She whirled around in fright and almost lost her balance at the sight of an old woman in a broad-brimmed straw hat, a long braid hanging down over her right shoulder.

"The wagons are rolling on the Death Trail," she said. Her clear, ocean-blue eyes looked earnestly at Camilla. Then, using a sturdy limb as a cane, she turned on her heel and vanished silently and astonishingly quickly into the forest.

Camilla stood midstream, too shocked to speak to her. She had no idea where the woman had come from; had heard nothing until she was practically at her back. She didn't even know if there was an entrance to the forest anywhere near the stream.

She hurried home in the twilight, dripping wet, her heart hammering in her ears.

5

Sune tried one more time. He'd found some dry twigs inside the hollow tree where he'd hung his hoodie up to dry, but couldn't get a fire started with his lighter.

He thought about his mother. She always backed him up, like the time he wanted to be a Boy Scout. His father had said it was a silly idea, that he'd started playing handball when he was seven, and he couldn't understand why his son wouldn't give it a shot.

Your son doesn't have the talent for it, she'd told him, after Sune did try. In the Boy Scouts, however, he earned every merit badge. Each time he brought one home, she proudly sewed it on his scout shirt.

Now his teeth chattered and his fingers were stiff from the cold, even though the rain had stopped. He'd waited over an hour before returning for the food he'd abandoned when the woman came running up and yelling at him. He knew he shouldn't eat it—he could get sick—but he was so incredibly hungry. His body, not his brain, steered him to the trees toward the clearing. To the food.

Another group of Asatro held their sacrifices at the old oak. It was their leftovers he'd been eating. He'd watched them from his hiding place as they gathered around the bonfire. He had never met them; they were the ones who had expelled the Asa group his father belonged to. That he also belonged to now. The thought slammed into his chest so hard he could barely breathe.

At first his father and the others in the group had been furious about the decision of the Asa and Vanir religious organization, Forn Sidr, to expel them. Now, however, they seemed to think of themselves as nobler, because they were more faithful to the original customs. Not like the hippie types who were more interested in getting high and drinking their homemade mead, as his father put it.

He had spent many nights in the forest since his initiation. Twice he had found food at the sacrificial oak. What he'd gathered up after the ceremony had lasted a week. The second time, he'd packed the food in big leaves, hoping that would help keep it fresh.

Several hours had passed after the horrific events of his initiation before he dared sneak out into the clearing. The cars were gone, and he'd held his breath; the silence and the sharp light from the clear, starlit sky seemed threatening. A few embers from the bonfire still glowed, but he didn't dare approach it to warm himself. He had no way of knowing if anyone had stayed behind to wait for him. At last he snuck around in the shadows of the trees over to the oak, where he knew they must have left a lot of the food his father had brought along.

He had tried to forget what had happened, to banish the image of the young woman smiling at him before she was killed. After the men had returned to the clearing without her, and the gothi had closed the circle and passed the oath ring around, they sat beside the bonfire, eating and drinking as if nothing had happened.

But so much had happened, and everything had gone wrong for Sune. Very wrong. He missed his mother. Every single night, he suffered from nightmares about her death. He saw white coffins and graveyards. He woke up bathed in sweat. He knew his mother grew weaker every day that he was away. But he also knew, full well, that he couldn't return home without reconciling with his father and the others. And he wasn't going to do that. Not after what he'd gone through that evening. He would never be a part of that; would never be like them.

He jerked around when he heard a car approaching on the narrow forest road, kicking over the small twigs and branches he'd arranged for the small fire before hiding in the tree.

They came looking for him every night. When they got too close, he picked up his things and ran. Like a hunted animal driven from its den, he hurried off to find another hiding place. He didn't know who it was on any given night. They might be taking turns searching, he thought. He hugged his knees.

The fear of being found made his skin tingle. He had to get out of this area, go somewhere they wouldn't be looking for him. He just didn't know where. If only he'd gotten the stupid fire started earlier. His clothes would've been dry by now, and he wouldn't be freezing.

He opened one of the leaves and gnawed on a cold pork chop, thinking about his mother again. Hopefully, his father was taking care of her. Sune used to go into her bedroom and sit and read to her when he'd come home from school. She wasn't strong enough now to hold a book. Once in a while she fell asleep and snored lightly with her mouth half open, but he'd just kept on reading. When she woke up, she'd smile and say, "I guess I dozed off for a moment."

His father didn't like books. They were a waste of time, he always said. But he wanted his son to do well in school, so he didn't complain when Sune read.

School, Sune thought, as he watched the red taillights of the car after it passed by. This was the final week of exams. How had his parents explained his absence to the school?

He swallowed the last of the pork chop, too quickly— and felt a sharp pain in his esophagus. He didn't have anything to wash the food down with. Normally he drank from the stream, but he couldn't go there now.

The car approached again, so he kept perfectly still. It drove by slowly, stopping several times while the driver peered out into the trees. Finally it left.

Sune had asked himself a thousand times if he

shouldn't just go home, but he realized that was no longer an option. He had defied the men, the brotherhood, by not receiving the ring and swearing an oath of silence together with the others.

6

Camilla closed the heavy front door, kicked off her running shoes, and barged into her husband's office in her wet clothes.

"When you gut a buck or whatever the hell it's called, you could clean up, you know. There's practically a lake of blood out in the forest."

Frederik looked up. "What is this, what's happened to you?"

"I fell flat on my face in a big puddle of blood."

Camilla didn't know much about hunting or forest management, though she did know that Frederik had been out several times lately hunting bucks. But she had no idea what happened after the animal was killed, except that it had to be split open on the spot and gutted to make sure the meat wasn't spoiled.

"As far as I know, there haven't been any bucks gutted

out there," he said. "We haven't hunted in over a week now. Where was it?"

"I don't know exactly. But there's a big tree, partly hollow, close to a clearing with a bonfire site. It looks like someone has been there."

Frederik stood up. He didn't work at home very often. Most of his waking hours were spent in the management offices at Termo-Lux, a window manufacturer. But the board of directors had just accepted his ultimatum: If he was to stay on as managing director of the family business, he had to have one day off a week to work on his film manuscripts—and also to see something of his wife, he'd added, when telling Camilla that they had accepted his demands.

She had met Frederik Sachs-Smith in California, where over the years he had established himself as a film scriptwriter. He'd already had a hand in several big Hollywood productions; she had considered him a mixture of upper-class bohemian and cool businessman. The scriptwriting was something he did simply because he enjoyed it. While doing research for an interview with him, she had discovered that he was a more-than-competent investor; he'd turned his inheritance from his grandparents into a sizable fortune. He didn't need to work.

When they fell in love, the plan had been that she and her son, Markus, would move in with him in Santa Barbara. But after the death of Frederik's brother and the announcement that his sister had chosen for personal reasons to step down as managing director, their plans changed. He returned to Denmark.

At first, Camilla didn't understand; Frederik had never hidden the fact that he had left Denmark to avoid becoming part of the family dynasty. He'd said numerous times that there had to be many others well qualified to head up the business. Gradually she came to realize that he had accepted the job for the sake of his father, not for the business. Walther Sachs-Smith had been forced off the board of directors of his own company the year before, as he had begun to prepare for his successor. Greed and a lust for power had driven Frederik's two younger siblings to betray their father, who all too late discovered what they were up to.

Which was why Frederik put on a suit and tie four days a week now, to lead the business his grandfather had established many years ago.

"It sounds like you've been out at the sacrificial oak," he said. "Which means it's probably pig's blood you slipped in. They buy it from the butcher."

"They? Who in the hell are 'they'?" Camilla bellowed. She began ripping off her jogging pants.

"The people who make sacrifices to the gods. They believe in Odin and Thor, and once in a while they meet out in the forest and perform rituals."

"Are they some of the people from over at the Viking Ship Museum?"

"No." He laughed and shook his head at her. "These people are believers. They're Asatro."

"Actually I think I saw one of them."

She tossed her blouse on top of the wet pile of clothes and grabbed a blanket off the Chesterfield sofa. The office looked exactly the same as it did when Frederik's father

41

moved out and left the house to them. Immediately they'd changed the property's name to Ingersminde, in honor of Walther's deceased wife.

"This old lady appeared out of nowhere and looked me straight in the eye. I almost had a heart attack—I hadn't at all heard her walk up behind me. It seems to me she could be one of those people. She had this long braid hanging down over her shoulder."

Frederik laughed harder this time. "That's Elinor. She lives in the gatekeeper's house; she has most of her life. She's completely harmless, and definitely not one of the Asatro or wights."

"Why do you let them run around and pour blood all over our forest?" Camilla asked. She nestled into the couch to get warm.

"The old Asatro has deep roots in this region, though no one in our family ever believed in it," Frederik said. "It attracts people interested in the Nordic gods and sagas. A lot of our country's history comes from this area."

Camilla struggled to remember some of what she had learned in history class.

"This is where Skjold drifted to shore in an unmanned ship the gods sent," Frederik continued. "He grew up and became king in Lejre. His was the strongest and bravest army. Did you know that?"

She nodded. Everyone who had gone to high school in Roskilde knew that story. They had heard a lot about King Skjold and his descendants, including the tale of his departure. When he died at a very old age, his body was carried aboard the ship he had arrived on as a baby and laid on his shield, together with piles of gold, jewelry, and valuable weapons. The ship was launched from shore; only the gods know where it ended up.

"I met a boy out there, too," she said. "I think he's about Markus's age. He was eating some food on the ground by the tree. But he could have been one of them, of course."

Frederik frowned. "I don't think the kids come by themselves. Usually they all meet down by the gate where they park their cars, and then they all walk in together. But I've seen their food lying around on the ground, several times. They share it with the gods or something, and that's fine. The animals out there can have at it, as long as there's no plastic or other garbage."

Camilla smiled at him and gathered up her clothes. "We certainly didn't have heathen worshipers like that when I was a little girl in Frederiksberg."

She kissed him. "At least not in my part of Frederiksberg."

7

Someone knocked on the office door and immediately Charlie was on his feet, growling. Louise jumped; she'd forgotten about the big German shepherd on the folded-up gray dog blanket beside Eik's chair. She waved and shook her head, warning Rønholt not to come in.

"Can I have a few minutes?" he asked, stepping behind the door.

The dog was still growling, even though Eik grabbed his collar and tried to force him back on his blanket. "Settle down. Down now; it's okay for them to be here, too," he said. Louise rolled her eyes and walked out into the hall.

Rønholt put his arm around her shoulder. "It's nice having you back," he said. "We've missed you. So how are you doing?"

"You're going to have to explain to him that he can't

bring that dog in here. It's totally crazy," she said, niftily avoiding the question, as they walked down to Rønholt's office. "I've tried to tell him, but it goes in one ear and out the other."

"That's not going to be so easy," Rønholt mumbled, staring down at the gray linoleum.

"What do you mean? You're not going to allow this!"

Rønholt still didn't look at her. "You have to admit he's being very decent."

"The dog?" Louise was incredulous. "You couldn't even walk into our office! If that dog's staying, Eik's going to have to move back to his old office."

"Not the dog. I'm talking about Eik offering to take care of it while his friend is dealing with his very unfortunate situation."

Ragner Rønholt closed his office door and gestured to her to drag the chair over to his desk. Louise could see he was finished talking about the dog.

"I'm having second thoughts," he began, looking a bit apologetic now. "I sent a case from Hvalsø over to you."

She broke in. "I've already talked to Mik."

"You're too close to it," he continued, ignoring her remark. "I was just thinking that coming back to a case would be good for you. You know, right back up on the horse, that sort of thing."

He was wringing his hands, so hard that Louise thought it must hurt.

"But not in Hvalsø. Of course you shouldn't be going back down there. Especially if the father of the missing boy is one of the…"

He seemed to search, in vain, for the right words.

"You're too close," he finally repeated. "I've told Olle to take over."

Louise studied her clenched hands. "You can't do this," she said. "I have no problem with working in Hvalsø."

And she meant that. She hadn't seen Lars Frandsen in twenty years, and she could hardly imagine what he looked like now. Back then, he had been rangy with thick, light hair, round cheeks, and a broad nose that wiggled when he laughed. A happy boy with a certain status, he was the butcher's son and lived in a large residential home on Præstegårdsvej, with an indoor pool and access to his parents' bar in the basement, where there were pinball machines and a billiard table.

Louise knew all of this because he was the guy Klaus hung out with the most back then. They had finished their apprenticeships at the same time, Lars with his father in Hvalsø, Klaus with the butcher over in Tølløse. When they attended butcher school in Roskilde, they took the morning train together, which was how Klaus had become part of Big Thomsen's gang.

"I just thought it might not be good for you to meet one of them after what happened," Rønholt added in a nearly fatherly tone. "It's better that I send one of the others to poke around."

Louise shook her head. "If anyone's going to poke around over in Hvalsø, it should be me. It doesn't bother me one bit to meet the butcher or anyone else there."

She gave him her stubborn look. "If I was that way, I couldn't walk around Copenhagen for fear of running into someone from the Eastern European mafia, not to mention the gang members I've put behind bars. If I'm scared or have problems confronting people, I should go into private security instead of holding on to this lousy-paying job."

She paused for a moment, then leaned forward. "I'll find that boy. Tell Olle the case is mine."

She met Olle in the hallway as he walked down from their office, carrying the few case files that Mik had mailed them. "Welcome back!" he said, and spread his arms.

He was about to keep chattering, so she broke in to tell him that Rønholt had changed his mind: She would continue with the case. "But it could very well be that we'll need your help," she added, smiling at her tall, balding colleague before walking past him.

Louise was about to open the door to the Rathole when she remembered the dog. "Can I come in?" she called out. She felt like an idiot, standing there waiting for the green light to enter her own office.

A moment later Eik said, "Come on in."

She hurried inside and sat down at her desk while Eik held the German shepherd's collar with one hand and pushed three dog biscuits across her desk with the other.

"Try giving him one," he suggested.

"Come on, Eik! You're the one who has to deal with this dog. He shouldn't be here. It's not right that I can't work without worrying about a German shepherd biting my ass."

"Charlie's not aggressive. He just has to get to know you. Give him a chance."

Eik went on to say that the photographer who had set up the camera blind in Boserup Forest had called while she was talking to Rønholt. "He'll call back."

Reluctantly, Louise grabbed one of the square dog biscuits and held it out. The dog growled from deep in his throat.

"Come on, give it to him!" Eik said. "Or else he'll think you're stringing him along!"

"This is bullshit!"

Eik broke out laughing. It flustered her that he looked so great when he laughed; she ignored Charlie's growling and held out the biscuit, which disappeared in a second. The dog began licking her hand.

"What did I tell you?" Eik said, gesturing for her to give Charlie another one.

The dog rested his big head on her lap. "Here!" She pushed him gently and dropped the biscuit on the floor to get him away, but as soon as he ate it, he was back.

"Oh, look. He loves you," Eik said. He folded his arms and looked on with obvious contentment as she gave Charlie the last of the goodies. Louise shook her head.

The phone rang. She wiped her dog-slobbered hand on her pants. "That's perfect," she answered when the photographer offered to meet them in the forest and show them the camera that had captured the boy. "We can be there in an hour."

Eik caught her attention. "Is the boy in any of the photos we haven't seen?"

Louise repeated the question to the photographer, and thanked him when he offered to look through the pictures before meeting them.

8

Charlie was asleep in the back of Eik's rattletrap Jeep Cherokee when they entered the forest west of Roskilde forty-five minutes later. They had passed the driveway to Camilla and Frederik's place, but trees blocked all views of the big manor house.

"You think this is it?" Eik asked as he signaled with his blinker. A red barrier closed off the forest road, and a sign expressly forbade all vehicles on the private property.

"I think it's a little farther," Louise said. She reached into the front pocket of her bag and pulled out the scrap of paper with directions. "There's a parking lot and a path leading to a small area with benches."

Several hundred meters down the road they saw the parking sign and pulled in.

"Don't even think it," Louise said when Eik made a move to let the dog out. Instead of opening the door, he reached out for Louise and pulled her close.

"Don't you think you two can be friends?" He hugged her, his odor filling her nose. She closed her eyes for a moment and enjoyed it, until she heard a car on the road slowing down. She broke away from him just before a light-blue Fiat 500 pulled in and parked beside Eik's dirty four-wheel-drive.

The photographer was in his late fifties and partially bald, his gray hair like a wreath gracing his round head.

"You're early," he said, smiling as he tapped his watch. "I thought we were meeting in two minutes!"

"Right, you're right, you're not late," Eik said. He walked over and introduced himself.

The photographer slung a camera over his shoulder and locked his car. Something about him made Louise think of her father, an ornithologist, who had the same energetic look when he took off with a pair of binoculars around his neck.

"You never know what you'll run into, so I always carry a camera with me," he explained.

Louise smiled at him. He took off, waving them down a slope instead of following the gravel path. "This way," he said, holding back a few limbs for them. "We'll circle around the edge of the forest until we hit a stretch that juts out into a field. That will take us to the camera."

Louise followed Eik. She swore when she stumbled over a root.

"I have three bases here in the forest," the photographer said. "They're placed to capture specific animals. For instance, the boxes I use to photograph birds are in a clearing farther in the forest, much higher up than the camera that caught the fox cubs."

He pointed around at the different types of trees and chattered about them as they worked their way around the forest.

"Can you tell us when the photo was taken?" Eik asked as they stopped.

The photographer pulled a folded-up sheet of paper out of his pocket. "I can tell you that it was taken on June eleventh at precisely six forty-seven a.m. The time is registered automatically when a photo is taken."

Eight days ago, Louise thought. "Did you find him in any of the other photos?"

The photographer nodded. "Five. I've written it all down for you."

He handed her the paper. "The first time he showed up was a week before the photo used in the paper. June sixth. But you have to look closely to see him. Let's go down here."

He walked onto a path hidden behind the exposed roots of a fallen tree. "The camera is right over there."

Louise approached the metal box screwed onto a tree stump. The hole for the camera lens was on the other side.

"It's focused on the fox den over there," the photographer explained, pointing to a thick tree trunk on a slope, its open roots just above the den's entrance. Eik headed for the small hole while the photographer checked the lock on the box holding the digital camera.

"The fox cubs were born in March, so they're three months old now," he continued. But Louise wasn't listening. Eik waved her over, and before she got there she spied the remains of a small campfire.

"Do you want to look through my photos?" the photographer called after her; she thanked him when he offered to mail them to her.

"And thank you very much for helping us on such short notice," she said. She gave him her card so he could call if he happened to see the boy again.

"What is it about this boy?" he asked. "Did he do something stupid?"

She smiled and shook her head, impressed that he had waited so long to ask. "We just want to find out why he's staying here in the forest and not at home with his parents."

"He's been here, no doubt about that, but not recently," Eik said as he squatted down beside the fire. "Him, or at least somebody."

The fire had been extinguished before burning out. A small pile of limbs lay beside it, along with an old can. Eik sniffed it.

"I think he was making soup out of stinging nettles," he said. He dropped the can back onto the ground. "But he didn't finish."

"Maybe he slept over here," Louise said, from the other side of the tree. The trunk was split, and when she leaned in close she saw that part of the tree was hollow. The hole wasn't big, but a boy could curl up and lie in it.

She got down on her knees and crawled halfway in, groping around on the ground. She found a few small limbs for the fire, but when her fingers touched something soft, she pulled her hand back and banged her head above the opening.

"There's something in there," she said when she backed out.

Eik pushed her aside and squeezed into the hollow space while flicking his lighter. He came out carrying a dark-blue sweatshirt, which he unfolded on the ground. Inside was a small pocketknife, a lighter, and a set of keys.

"It's cold and damp from the ground," he said. "But we can't know how long it's been here. Possibly only one night. It's not much use to us."

He studied the knife. "It's his," he said, handing it over to her. "His name is engraved on it."

He sat on the ground and studied the small, primitive camp.

"Let's take these things back with us," Louise said. She began packing it all in the sweatshirt.

"No, wait," he said. "If he still lives here, he'll need his knife and the warm sweatshirt. There's no reason to make things harder for him."

Louise brought out her phone and took a picture of the engraved name on the knife. Then she rolled up the old sweatshirt with everything inside and laid it in the hollow tree. "Let's drive over to his parents and give them the news before we inform social services."

9

Neither of them spoke until they arrived in Hvalsø.
Louise gave him directions at the roundabout,
steering him out of town and over the hill before the as-
phalt road turned to gravel.

"Why oh why is that boy living out in the rain and
mud instead of relaxing in his nice, warm room at
home?" Eik asked.

She shrugged. It wasn't unusual for kids to run away
from home. Or for them to return, either voluntarily or
when they were found.

The butcher's house was one of the last on the road.
An old friend from school had lived in the first house, and
they had often ridden horses on the gravel road leading
into the forest.

She motioned for Eik to pull in. On the right side of
the driveway stood a big chestnut tree, like a giant parasol

shading most of the farmyard. The three-winged house had stable doors on every wing and a thatched roof overhanging the windows, like thick hair over a forehead. A white van was parked by the green front door.

Louise took stock of the place a moment before walking up to the door. She was fairly confident that the butcher didn't know who had turned him in about the meat back then, yet she had butterflies in her stomach when she grabbed the heavy knocker and let it fall against the brass back plate.

A moment later the door opened. There he stood, only slightly taller than her. His ranginess had vanished and his round cheeks had spread to the rest of his body. The open expression on his face suddenly closed; clearly, he'd been expecting someone else. He casually stepped back and looked expectantly at her without speaking. She could tell he didn't recognize her.

Something in his eye jogged her memory. She knew Klaus had been with him the evening before his death. That Lars had agreed to come by and help him carry their double bed upstairs while she was in Roskilde, at the Gnags concert with Camilla.

Louise had completely forgotten that. Just as she had repressed all the too-painful details. She didn't even know if the bed had been moved upstairs, because she didn't go inside the house after she found Klaus hanging in the hallway. And she'd never returned.

Her little brother Mikkel, her parents, and Camilla had packed her things and taken them to Lerbjerg. Klaus's parents had dealt with all his belongings. They told Louise that she was welcome to anything they had bought together, but she had politely declined. All of it had been recycled.

A shadow passed over the butcher's face when he finally recognized her. He lowered his eyes to the level of her throat to avoid eye contact. He still hadn't said anything and she couldn't find a way to get started, until Eik saved her by announcing that they wanted to talk about his son.

"Police," the butcher said, nodding as he stepped aside. "I don't know if my wife is awake. She's not doing so well. I thought you were the nurse; it's been over an hour since I called."

"I'm very sorry to hear that," Eik said.

"Have you found him?"

The butcher looked up at Eik, who was already halfway into the hall. He seemed uneasy, fearful.

"No, we haven't found your son yet," Louise said. Quickly, she stepped inside. "We'd like to talk to you about him, and why he might possibly be hiding in the forest close to Roskilde."

The butcher got in her face. "Let's get something straight right now. If you've been listening to that schoolteacher, you need to know he's full of shit. I don't want to hear it. My son isn't hiding. Why the hell should he be?"

Louise was so surprised by this outburst that for a moment she stood speechless, staring at the Thor's hammer hanging from a silver chain around the man's neck.

Eik walked into the kitchen and asked where they could sit and talk. The butcher turned his back on Louise and motioned them into the living room, where a big flat-screen TV took up most of one wall.

"I'm not listening to more gossip," he said. "The whole town's talking. They even talk about it while they're fucking standing in line in my shop. And they stare. Like it's my goddamn fault, all of it. That my wife's sick, that my boy couldn't handle it. I'm not going to fucking take it anymore. And now you show up…"

He sank down into his soft leather easy chair, his back to the windows with a view of the fields behind the house.

"Your son is handling it better than a lot of people would," Eik said, sitting on the sofa across from him. "We have reason to believe that he's doing fine. But we need to ask you and your wife a few questions."

"Have you talked to him?" the butcher asked. He sat up; suddenly he looked very pale.

"Would you please see if your wife is awake and able to speak with us?" Eik said. Louise kept her mouth shut and walked over to the window behind the dining room table. The lawn looked more like a meadow, separated from the field behind by an uneven stone fence.

The butcher walked over to a door across the room, knocked lightly, and went inside. Louise glanced into the room, but it was dark. He closed the door, and she turned back to the view outside, disquieted by the atmosphere in this house.

She knew Hvalsø all too well. Knew how it felt when the town talked about you, whispered behind your back. Even though she had an instinctive aversion to the butcher, she couldn't help but feel sympathy for him, too. And anyway, Klaus must have had a reason to be friends with him.

"You can come in," he said from the doorway.

The first thing Louise noticed was the metal pole with the IV bag and the clear plastic tubing that disappeared underneath the thick comforter. A tiny, frail woman lay buried in pillows.

Eik stood beside the bed and introduced himself. Louise joined him and was about to offer her hand when she froze.

"Jane," she said, her voice hoarse. She crouched down, her eyes now level with her old schoolmate. "Is it you?"

The woman was a shadow of the schoolmate Louise had played handball with, but after Louise hooked up with Klaus they'd gone their separate ways.

She stopped before her voice broke. Why in hell had she not read up on the case properly? She should have checked to see if the boy's mother was someone she knew.

"Yes, it's me." The voice seemed to come from deep down in the pillow. "I'd recognize your voice even if I couldn't see you."

Jane's eyes were sunken, her face so thin that her cheekbones stood out like two sharp corners. Not much remained of the grocery manager's beautiful daughter, but she lifted her hand up a few centimeters from the comforter and smiled at Louise.

"Lars says you have news about Sune." Her eyes blurred, and a moment later a tear ran down her cheek.

Louise took her hand and stroked it with her thumb. "We think we've found him." She pulled her phone out with her other hand and showed Jane the photo of the pocketknife from inside the hollow tree. "Or at least we found where he's been staying some of the time," she said. She asked if the knife belonged to their son.

It was overwhelming to see the relief flooding into the mother's face when she saw the knife. The father's reaction wasn't as clear. Relief. Fear. Confusion, maybe.

"It's his old knife," Jane said to her husband. The tears came freely now; she turned her head to the side and let them fall on the pillow. Then she closed her eyes, and it seemed as though she withdrew into herself.

Louise let her rest. A somber silence fell over the room.

"I just don't understand what he's doing out there," Jane said a few moments later, her eyes still closed. "Is he hiding from someone?"

Her husband broke in. "None of us understands this. We've been preparing ourselves for anything after he disappeared. Someone could've stolen his knife," he added.

Louise and Eik glanced at each other. What the hell was it with him? Louise thought. Could it be some mental wall he'd built, to shield himself from the family's problems?

Eik asked if they could borrow a few chairs and sit down.

"Sure," the butcher said, bringing in two dining room chairs. They sat beside the bed. Jane looked up at the ceiling with her hands folded on the comforter.

"Our son has been very deeply affected by my illness," she said, turning to them now. "But all the time he's been missing, I've never believed he would go so far as to take his own life."

Her husband quickly jumped in. "No one's said he did." His tone made it obvious that they indeed had talked about it, possibly even prepared themselves for it. "But you do read nowadays that a lot of teenagers play around with the idea," he continued. "It's the ultimate punishment for parents. The school principal even said that on the phone."

He sniggered. "It's almost like they blame us already. That it's our fault he might have done it."

"Lars, please!" his wife whispered. "Don't be so angry."

The butcher suddenly hid his face in his hands and bowed his head.

"It's not always easy living in a small town, with people gossiping," she said, to excuse her husband.

Louise looked away when her old school friend made eye contact with her.

"At any rate, not when you have a shop, and everyone thinks they know you," Jane continued. "And Lars is right. You get the impression that people think my illness is why Sune isn't doing well, that maybe he even..." She closed her eyes.

"But luckily there's no reason anymore to believe that your son chose that path," Eik said. He asked if Sune had been a Boy Scout.

"Yes," his mother said, with a hint of pride. "He has all the merit badges you can earn. He never cared about hanging out at the gym with the other boys."

Louise noticed that his father was about to say something, but he stopped himself.

"Does this mean he's coming home?" Jane said hesitantly, as if she was afraid it was too early for optimism. "Not a moment has gone by that I haven't thought about him. What hurts the most is that we might never say good-bye to each other. I've planned it all; I know exactly what I want to say to my son, the words that will help him when I'm gone. But now that he's not here, I haven't been able to say any of it to him."

She turned to Louise, who had to muster every bit of willpower not to lower her eyes. She'd known this woman well, and it was heart wrenching to see her this way. *Be professional*, she scolded herself. She tried to focus on what was in front of her: a dying woman now hoping to be reunited with her son.

"We found a campsite in Boserup Forest, where your son probably has been staying since he disappeared," Eik said. Louise straightened up in her chair, thankful once again for Eik.

"Fine," the butcher said, preparing to stand up. "I'll go out and get him."

Louise and Eik said nothing, and eventually the parents sensed that something was wrong.

"He's not there anymore," Louise said. "The camp's been abandoned."

"Did he have any money when he disappeared?" Eik asked. "Cash, credit card?"

Both parents shook their heads. "He had a debit card, but it's in his wallet," his father said. He leaned back in his chair.

"We're going to ask Roskilde Police to initiate a search for—" Louise said.

"I'll find my son myself," the butcher said. "Sune has been through enough. I don't want him hunted by the police, too."

Louise nodded and handed him her card. "I don't know

if you have anyone to help you search, but call me if you don't find him. And I'll notify my colleagues in Roskilde."

Jane reached out for her hand. "Thank you for helping," she said, smiling broadly now. "I can't tell you how relieved I am. I've been so unhappy. I might leave this world at peace with myself after all; that means more than I can ever say. I'm sure you know what I'm talking about. It's so important to be able to say your good-byes."

Louise squeezed Jane's hand and nodded. She wasn't sure she could help her old friend. All she knew was that Jane's son had been staying in the forest, and right now she had no idea where he was.

She felt the butcher's eyes on her back all the way out to the hall, and when she turned to say good-bye he was right behind her. She lowered her hand when she saw the expression on his face.

"I can't believe you'd stoop so low, putting René behind bars," he said, his voice low. "He helped you, and that asshole got what was coming to him."

"René killed him," she snapped. "Shot him. It was completely unnecessary."

"That's not what I heard."

"So what did you hear?"

The butcher retreated a step and looked on her with scorn. "I heard he saved you from that asshole fucking your brains out."

"He told you that?"

"You hear so much," he said offhandedly, but then continued. "It's hard for him to tell what happened, sitting in jail. But I have a visitor's permit. I'm going in to see him tomorrow."

Louise was enraged. She could imagine them sitting together and talking about her. Only moments ago she had almost changed her mind about Lars Frandsen, but now she remembered very clearly why she had hated him and his gang.

10

Louise felt dizzy when she walked out of the house. Eik stood smoking a cigarette, enjoying the view of the forest. She asked him to unlock the car, and just as she was about to get in, Charlie jumped up right behind the front seat. He looked at her and cocked his ears forward, as if in anticipation.

"You'll just have to wait to get out and run," she snapped. She was still enraged. She'd let the man provoke her. She shouldn't have reacted when he mentioned René.

"Damn it," she said under her breath. She vowed that from now on she would be better prepared.

Eik walked over to her. "What are you mumbling about?"

"Nothing," she said. "You were good in there. I'm sorry; it threw me off to see it was Jane lying in bed. We knew each other."

Eik put his arm around her. "I figured it was something like that." He kissed her hair.

Images from the past kept popping up now, after seeing Jane. Happy images. Despite her anger, Louise could suddenly recall what it was like being an eighth-grader in love.

She had been crazy about Klaus. She'd stood by the outdoor handball court in every kind of weather to watch him play. She'd hung out in the gym's clubhouse, just to see him walk out of the locker room.

It all seemed so ridiculous now, but back then it had been a matter of life or death. Teenage love had been a force she couldn't control, no matter how hard she tried. She could still remember her heart jumping when he looked at her and smiled.

They started going together after a party in the gym. Maybe she'd been drunker than she thought when she walked over to him. And it had felt like the most natural thing in the world when Klaus put his arm around her and whispered in her ear, "Finally."

Eik backed out of the courtyard and drove down the bumpy gravel road, out to the highway. "You want to go out to eat tonight? Jonas is welcome to come along, of course. We could go to Tea; they make the best Peking duck in town."

She smiled and said that Jonas was going to a movie with a friend and would be staying all night with him afterward.

Eik grinned. "It's not like I have anything against it being just the two of us." He leaned toward her. "We can have coffee at your place afterward."

She touched his cheek, felt the stubble grazing against the palm of her hand.

"There's something I have to do first," she said. She told him to turn right before they reached the roundabout.

"There's no hurry, it's only five."

"This is something I have to do alone."

She pointed at a side street ahead. "Would you please drop me off there?"

Eik's expression became serious. When they reached the street, he stopped and turned to her. "Are you sure this is wise?"

She saw the doubt in his face. He couldn't possibly know where she was going, but he wasn't dumb; she'd told him about losing a man she'd loved. She touched his cheek again and nodded.

"I haven't spoken with Klaus's parents since he died, and now I have to. They deserve to know what René Gamst told me. If their son didn't commit suicide, they should know. But going out to eat Peking duck tomorrow or this weekend sounds fantastic."

She loved the thin pancakes and the pungent hoisin sauce. It was one of Jonas's favorite foods, something he and his father had made together. Jonas had diced the cucumbers and spring onions; his father had been an expert

66

at the crisp skin. Suddenly Louise missed her foster son terribly. His relaxed face, the thick, dark hair that fell into his eyes.

"Of course," Eik said, jolting her out of her thoughts, the chaos of emotions from the past and present bouncing around inside her. All the things she had pushed away, repressed.

She didn't even know if Lissy and Ernst still lived in the white house on Skovvej. Back in the eighth grade, Louise always bicycled past as slowly as possible on the way to Lerbjerg, to see if Klaus's scooter was parked in the drive, or if he was helping his father behind the house.

She studied Eik's face in profile for a moment before getting out of the car. She shook her head when he asked if he should wait for her.

"I'll take the train home," she said, and smiled at him.

"Shouldn't we check to see if they still live here?"

"I have to do this alone," she repeated. She was beginning to wonder herself if this was such a good idea.

Eik watched her a moment, then nodded and blew her a kiss.

She stood on the corner as he made a U-turn and drove off toward Copenhagen.

11

Louise walked the last stretch with her hands in her jacket pockets, her eyes on the sidewalk. *Step on a crack, you'll break your mother's back*. It was as if the lock on her trunk of repressed memories had been blown off. The old children's rhyme kept running through her head, in time with her steps.

It was a game she'd played with her girlfriends at school. They had upgraded it to a teenage version—whoever stepped on a crack had to tell the others a secret. Louise had revealed that she was secretly in love with Klaus, and instantly she'd seen that she wasn't the only one; he was one of the boys many girls in school had their eyes on.

Suddenly she spotted the freshly painted picket fence and house, which looked exactly like it had all those years ago. Well kept, though not renovated. A café curtain still hung in the kitchen window.

She breathed deeply. Did they still live here? Anyone younger probably wouldn't have hung that curtain. She crossed the street and stopped at the gate, her legs refusing to take her another step.

Pull yourself together, she thought. Their name was on the mailbox. But she still couldn't move.

In her mind's eye she saw Klaus's scooter and the birdhouses his father had built, a hobby that had given him something to talk about with Louise's father. The two men were always showing each other something or telling stories that had to do with birds. She had completely forgotten about those birdhouses. She looked around; they hung from every tree in the yard, more numerous now than back then. Many were ornate, too. One on the big tree in the middle of the yard was a precise copy of a Swiss hut. A newer model, she thought. Surely he wouldn't have had time for that level of detail back when he'd worked at the sawmill.

She heard a voice from the woodshed. "Louise? Is that you?" Ernst, Klaus's father, walked over to her and opened the gate. "Come in, come in!"

She tried to smile at him; she wanted to say something, but her mind went blank. Over twenty years had gone by without them hearing a single peep from her. Not that she'd heard from them, either. Finally her feet moved, and before she knew it the words flew out of her mouth.

"I don't think Klaus committed suicide."

Instantly she realized her mistake. She should have said that it was so nice to see him again; that he was looking well.

Ernst stiffened for a second, then laid a hand on her

shoulder. "Come inside. It wouldn't surprise me if Lissy had a cup of coffee waiting for us."

Louise followed him around the corner of the house to the back porch, where a half-finished birdhouse stood on his workbench. They entered the house through the laundry room to the smell of newly washed clothes and freshly brewed coffee. She took off her shoes, and he led her into the kitchen. She couldn't remember exactly how it had looked back then, yet a sense of security and familiarity overcame her. Which made it even more difficult to say what she was there to say.

Klaus's mother appeared in the doorway and welcomed Louise with open arms, as if she were a long-lost child come home.

"Now, this is a surprise!" Lissy said.

Her hair had turned gray, and her figure was rounder now, but her eyes were still lively. And she had the same habit of drying her hands on her apron. Without another word, she opened a cupboard and brought out coffee cups.

"Do you use milk or sugar?" she asked as she walked over to the refrigerator.

"Milk, thank you."

Ernst led her into the living room. At once, she noticed the photos covering the bureau, of Klaus and his younger sister. They appeared together in several shots, then a few were of an older Heidi. Alone. What looked to be the most recent showed her with a little boy on her lap.

"Our grandchild," Ernst said. "Jonathan. He just turned three."

Farthest to the left in a silver frame was a photo of her and Klaus. Her hair was tightly curled, a permanent gone wild in Salon Connie. She'd forgotten that.

Louise managed to say that their grandson was a real cutie before her throat tightened up from the grief that revisited her. They sat in awkward silence, waiting for Lissy. The moment she stepped into the room, Ernst told her what Louise had said out on the sidewalk.

"You don't think it was suicide," he repeated. "But isn't it hard to know what happened after all these years?"

Before Louise could explain, Lissy said, "I've never believed it was his own idea." She looked at Ernst. "We've talked about that."

Ernst nodded almost imperceptibly, then stared down at his hands.

Louise set her coffee cup down. "So what you're saying is, you've known all along?"

"Don't think that we've *known*," he mumbled.

"We have our theories," Lissy said, her voice more assured.

"But you didn't do anything about it?" Louise said. "You should've said something."

"No one knows for sure what happened that night," Ernst said. "That's why it was hard to make serious accusations. And no parent wants to think that their child took his own life."

"You know this town," Lissy said. She studied the fingernails on her right hand, then looked up. "You know how it is when everyone turns against you. And it's right what Ernst says: We didn't know what happened. We just couldn't make sense of it. He was so

71

happy, all he could talk about was you two and your house. He was starting a new life, and he'd settled his debt, too."

"What debt?" Louise asked.

"He owed Ole Thomsen for a motorcycle. And it turned out he even had to pay interest. It ended up being expensive, more than he could pay from what he earned as an apprentice."

Of course, Louise thought. Thomsen wasn't above squeezing his friends.

"We helped him out. We paid off Thomsen so Klaus wouldn't have to have anything to do with him and his gang."

Louise hadn't known about that, either.

"But it's hard to turn your back on old friends," his father said. As if an explanation was needed for his son's problems with leaving the gang. Louise had never understood what he had in common with them.

Louise also didn't understand why his parents hadn't acted if they suspected wrongdoing. *She'd* never doubted that Klaus had taken his own life. The only question for her was why.

"I'm not sure if you've heard what happened out at the gamekeeper's last month," she said.

They both nodded. She told them what René Gamst had said just before his arrest. That someone had put the noose around Klaus's neck.

Several moments went by before Ernst said, "There was a bunch of them out at your house that night."

Louise's skin tingled. She'd never heard how much people knew about that night, and she'd never asked. She wasn't sure she wanted to know, to have the images of Klaus's last hours swirling around in her head.

She'd been told about the beer drinking. Her brother had seen empty bottles on an upside-down beer case— a makeshift table Louise and Klaus ate breakfast on that first morning in their house. Klaus had spread a newspaper and set out paper plates and plastic tableware they'd bought at a gas station.

Ernst continued. "Every one of them said that they left around one thirty that night."

"You can't believe anything they say," Lissy said, "you know that. All their explanations. It was the same way back then in Såby."

"Såby?" Louise said.

"That's something else entirely," Ernst said.

Lissy brushed him off. "It's not something else, not at all. And then there was Gudrun at her store. No one believed she stumbled and fell on her way to the bathroom that night, not with those injuries. And why would she use the store's bathroom? She had her own, right beside her bedroom."

Ernst clenched his hands so tightly that his rough knuckles turned white. "We don't know anything about what happened to Gudrun. The police chief said she fell."

"What about everything missing from the store?" Lissy said. "The alcohol and cigarettes."

Louise broke in. "Wait, you're talking about the Gudrun who ran the convenience store at the gas station; the woman who died?"

Everyone in Hvalsø had known you could knock on Gudrun's back door and buy beer and cigarettes at night.

Louise had done it herself, several times, when they'd run out of beer at a party. Gudrun had been a sweet old lady, well-liked by everyone, and the whole town had gone into mourning after her adult daughter showed up for lunch that Sunday and found her mother on the floor in the store's back room. At first it was rumored that she'd been beaten and robbed, but the police said there was no sign of assault. The items missing from the store had been attributed to Gudrun's back-door business, which she'd kept off the books. Of course, that was easy to claim; she wasn't around to dispute it. Nobody knew for sure what really happened that night.

Lissy wouldn't let it go. "I heard from down at the clinic that her skull had been fractured. A few ribs, too. And the injuries to her face."

"The police said it was bad luck how she fell; how she hit her head on the counter," Ernst said.

"She was beaten," Lissy said, annoyed at her husband. "And she could hardly knock herself in the head from behind and fall on her face and crack her ribs, all at the same time. They said she must have lost consciousness right off the bat."

"That may be, but we still don't know for sure."

"Who was in charge of the investigation?" Louise said.

"The chief of police did the talking," Lissy said. "I don't know who was actually out there doing the investigating."

The police chief back then was Big Thomsen's father, old Roed Thomsen. He'd retired just before Louise had finished at the police academy. He had always been well respected, was one of the town's leaders—he probably still was, Louise thought. Hadn't he been president of the Hvalsø Sports Association? She was never around him. Her parents didn't belong to the town's elite. Her family would always be regarded as outsiders, no matter how long they lived there.

"What happened out in Såby?" Louise asked.

"The school janitor was killed by a hit-and-run driver. They never found him."

"For God's sake, Lissy!" Ernst said. "There's no reason to start in on things we don't know about."

She ignored her husband. "Did you know him?"

Louise shook her head.

"But then you never played handball, did you?"

"I did, yes. But I don't remember the janitor out there."

"He lived in Vestre Såby with his wife and two small children. There was a handball tournament that weekend, and as I recall he left for the gym early Saturday morning to let the cleaners from Roskilde in. There'd been a dance the night before."

"None of this matters now," Ernst said. He looked at Louise. "A paper boy found him in the ditch. They never did catch whoever ran him over, even though the police questioned everyone around there. The chief of police finally gave up."

"Of course he gave up," Lissy said. "He knew who was out there in the middle of the night, running the intersection with their headlights off."

Ernst sighed. "I don't know why you're digging all this up."

"I'll tell you why, because it's so easy to see what goes

on around here." Suddenly Lissy sounded tired. "You've always been afraid of the bigwigs in this town; you'd rather just shut your eyes. But I'm not going to keep quiet anymore, not about anyone who might have been involved in Klaus's death. And that's that! Not after hearing this from Louise."

Chills ran down Louise's spine. Her joints suddenly felt stiff and sore, as if she'd been sitting motionless too long. But she couldn't move. "Who drove around at night with their headlights off?" She looked back and forth between Klaus's parents, though she felt she already knew the answer.

Lissy avoided her eyes, and Ernst folded his hands in his lap again, perhaps considering her question. Finally he looked at her. "Thomsen and his crowd. Klaus was with them the night the janitor died." He didn't look away this time, as if he wanted to show her that he realized he'd let the cat out of the bag.

Louise opened her mouth, but no words came out.

"They shut their lights off and crossed the intersection," Lissy said quietly.

"It was a sort of test of their manhood," Ernst said.

Louise was familiar with the Såby intersection. When you crossed the highway to Holbæk, the road continued on to Torkilstrup. A large building blocked the view on the left side of the road, and if you didn't stop at the intersection, you couldn't see traffic coming from Roskilde. A gas station on the other side of the highway made it difficult to see cars coming from Holbæk.

"They didn't stop, they just hoped there weren't any cars," Louise said to no one in particular.

"When it happened, Klaus didn't say anything about being out there that night," Ernst said. "Later, he talked about it, but he claimed he hadn't seen anything. I told the chief of police what these kids were up to, but he said they had nothing to do with the accident. Monkey business, as he put it, is a lot different from killing a man. He also said the janitor was thought to have been drunk, and the question was whether he'd even been hit by a car."

"And two days later you got sacked at the sawmill," Lissy said. Ernst nodded.

She looked at Louise. "That's how things are done here. You must know that. The chief of police plays poker with the owner of the sawmill."

"Yeah, but I got my job back," Ernst said.

Lissy nodded. "You did. After he was sure you weren't going to raise a fuss."

"We don't know that," he said, shaking his head at her. "That's why you're better off keeping your suspicions to yourself. We don't know anything. We're guessing."

"No," his wife said. "We're putting two and two together; that's something else entirely."

"We won't know anything unless one of them starts talking," Ernst said. "And none of them will. They don't dare."

Lissy folded her hands in her lap and slumped in her chair. Louise felt she had to say something. That she had reopened old wounds, and what for? For her own sake. She leaned forward.

"If you're talking about Big Thomsen and his crowd, I promise I'll do everything in my power to get René

Gamst to talk. And if there's anything we don't know about Klaus's death, I will dig it up."

She got up and gave both of them a hug.

Five minutes later Louise stood out on Skovvej, trying to remember precisely what she had told Klaus's parents she would do. All she could think of was the trail of death Big Thomsen's gang seemed to leave behind them. A shadowy and vague trail. Her teeth were chattering, even though the June sun still stood high in the sky.

She headed to the station to take the train back to Copenhagen, but the thought of walking down the main street of town exhausted her. Instead she began walking toward the old sports complex.

Why had he never told her about the debt? Louise formed the words on her lips: Klaus owed money to Thomsen. A debt she'd known nothing about, but which hung around even after he'd paid it off.

She stopped and closed her eyes for a moment, imagining the old farmhouse out in Kisserup. The rafters under the ceiling, the doorways that Klaus had to duck his head to get through.

How many had there been in the house that night?

Feeling weak in the knees, she dragged herself over to a boulder at the end of the street and sat down.

The images kept popping up. She knew she should be focusing on the missing boy, because there was nothing she wanted more than to see Jane reunited with her son.

The smartest thing by far to do right now was to take the train back to the city. To Eik.

She snatched up her bag and was about to loop it over her shoulder when she realized that all this wasn't about her sorrow and shattered emotions. An anger was building up inside her, so black that she had to do something about it.

She made her decision. She would find Jane's son, but if anyone had been involved in Klaus's death, she would find them, too.

12

Camilla turned onto Skovvej and immediately slowed down. Even at this distance, she recognized her friend sitting on a boulder, her long, black hair whipping in the wind.

"It's so good to see you again!" she said when Louise got in the car. "Can you spend the night with us?"

Camilla had been surprised when her friend had called, wanting to know if she could pick her up in Hvalsø. Frederik had gone to Copenhagen—he was bringing dinner back—and she had just sat down to work on an article due the next day.

She had covered a pony show at the Roskilde Riding Club that weekend. Her former editor at *Morgenavisen*, Terkel Høyer, would die laughing if he knew what she was writing about as a freelancer. And when Louise called, she decided that the piece wouldn't suffer one bit if she waited until early the next morning to write it.

She turned the car around in a neatly kept driveway to head back to Roskilde.

"Would you mind driving me to Holbæk?" Louise asked.

"Holbæk! What on earth for?"

"I need to stop by the jail."

"The jail! Why?" She drove down the main street and under the viaduct. Louise didn't answer.

"An interrogation?" Camilla asked. Still no answer. She was used to this; she had covered crime for *Morgenavisen* while Louise had been in Homicide. Some things they couldn't talk about.

But Louise turned to her and told her about visiting Klaus's parents and what René had said to her at the gamekeeper's.

"Honestly, Louise!" Camilla said. "He might have just been throwing that out at you."

She was dismayed that her friend had told all that to Klaus's parents without knowing whether it was true or not. It also hurt that Louise had clammed up after the episode at the gamekeeper's, only now telling her what had happened.

"I don't think so," Louise said, her voice small.

"He might've wanted to hurt you." Something in her friend's voice made Camilla want to put an arm around her shoulder. She glanced over at her, but Louise kept staring down at her phone.

"Can you even get in to see him at this time of day?" Camilla wondered if the assault had thrown her friend's thinking out of whack.

"Mik gave me the green light to talk to him about a

boy who's been missing for a while. He's been hiding in your forest, as a matter of fact."

"What in the world does he have to do with a missing boy?" Suddenly she realized Louise must be talking about the boy she'd seen. She thought about his wet hair, how he'd run off.

"Nothing," Louise answered. "But the boy's father is visiting René tomorrow, so if I'm going to find out whether the family has problems, I need to talk to René now."

"And while you're at it, you'll pressure him to tell you what happened back then," Camilla said, nodding. This was more like the Louise she knew.

"I'm going to give it a shot," Louise admitted.

"What about this boy?" Camilla turned off the freeway. "How is this all connected with those men from Hvalsø?"

"It's the butcher's son. You don't seem all that surprised to hear that he's been hiding in your forest. Don't tell me you've seen him."

Camilla nodded. "But he ran off before I could talk to him. Is he mixed up in something?"

Louise shook her head. "I don't think so, but he might be emotionally unstable. His mother is dying; he's had a difficult time handling that. He's been very unhappy for a long time. Anyway, he ran off. How did he seem to you?"

Camilla tried to recall how the lanky boy looked. "Pretty ragged, I'd say. It was raining and he was obviously cold. I thought something was wrong. I even thought about calling the police in Roskilde, but then I got distracted by what happened with all that blood."

"Blood?"

"It was so gross. I took off after the boy to ask him why he was running away, then I fell and got covered in blood, head-to-toe. Frederik says it's something to do with the Asatro, the sacrifices to the gods they make out in the forest."

She glanced over and saw a smile on Louise's lips. "Don't sit there laughing at me. I thought it was an animal they'd shot. It was just so disgusting."

"When did this happen?"

"A few days ago."

Camilla remembered her wet jogging clothes, still in the plastic sack. She should probably throw them away.

They drove past the train station. "Where do you want me to let you off?"

"In front of the police station is fine. Mik's coming down to meet me."

"I can wait for you. I just need to tell Frederik if you'll stay and eat."

Louise opened the car door. "Thanks, but I have to get back to Copenhagen. I hope I haven't ruined too much of your day."

"Of course you haven't," Camilla replied at once.

"Can you give me a description of the boy?" Louise asked, out on the sidewalk now.

Camilla thought for a second. "Light hair, maybe on the brownish side. A bit awkward, I think. Thin. But I didn't see him up close. Straight hair; he needed a haircut. Jeans and a dark T-shirt. I don't know if it was black or dark blue, but something was printed on the front."

"That sounds like him," Louise said, nodding. She

turned when she heard Mik calling out to them from the doorway. "Thank you so much for the lift, Camilla. Talk to you later. I'll call this weekend."

"Driving Miss Daisy. Just let me know when you need a chauffeur." Camilla waved good-bye.

She watched her friend cross the street and walk into the police station. Something in Louise's voice had made her uneasy. A hint of anger. Fear, maybe.

13

"Do you want me to follow you over to the jail?" Mik asked.

Louise had been hungry in the car, but now her stomach was doing somersaults at the thought of meeting René Gamst. She hadn't seen him since his arrest. "No thanks, I'm fine. Just so they know I'm coming."

She let him hug her, but she couldn't tell whether it felt nice or not. She felt safe with Mik. Once he had wanted to take care of her, and even though everything else between them had disappeared, that seemed to still be there.

"Why won't you let me grill him about the boy's relationship to his parents?" he asked, his voice serious. "You're so hard on yourself when you don't need to be. You don't have to be the one who goes in there."

"It's my case," she said. "I do my own interrogations."

She looked away; she hadn't needed to say it that way. "Thanks, Mik. It's sweet of you. But I'll be okay."

"I'll be waiting in my office," he said. He waved his phone in the air. "Just call."

"You really don't need to wait."

She knew that he'd begun dating a nurse named Lone. Jonas had told her; Mik and her foster son were still close. Mik had given him the deaf Labrador, much to Louise's dismay, and he and Jonas talked together at least once a week under the guise of Mik wanting to hear about Dina. But from what Louise could hear, the conversations were just as much about Jonas and how he was doing. And now that Louise accepted the fact that Mik had dropped her because of her indifference, she was enormously grateful for his contact with her boy. Jonas didn't have anybody besides her and Melvin to talk to about homework, music, and girls.

She took Mik's hand and gave it a squeeze before heading for the jail.

Holbæk Jail had twenty-three cells. René Gamst was awaiting his sentence, but no one knew when it would be handed down. Only then would he be transferred to a prison.

Louise felt self-conscious, as if she were a caricature, when she straightened up before walking in to show her ID. It was seven thirty. A TV blared somewhere, but no one was around. She knew she had to steel herself, otherwise she would be far too vulnerable when René entered the interrogation room.

"Sign here first," the guard said when she began walking past the visitation rooms. Beds, chairs, and condoms.

"Of course," she said, and turned to sign her name and time of arrival. "Is he in there?" She nodded toward a room at the end of the hall.

"No, I'll get him," the young guard said. "But it's open; you can go on in."

He ducked through a doorway at the back of the office, and Louise walked to the interrogation room and closed the door. A table and two chairs. That was it. White light blazed from the long fluorescent in the ceiling; the window was hidden behind venetian blinds.

The lighting reminded her of the barn at the gamekeeper's. She couldn't stop it—suddenly she was back at the assault. She felt the rough hands on her naked body, the pain from broken ribs. And when she pulled the chair out from the table, she heard the heavy breathing that had wheezed like bellows on her neck. That was when René Gamst had entered the barn. At first he was nothing more than a silhouette approaching, but then she recognized him as he stood a few meters behind them, holding a shotgun.

Relief streamed through her when she made eye contact with him, but then he glared at her exposed genitals. She saw the bulge in his pants. He could have stopped it right there, but he'd waited, which had made her humiliation complete.

Louise closed her eyes and composed herself when she heard footsteps in the hallway outside. She blinked rapidly to erase the image of René's eyes on her naked body. She straightened up in her chair and rested her arms on the table, while finding an expression to mask the chaos inside her.

René Gamst was astonished to see her. Then his face relaxed, and he stared at her without a word.

Louise wanted so much to stare back, but she couldn't. She concentrated on her folded hands resting on the table as fear slammed into her gut. The fear of not being able to go through with this; that she would have to leave without talking to him.

Gamst sat down on the other side of the table and crossed his arms on his chest. Neither of them spoke. She looked up at him, noticed his confident, superior attitude. Thoughts about the janitor from Såby and Gudrun at the convenience store ran through her head. She gave a start when he broke the silence.

"You're welcome." His voice was hoarse.

Something in his eyes made it clear that he remembered what he'd seen in the barn that night.

"For what?" she asked, without thinking.

"Aren't you here to thank me for shooting that bastard?" He looked down at her breasts. "They said my lawyer didn't need to be here because this wasn't going to be about my case."

"Excuse me, but do you really expect me to thank you?"

He grinned, obviously enjoying this. He tilted his head. "Sure, don't you think you should?"

"You are one of the biggest fucking assholes I've ever met. You made sure you got a good look at everything before you shot. And you didn't shoot to save me."

Rage boiled up inside her; suddenly she felt in control.

"You shot him because he'd raped your wife. It was revenge."

He stopped smiling, though he didn't look particularly ruffled. He shrugged and asked her for a cigarette.

Louise shook her head. Had she been interrogating anyone else, she might have had cigarettes and coffee on hand to help get things going. But Gamst wasn't just another prisoner, and she had no interest in getting friendly with him. She simply wanted a few answers.

"What did all of you do to him?" She stared into his brown eyes.

"To who? What the hell are you talking about?"

"What did you do to Klaus? Back then out at our house?"

Gamst's smile returned. First as an arrogant shadow in his expression, then to his lips. "Aren't you on the police force? Aren't you the ones who are supposed to figure these things out?"

Her rage felt like armor; there was no way he could humiliate her now. She would make him talk. "What happened out there?"

"What happened? What happened! Who said anything happened?"

"You did. You're the one who said that Klaus didn't put the noose around his neck."

"He was a pussy! He was scared of his own shadow."

She startled him by slapping her palms on the table, leaping to her feet, and leaning over the table. "Goddamn you. Tell me what happened!"

"Why should I?" He seemed like he was trying to appear unaffected by her outburst.

"All right then. If you're not going to say anything, I'll pay a visit to your wife and pump her for every last secret in your miserable, shitty little lives."

His shoulders tensed up at the mention of Bitten. Now she had his attention. He leaned back in his chair but didn't answer her.

Louise paused a moment before changing directions. "How's the butcher's relationship with his son? How are they getting along?"

"Why the hell are you asking me that?" Finally, he looked a bit flustered.

"Because I want to know. Are they having marital problems?"

"Not that I know of," he said.

Was he telling the truth? His eyes darted off to the side before he answered. She knew that the rule about linking truth with looking one way and lies with the other was shaky, but he did glance away.

"So. There aren't any problems. Except that the mother is dying, of course," she added sarcastically.

"Why are you asking me about this?" He couldn't hide his curiosity, even though he tried to sound indifferent, which she also noticed. He clearly didn't know the boy had disappeared.

"You don't know anything about any other problems?"

Quickly he shook his head. He looked confident again.

"Fine. I'll ask Bitten about that, too. I'm sure she'll tell me if the father and son aren't getting along. I might need to use some pressure, but then I can mention her affair with Thomsen. She doesn't like talking about that."

She walked over and rang for the guard.

"You better fucking leave my wife alone," she heard from behind.

Louise sensed he was standing up now. She calmly turned around and leaned back against the door.

"And if I don't?" She enjoyed watching Gamst fumble around for words.

"Just leave her alone!"

"Then start talking! Tell me what happened back then."

He didn't answer.

The door opened behind her. "Tell me what happened," she said, calm now.

When he still didn't answer her, she turned and walked out.

After the guard closed the door, Louise slammed her fist into the wall. An overwhelming fatigue hit her as she walked away; for a moment she thought she was going to fall. The guard noted the time of the interview's conclusion and she signed out, angry as well as exhausted.

Yet she felt that even though he hadn't talked, she'd won the first round. It hadn't been pretty, but she'd emerged victorious.

14

Camilla stuffed everything down into a large IKEA sack. The blanket, the water bottle, a Ronson storm lighter she'd swiped from Frederik. The bag with sweet chocolate biscuits, rye bread, liver pâté, a half liter of cola, a large chocolate bar, and a Danish salami. She had also been in Markus's room and robbed his stash of candy, plus a warm sweater she'd found in the bottom of his closet.

A little bit of this and that, maybe not the most vital necessities for survival out in nature, Camilla thought as she entered the forest with the sack over her shoulder. It might not be the wisest thing to do, helping a runaway boy stay away from home. On the other hand, she couldn't stand the thought that sorrow had driven him from his family. He may be sick at heart, but she was determined he wouldn't starve. She couldn't get the image out of her head of the sopping-wet boy sitting on the ground, wolfing down cold leftovers.

Farther down the broad forest path, she peered around. She had no idea where to look for him, so she decided to start from where she'd seen him. By the big oak.

The evening sun sat just above the treetops; the heat of the day had disappeared. She stopped to check where to leave the path. There hadn't been another path; she'd simply run after him. Suddenly she was unsure. The shadows made it difficult to recognize anything.

Camilla lifted the IKEA sack and continued on. She thought about Louise, then realized that she'd forgotten to bring her phone along. She would have to wait to call and ask how it had gone.

The path veered off to the left. She stopped again; she was sure that she'd gone too far. Irritated at herself, she retraced her steps and left the path. Immediately the big sack caught on a limb. She jerked to free it, and the limb whipped back against her shoulder. "Damn it!" she yelled. She pushed through the trees, one arm in front of her now, and yelped in fright when she almost stumbled over someone sitting on the ground. She dropped the sack and leaned against a tree trunk for a moment.

"Sorry," she said. "You startled me!"

The dark-haired woman below her wore a long, brown linen dress. A blue embroidered shawl hung around her shoulders and down her back, held together by a bronze clasp.

"Don't be afraid," the woman said, her voice calm. "I should have warned you, but at first I thought you were an animal, and I didn't want to frighten it away."

"What are you doing?" Camilla asked. A small parcel wrapped in aluminum foil and a long stick lay in front of the woman, a rolled-out sleeping bag behind. She'd brought along a thermos in a woven basket.

"I'm preparing my night sitting," the woman said.

Camilla guessed she was in her mid-fifties. Her hair was short and her eyes sparkled. She invited Camilla to sit down with her.

"What on earth is a night sitting?" Then she understood. "Are you one of the Asatro?"

The woman nodded and reached for her thermos. "And you are the new lady at the manor, I'm guessing."

Camilla sat down in front of her. "'Manor' is probably an exaggeration, but yes. We've taken over Ingersminde from my husband's parents."

For a moment the woman stared blankly out into the trees. "I've been coming out here for eighteen years now." She looked around as if they were sitting in her living room. "I live over in the lockhouse. It's the little yellow house on the way to Roskilde. Just ask if you want to know where to pick wild strawberries or find chanterelles."

The woman smiled. "I've been a member of the local Asatro for many years now. We meet out here twice a month. The evil has returned."

Camilla sat quietly. She wondered if the woman might be a little bit crazy. It wasn't so much what she said as her hoarse, foggy voice, which sent chills down Camilla's spine. They weren't very far from St. Hans Psychiatric Hospital. She could have escaped.

Then the woman seemed to return to the present. "I'm

sorry. I just thought I heard something." She offered Camilla a cup of warm mead.

"So what does your group do out here in the forest?" Camilla asked. She held on to the clay mug, which had a small foot.

"We pay tribute to the forces of nature," the woman said. She smiled again and raised her mug to the sky. "And we make sacrifices to the gods."

She slurped a bit as she drank. Then she carefully laid the mug down in a small depression in the ground.

"What happens?" Camilla asked.

"You have to sacrifice something to the gods if you want their help. Or if you have need of strength. It can be anything. Do you never pray to God?"

Camilla shrugged. Did she? "I do," she said, and nodded. "When there's something I really want, or if there's something I'm very upset about." It was true—she did in fact send up a prayer once in a while.

"Then you understand," the woman said. "The only difference is that we bring along a little gift that we set out here with our prayers."

"What sort of gift?" Camilla was thinking about the pool of blood.

"A silver coin, for example." She reached into her pocket and brought a few coins out. "Or home-brewed mead."

"What about blood?"

The woman nodded seriously. "It can be blood, too," she admitted. "The most powerful sacrifice you can make is your own blood."

Camilla felt the silence of the forest creeping in on

them. Several moments later she asked, "You said the evil had returned. What do you mean?"

The woman looked out through the trees again. Her shoulders sank. "In the old days, the priests used to drive a wagon around with a naked woman, to guarantee the fertility in the area."

She pulled her shawl tighter and spoke in a near-whisper. "Now they bring women out here to celebrate their own fertility."

"Who does? Surely not the priests!"

The woman shook her head. "The others."

Camilla raised an eyebrow.

"Once, we were one large group of Asatro that met out here in the forest. But after we became an official religion, we began disagreeing about what we stood for, how we should practice our beliefs."

Camilla nodded, urging her to go on.

"One small group in our community was expelled; their beliefs had become unhealthy." She sounded ashamed that anyone who believed in the Nordic gods could behave in such a manner. "They worshiped Loke and glorified evil. They violated what we consider holy by taking it to extremes, using our beliefs as an excuse for their primitive and bestial behaviors."

She shivered as if she were suddenly freezing.

"What sort of behaviors?" Camilla asked.

"They make every effort to replicate the old stories in Nordic mythology. They take the rituals very literally."

Camilla was about to pour the warm mead out on the ground when the woman called out. "Wait!"

She jerked her hand back. "What?"

"Remember to warn the wights before you pour any-thing hot out onto the ground. They like a sip of beer or something to eat, but you mustn't scald them."

"The wights?"

"The small folk. We have to take good care of them. They make sure nature flourishes. They protect it. You must also remember to ask permission before you pick a flower." She pointed out at the forest floor.

Hello, St. Hans Hospital, Camilla thought. She stood up, wanting to leave before she disturbed the forest. "Is that the way to the sacrificial oak?" She pointed.

The woman nodded and immediately closed her eyes. She appeared to have retreated into herself.

Twilight had deepened, shadows lengthened, and now it was impossible to make out anything in the trees.

Camilla continued toward the clearing, which lay a bit farther ahead. She didn't know what to think about the woman. Apart from nearly scaring Camilla to death, Camilla didn't think she would hurt a fly. Sitting out in the forest all night in communion with nature, to receive signs from the old Nordic gods, was hard to take seri-ously. But that was her business. Camilla stepped into the clearing and walked to the partly hollow tree.

She thought she heard a car, but when she stopped to listen, all she heard was the forest silence. The birds were quiet now, and the breeze had died down. She lay the blue sack on the ground. She thought about taking some things out so the boy could spot them from a distance, but the sky looked threatening. If it rained, a wet blanket would do him no good. Instead she wrapped two elastic cords around the sack to close it tightly, hoping he would be curious enough to look inside.

Maybe she should have written a note to him, she thought as she returned to the path she guessed would lead her back to the house.

Thoughts about the boy and the Asatro flitted around in her head. She came to a forest road she thought she recognized. A few meters down the road, she stopped. She heard the motor and spotted the headlights at about the same time: A car was approaching from farther in the forest. For a moment she was frightened, until she realized it had to be Frederik, out looking for her. She should have been back long ago. He teased her constantly about being the only person he knew who could get lost in a closet.

The headlights were close now, the engine growling. She waited. The car appeared from behind a rise and rolled silently down the road in neutral. She started waving.

The driver put it in gear and floored it, and a moment later Camilla was blinded by the headlights. She waved again even though it was less than fifty meters away, but instead of slowing down the car shot out, a dark shadow behind the twin lights.

"WHAT THE HELL—"

The car rammed into her and flung her off the road. Everything went black.

15

Sune hid behind the tree stump when the dark-haired woman with the basket and sleeping bag under her arm appeared in the clearing. For a moment he prayed that she had come to make a new moon sacrifice; his stomach began cramping up at the thought of the leftovers. But she walked by the bonfire site and back into the forest. It was twilight, so he didn't dare follow her.

He was so hungry that sometimes it felt like worms were crawling in his guts, robbing him of vitamins, minerals, all nutrition. He'd just been down to the creek to drink. He missed being able to gulp down a whole glass of water. It wasn't the same, scooping it up and drinking out of his hands. He'd tried sucking water up directly from the surface of the stream, but other stuff streamed into his mouth that he had to spit out constantly.

Just then a deer walked into the clearing, close enough

for him to make out the three-pointed white markings on its chest. He loved the thought of being at one with nature; he recalled the old myths about the boy who was sent out into the forest to live with his father...

But *his* father wasn't here. He was alone.

At first he imagined the animal had smelled him when it whirled around and sprang back into the forest. Then he saw the blond woman, the one who had tried to catch him when he was eating the leftovers from the last Asatro sacrifice.

She walked over to the sacrificial oak, slipped a big sack off her shoulder, and dropped it where he'd been sitting the first time he saw her. She stood around awhile as if waiting for something. He held his breath when she appeared to be staring directly at him, but then she strode off, leaving the sack behind.

Who is she? he wondered when his heartbeat returned to normal.

He waited until darkness fell to step out of hiding. He stood a few moments before sneaking over to the tree. He was in arm's reach of the sack when he heard the car; it was close, very close. He ducked into some bushes, and instantly his clothes were soaked from the evening dew covering the long, thin leaves. He kept his face down while the car drove slowly by on the forest road. It stopped. A car door opened.

Sune pressed himself even closer to the ground and lay perfectly still. A snail crawled up onto his hand. The door slammed again, and they took off. He got up on his elbows and crawled over to the big tree and the sack on the ground.

Suddenly they were back, their flashlights searching around and between the trees. If they walked into the clearing, they would find the sack she'd left.

They came looking for him almost every night. Never in the daytime, when someone might see them. Sune knew he couldn't keep hiding here forever, but he had nowhere else to go.

He missed his mother so badly that once in a while it overshadowed his hunger. He missed the evenings sitting with her in the living room, reading. Not saying a word. Just being together. But that was before her illness. Back then, she had taken care of the housework, reminded him of where and when he had to be somewhere, checked his homework. Everything.

It wasn't like that anymore.

He couldn't know if she still lay in bed with all the extra pillows. He wasn't even sure she was still alive. He could barely swallow the lump in his throat when he thought about it. When he curled up inside the tree and tried to fall asleep, he prayed to the gods. Prayed that she knew why he had to keep hiding. If she was aware of everything that had gone on out here, he was sure she would understand.

He wasn't afraid anymore to be confronted by what had happened. He didn't mind being held responsible, either, even though he had nothing to do with the girl's death. He knew he would have to pay; if you broke an oath, you would be held responsible. The others would turn against him. All of them.

The headlights disappeared and the darkness returned. The only thing visible was the clearing, where the silvery new moon cast a ghostly, surreal luminescence over the sacrificial oak. It looked like a giant rising up from the forest floor. Sune thought about Odin, the god who had hanged himself from Yggdrasil, the world tree, and had hung there for nine days to gather his strength.

He kept crawling toward the sack.

What was the blonde up to? He realized it could be a trap. Could she be in cahoots with them? But his stomach was screaming. He was driven by a hunger growing out of control.

He heard the car's engine again, though farther away now. It revved up, the sound split the forest silence, and he decided to go for the sack. He ran as fast as he could, grabbed the sack, and ducked back into the bushes. Then he heard tires whining and a sound like an animal crying out, followed by a thunk. He thought about the deer with the markings on its chest.

The silence returned. He held the sack close to his body, which covered up his rapid breathing.

Far off through the trees, the headlights glared and moved away from him. Soon it was dark again. He groped his way back to the tree stump and knelt in a small pool of clear moonlight.

His fingers were stiff, but he managed to tear off the paper around the roll of sweet biscuits. He stuffed them greedily in his mouth, the crumbs flying. He felt around for the blanket with his other hand, then carefully pulled it out of the sack.

After wrapping himself up in the warm wool, he leaned back against the tree stump and sorted through the rest of what was in the sack.

16

Louise's phone alarm startled her. She stared confusedly at the dark-gray ceiling for a moment before realizing she was in her childhood bedroom, in Lerbjerg. Slowly, everything came back to her.

She had taken the train from Holbæk after the meeting with René Gamst. Exhaustion had won out over anger as she walked to the station and sat down in the Copenhagen train, but when they reached Vipperød she called her father and asked him to pick her up at Hvalsø station. She wasn't ready to go home just yet. First she had to stop by the Starling House and talk to René's wife.

Louise swung her legs off the bed and sat a moment. She'd told her parents that Jonas was staying with a friend; that it was convenient for her to stay there because she had an interrogation in the area the next morning. She took a quick shower and hoped that Bitten hadn't already left to drop her daughter off. René's wife worked for Hvalsø Kommune, the local government.

She finished her shower at twenty past eight, and soon after wrestled her mother's green bicycle out of the old horse stall and pedaled angrily into the forest, thinking about René's scornful words.

Camilla could be right: He might have wanted to hurt her. At least that could be part of it. But Klaus's parents didn't believe he'd committed suicide, either. And others had to be punished if it turned out they were involved.

Louise hopped off the bicycle and leaned it against a tree. She walked down an uneven stone pathway to the old forest ranger's house. Hollyhocks lined an outer wall with small-paned windows, their tops leaning over toward the thatched roof's overhang. She knocked on the stable door and glanced around but saw no sign of anyone apart from the pink child's bike lying on the lawn.

She knocked again and stepped back. She heard a noise inside the house, then Bitten opened the door and stared at her in obvious surprise. She was wearing one bath towel and drying her hair with another.

"Yes?" she said. She seemed uneasy about her unannounced morning visitor.

"I'd like to talk to you for a few moments," Louise said.

The last time they had spoken together, a sort of confidentiality had arisen between them. But of course that was before Louise put her husband behind bars.

"This isn't such a good time," Bitten said, but Louise was already halfway in the hallway. She pushed Bitten into the living room. Before they reached the sofa, she noticed a dark shadow in the bathroom doorway. Big Thomsen stepped out. He had just taken a shower; a small pool of water formed at his feet while he wrapped himself in a dark-blue bathrobe.

Louise guessed that Thomsen had appropriated René's robe, seeing that it barely covered his stomach and stretched tightly across the shoulders.

"What do you want?" he asked. He stood behind Bitten, acting as if he were master of the house.

"I just want to hear how Bitten is doing," Louise ad-libbed.

"She's doing just great," he said. He grabbed Bitten's narrow hips, pulled her back, and began grinding against her ass. He stared into Louise's eyes. "I'm making sure she don't get lonely."

René's wife turned pale. Her eyes darted over the furniture and the complete mess in the living room.

Louise followed her eyes and noticed several things that hadn't been there before. An overnight bag beside the woodstove, a large, wide leather chair with footstool, an enormous flat-screen television.

So. Big Thomsen had moved in and taken over Gamst's wife while he sat in Holbæk Jail. For a moment she stared at Bitten, trying to get a read on her thoughts.

"It won't bother me one bit, you talking to her while I'm here," Thomsen said. He walked over to the coffee table and picked up his iPhone. "But you can see for yourself that she's fine."

Bitten said nothing, her eyes glued to the floor.

Louise ignored Thomsen and kept watching her in the hope she would look up. She couldn't believe that René's wife had voluntarily allowed Big Thomsen to move in. On the other hand, it seemed as if she were resigned to the situation. But surely she had something to say. She knew Bitten had been having an ongoing affair with her husband's friend, but it was her impression that the woman had been pressured into it, that Thomsen otherwise would have fired Gamst.

Thomsen worked for the Bistrup Forestry District besides owning three semis. Gamst drove for him. Louise had once asked Bitten why Thomsen even bothered working for the district. She'd explained that he just loafed around in the forest; he made his living from the trucks but was too lazy to drive long distances.

"Call me sometime today, okay?" she said. She headed for the door when Bitten didn't answer.

"Why the hell should she?" Big Thomsen snapped at her. "Nobody here owes you a thing."

"I've heard enough out of you." Louise whirled around and glared at him. "Bitten can answer for herself."

"You keep your nose out of our business," he sneered.

Bitten's expression was blank, her arms hanging limply at her sides.

"No!" Louise spat out. "There is no 'our' business. I will have nothing to do with you. You will not interfere with my work and you will stay out of my investigations. I couldn't care less what strings you pull or who you try to shut up."

She slammed the stall door and stood under the trees to calm herself. She breathed the morning air deep into her lungs. Damn it, she thought. She'd lost her temper.

Not that she regretted it, but she'd just made things a little more difficult for herself. Especially if Thomsen started asking about this investigation he was supposed to stay out of. Her chances of asking Bitten about Sune, about why he was hiding in the forest, had also taken a hit.

The morning sunlight poured in from above the tree-tops. Louise was certain that Thomsen stood inside watching her, if he wasn't already calling around on his phone.

She pedaled away, but her legs felt heavy, as if they held all her animosity toward him. She rode behind a mountain of firewood and stopped, leaned against the wood, and closed her eyes.

What the hell had happened to Bitten? She was thirty-one, with a young daughter. Despite that, she didn't seem to realize she had the right to say no. Or was it Louise who didn't get it?

What was going on around here? Not just with Bitten. Everyone seemed mixed up in something or with some-body, and Louise couldn't connect the dots, didn't under-stand the games they were playing. But even if she had to show up at Bitten's job, she was going to pressure her and find out if there were problems between the butcher and his son. And if René's wife knew anything about Klaus's death, she would get that out of her, too.

Louise put Thomsen out of her mind and checked her phone to see how late she would be. She'd better call Eik, she thought. It annoyed her that he still considered a text to be something the devil thought up. If you needed him, you had to call.

Three messages. Two were from Jonas who, being the

responsible boy he was, had gone home to be with Dina instead of sleeping at his friend's, after Louise told him she was staying in Hvalsø. He'd walked the dog and was on his way to school now.

That warmed Louise's heart. She missed him. Overnight, it seemed, he'd grown up into a mature teen. She knew it wouldn't be long before parties and friends began to pull at him more strongly than the yellow Labrador, whom he'd taken good care of as he'd promised.

The last message came from a number Louise didn't have on her phone. *C was hit by a car, call. Frederik.*

17

"The asshole meant to hit me," Camilla told Frederik again, in the car on the way home.

The X-rays had taken an eternity, and it had been the wee hours of the morning before the doctor finally examined her. Only then had he decided to keep her under observation for a day, to make sure she hadn't sustained a concussion.

Camilla's entire body had hurt too much for her to complain about waiting. Everyone in the emergency room had been in the same boat. Several slept on hard chairs, and a mother had left despite her son's considerable pain from a fall on his trick two-wheeler scooter. She'd sat straight in her chair and waited patiently for eight hours as blood soaked through the tall teenager's pants at the knees and tears ran down his acne-covered cheeks.

The emergency room nurse had walked around with her eyes on the gray linoleum floor, avoiding contact with the many people waiting. "These poor people," Frederik had said, after trying several times to get someone to help. "My wife was rushed here in an ambulance and still no one has time to look at her. HEY! ANYONE HERE?"

But nothing happened, apart from an elderly lady with a scarf tied neatly around her head, who looked up from her magazine and said her husband had fallen down the stairs at the train station.

It had to be tough, working here every day under this kind of pressure, Camilla thought, when the doctor sent Frederik home and told him to come back for her the next day. They had waited for the doctor all morning, with compelling reasons to protest cuts in the national health care system going through her head.

"We can't know he ran you down on purpose," Frederik said. Without saying it directly, he was critical of her for not having reflectors on her bicycle. That, of course, annoyed Camilla even more.

"Oh we can't, can we? Well, I can. I can goddamn tell when a driver turns his brights on right in my eyes. I was standing in the middle of the road. It wasn't like it was dark when he sped up to hit me!"

Frederik nodded while concentrating on traffic. "Whether he tried to hit you or not, there's no doubt he was driving way too fast," he said. "And we don't allow unauthorized vehicles. But right now, I'm just relieved you weren't hurt worse."

Camilla cooled down. She knew he was right. The doctor had said it was a miracle her injuries weren't severe. He'd added that the next few days she would probably feel like she'd gone twelve rounds in a heavyweight fight. But no bones were broken. Her black-and-blue eye looked bad. The doctor thought she must have hit a tree trunk after being flung into the air. The right side of her face was swollen, closing up her eye. Camilla had been shocked when the nurse handed her a mirror.

"Tønnesen went out and put the chains up so nobody can drive into the forest now. Once in a while, someone ignores the signs and drives down to the creek. But this happened on one of the small roads, and I'm thinking we may have a poacher. What did the car look like?"

Camilla thought for a few moments, then shook her head. "It was bigger than most cars, but I don't know if it was a van or a four-wheel-drive. It came at me like a big, black shadow."

That's all Camilla could remember. She had no idea how long she had been on the ground. Didn't know whether it was Frederik's voice or the ambulance's siren she'd heard first. Her entire world had consisted of pain. She'd cried when they lifted her up on the stretcher.

"By the way, how did you find me?" she asked Frederik.

"I didn't. It was Elinor. She came up to the house and demanded I follow her. I didn't realize until I got out there that there'd been an accident."

In her head Camilla saw the old lady with the long gray braids. She shuddered.

She put her hand on Frederik's thigh and moaned loudly when they took a sharp right just after the Viking Ship Museum. "It was a good thing you went with her," she said. She asked if he'd spoken with Louise.

"She and Eik have already looked around out there. They went back to their office, but she insisted on coming out to stay the weekend. She just had to pick up Jonas and the dog."

Camilla nodded. She was happy that her friend had investigated the scene instead of showing up at the hospital with flowers and chocolate. "And Eik! What about him? Is he coming, too?"

She couldn't figure out if Louise still had something going with her colleague. Camilla liked him, a lot. Louise and Eik as a couple—that she hadn't seen coming, but they got along very well. Though Louise hadn't mentioned him since that night at the gamekeeper's. Maybe it was a good idea to get him back in the picture, now that so much from Louise's past was flaring up again.

"Anyway, I'll call and ask," she said.

"Shouldn't you maybe—" Frederik began, but Camilla had already called the National Police Department and asked to speak to the Search Department.

"Eik sounded happy for the invitation," she said a few moments later. "He'll see if they can't take off early. What about Markus?" They turned into their driveway. "Is he home this weekend?"

"I don't really know," Frederik said. He shrugged.

Lately it was as if someone had stuck a rocket up Markus's rear end. Her fifteen-year-old son was out constantly with his friends, and on the rare occasions he was

112

home, he lay around on his bed wrapped up in Facebook while his TV blasted away. It was more or less impossible to come into contact with him. At least for her.

They drove up to the house. Camilla swung her legs out of the car. "Oh shit," she moaned.

Frederik came around and pulled her up. Unable to stand straight, she hobbled slowly toward the house.

"We better get you in bed," he said. Despite her weak protests, he carried her up the broad steps to the front door. "If you take a few of the pills the doctor gave you and rest awhile, maybe you'll feel better when Louise comes."

Camilla relented; it was too painful to walk anyway. Frederik carried her to their second-floor bedroom. He helped her out of her clothes and tucked her into bed. He sat for a while, stroking her cheek. Then he fetched a glass of water and handed it to her.

"Thanks," she whispered, and kissed him. His longish hair fell over her face, his stubble tickling her chin.

She swallowed the pills and nodded when he said he would check on her later.

18

Sleep, pain, awake. Sleep, pain, awake. Short sequences of each state wove in and out of each other.

Camilla's head spun as she lay with her eyes closed, waiting for the pills to work. Maybe she'd dozed off, she wasn't sure, but suddenly she sensed someone standing beside the bed.

She opened her eyes to a wrinkled face staring down at her. It was the old woman from the forest.

"The wagons are rolling on the Death Trail," she said with the same weird little-girl voice that had nearly scared Camilla to death down by the creek.

She froze, so frightened that she almost began whimpering. She stared back at the narrow mouth mumbling the same message again and again. Finally the old woman backed away, but instead of leaving, she walked over to the window and the small dent in the wall next to where Camilla had placed her large wardrobe.

Camilla realized she was holding her breath; she let it out slowly. Her heart was pounding. She stared in shock at the bowed back of the woman, then threw her comforter off to the side and, despite her pain, hopped out of the door in her short T-shirt and panties. She made it down to the kitchen and plopped onto a chair before finally moaning loudly.

Frederik must have heard her staggering around, because he came to the doorway looking very worried. "Couldn't you sleep?"

"She's up in the bedroom," she managed to say. She hunched her shoulders. "How did she get in?"

"Who? What are you talking about?" He walked over and put his arms around her. Camilla knew that he thought she'd been dreaming.

"The old woman from the forest. She's up in our bedroom!"

"Elinor?" Frederik didn't seem all that surprised. "Oh no! Not again."

"What the hell do you mean, 'again'?"

"Are you cold?"

Frederik was already on his way to the living room. He came back with a blanket and covered her with it.

"What do you mean, 'again'?" Camilla repeated. She pulled the blanket tight.

"Elinor lived here back when it was a home for girls," he said. "Mom said she couldn't have been more than two years old when she came. Sometimes she forgets she lives in the gatekeeper's house now. She's harmless, and besides, she's part of the history of the place. It's nice when she shows up, too."

Camilla didn't totally agree with that last part.

"I'll call Tønnesen," he said. "He can follow her home."

Camilla drew the blanket around her again and closed her eyes while he talked to the manager.

"She kept saying that the wagons are rolling on the Death Trail," she said when he came back. "What does she mean?"

Frederik shrugged. "No idea, but it's what they call the path here from the house down to the girls' graves, and then on to the sacrificial oak. It's always been called that."

"Girls' graves?" Camilla sat up in her chair, but Frederik was on his way upstairs to get Elinor.

The front door opened, and Camilla was about to call out to Tønnesen when she heard dog feet galloping over the tiles in the hallway. A second later two dog snouts were sniffing her legs.

"What in the world, whose mutt is this with my favorite dog?" she cried out. She tried to cover her legs with the blanket before the big German shepherd slobbered all over them.

"Get that dog out of here," she heard Louise say. Someone whistled, and the dog turned and ran out of the kitchen with Dina on his tail. Her friend appeared in the doorway.

Louise looked as if she was about to say something about her face, but she held back at the last second and instead mumbled, "Jesus." She hugged Camilla very carefully. "It's going to be a while before you run your next marathon."

"It's not so bad, really," she said. But her friend was

right. The pressure on her eye was excruciating, and water kept running out of it.

Louise stroked her hair. "The car must have hit you at a relatively high speed. I called the hospital, and they told me that you'd been knocked several meters from the impact."

"You've talked to them?" Camilla tried to smile, even though it felt like she was grimacing.

"Of course. I wanted to know what happened. Though I had to say it was in connection with a police investigation, otherwise they wouldn't have told me."

"Have you reported it?" Eik asked. He'd just come back inside. He sat down on a kitchen chair. "Louise and I were out in the forest, but we couldn't find anything except tire tracks where the driver definitely floored it."

Camilla nodded.

Frederik said something out on the stairway, then came into the kitchen with Elinor on his arm. Both Louise and Eik rose so she could sit.

But Elinor didn't want to sit down. She stood beside Camilla's chair, her lips moving as if she were talking to herself, her hands in the pockets of her loose summer jacket. She didn't look at anyone, she simply stood mumbling.

Camilla didn't know what to do. She had the strange feeling that the old woman was keeping an eye on her, and she didn't like it. She closed her eyes and rested her head on the back of the chair. Louise asked what the doctor had said before releasing her. Finally the pills began to work; her body tingled pleasantly as the pain subsided.

She tried to smile again when Tønnesen walked in and

caught sight of her face. Elinor livened up, and without so much as a glance at the others she took the manager's arm and walked outside with him.

Frederik smiled in resignation, then he shook Eik's hand before giving Louise a hug. "Where's Jonas?" He looked around.

"He's already upstairs," Louise said, nodding at the stairs and Markus's room. Camilla asked how their estate's manager had become the caretaker for the old crone.

"Elinor came here in 1922, back when the house was an orphanage for girls," Frederik said. "When the orphanage was shut down, the district wanted to move Elinor to a closed institution—they didn't have anywhere else to put her. But the old manager and his wife wouldn't hear of it. They took care of her until my grandparents bought the place several years later. They let Elinor live in the gatekeeper's house. Since then it's been one of the manager's duties to take care of her, and in fact I think Tønnesen enjoys it."

The woman must be over ninety, Camilla thought.

Frederik offered Eik and Louise a beer. "Or would you rather have coffee?" he asked from beside the refrigerator.

They both shook their heads, and Camilla nodded when he asked if she'd like some elderberry juice. "I don't think alcohol is the best thing for you," he said, smiling at her.

She felt better now that the pills were working, and wanted to hear more about Elinor and the history of the estate. They helped her to the sofa. "How much do you actually know about it from back then?" she asked.

"I have photos." Frederik walked over to the book-shelves and opened a drawer below. "My parents took over the estate in 1972, from my grandparents. They'd owned it since 1954, when the orphanage was shut down. My mother was very interested in the history of the place; once in a while she scared the daylights out of us with some of the stuff she dug up. I remember having night-mares for a whole week about the big tree in the front courtyard burning."

"Why?" Camilla asked. She'd never known her mother-in-law, Inger Sachs-Smith, who'd died shortly before she met Frederik.

"It's a warden tree," Frederik said, as if that explained everything.

"And what the hell is that?" She sat up and looked outside.

"It's also called a fire tree," he said. "According to su-perstition, the manor will burn down if you chop a limb off the tree or fell it. Mom thought that was fascinating; also the sacrificial oak."

He told Louise and Eik about the big partly hollow oak tree in the forest. "The tree is a sacred object that ap-pears in several of the old legends and myths from this area. The manager back then was very interested in the old tales, and he reinstated the old traditions. They be-came a part of the estate's history."

Eik was looking out the window at the yard. "Isn't there something about the warden trees, that you take a chunk of the timber frame from the house and graft it onto the tree?"

"Mom said that they removed a section of bark and

drilled a hole in the trunk of the tree, and it was filled with a plug from the timber frame," Frederik said. "Then they replaced the bark and it grew back. That was a hundred and twenty years ago, and I'm sure no one has touched a limb on that tree since. As far back as I can remember, there's been a lot of respect for it and the old superstition. When I was a kid I was afraid lightning would hit it, or something else would happen, something out of our control. I really believed that all hell would break loose!" He laughed.

Camilla leaned forward when he opened the old photo album. The manor was easy to recognize, majestic and white, though without nearly so many trees and bushes as now. The forest was visible, of course, but the area around the yard was much barer.

"Is that the Death Trail?" She pointed to a path in the photo that entered the forest on the manor's gable side.

Frederik nodded. "It was called that in the old days, because they used it to haul the dying down to the sacrificial oak on wagons. The director of the orphanage revived the old tradition. Back then, a lot of the young orphans were weak. They didn't make it. They're buried down there."

He pointed to the spot where the path vanished into the forest.

Camilla hunched her shoulders. Though all this had happened many years ago, the thought gave her the jitters.

"When a girl was dying, the director brought the wagon around, wrapped the sick girl up, and drove her down that path, past the graves, to the sacrificial oak. He made a sacrifice of the sick girl's blood so the gods would accept her when she passed away."

"Is that the director standing there?" Louise asked. She pointed to a man at the edge of the photo standing straight as an arrow.

Frederik nodded again.

In another photo he stood surrounded by girls in identical dresses. Obviously they had been dolled up for the photographer. It all looked so pompous, but the girls did have big smiles on their faces. One of them must be Elinor, Camilla thought.

"Right when Elinor moved here, one of the small girls became very sick," Frederik said. "The director laid her in the wagon and drove down to the sacrificial oak, where prayers were said for her. They held a vigil at her bed for several nights after that; everyone thought her time had come, but the girl didn't die. Then an influenza epidemic hit the orphanage. It went on for over a year, and many of the very young girls died. It was said to be the gods' punishment for not getting the girl."

He smiled faintly. "That was one of Mom's favorite stories. She told it to us when we were kids, and my sister got very wrapped up in it. She pretended she was the girl who didn't die, the one everybody else shunned because she'd caused so many of the other orphans' deaths."

Camilla could hardly imagine her sister-in-law in that scenario. When she first met Rebecca Sachs-Smith, she'd been a businesswoman with a heart of stone. She'd changed somewhat when her daughter had been kidnapped, but even then Frederik's sister didn't seem to fit the role of victim.

"According to Mom, this sad story ended with the poor girl drowning herself in the fjord. Mom was serious when she claimed that you could see the girl once in a while, walking around the house or standing out in the yard, dripping wet, as if she'd just walked out of the water."

The quiet in the room was intense for a moment.

"Quite a place you've settled into," Louise said. She smiled at her friend, now lying on the sofa with the blanket over her.

19

They sat for a while, no one saying a word, absorbing the history of the place.

"Can we find the spot where the girls are buried?" Eik asked. He stood up. "The dogs need to get out, and who knows, I might be lucky enough to meet the girl who didn't die. You want to come?"

He held his hand out to Louise.

"What about food?" she asked them. "I can drive into Roskilde and do some shopping. Will it be too late if we take a walk first?"

It was almost eight.

"We'll take care of dinner while you're gone," Frederik said. "I'll get the boys to make a salad, and I'll light the grill."

He found a map and spread it out. "The Death Trail enters the forest here, but the part of the trail close to our house is overgrown with weeds and bushes. It's probably easier for you to find the graves from the sacrificial oak."

He picked up a red felt pen and marked the route for them on the map. He drew a circle. "There's a clearing here. The Asatro's bonfire site is in the middle, but if you walk behind the tree you'll find the Death Trail. Just follow it to the graves. It'll take about ten minutes."

"Sounds good," Louise said. "We'll find it."

Eik stood outside with the two dogs, who were jumping around when she came out. Louise smiled when the retired police dog rocketed off, as if he'd completely forgotten that one of his back legs didn't work. The German shepherd was as friendly as he could be now that he was out of the office, which he considered his territory to guard. He hadn't growled or bared his teeth at Camilla, Frederik, or Markus, and it had been love at first sight with Jonas and Dina.

They strolled toward the old oak. Louise enjoyed holding Eik's warm hand, the way he held her fingers and stroked her hand with his thumb. The peaceful forest, the sunlight and sound of the dogs running ahead, all so beautiful and quiet. Once in a while they stopped and kissed, and she rested her chin against his leather jacket as he held her. Louise wanted to melt away into the moment.

It wasn't difficult to find the sacrificial oak or the narrow path. Louise let go of Eik's hand and leaned her head back to take a good look at the old oak. The trunk was so large that they couldn't have reached around it even if Camilla and Frederik had come along.

"If you've got any aches or pains, you should crawl into the hole," Eik said. He pointed to the trunk. "These old trees can heal you, and they also say that the old hollow trees can improve a woman's fertility if she's having trouble getting pregnant."

"I'm not getting into any tree," she said. She started toward the path. "Where'd you hear about that?"

He let go of her hand when they reached the path. "Those things interested me when I was a kid."

Why did that not surprise her?

Eik held a limb back, but twigs caught and pulled at Camilla's hair as she fought through the underbrush covering the two wheel ruts of the trail.

"Let me lead the way," he said. He tromped through to make a path.

The dogs were already far ahead. The thick underbrush closed behind them, as if they had been swallowed.

Suddenly a clearing appeared. A gnarled tree stood in the middle, its crown spread out like a toadstool. The sun was hidden behind the forest, but the evening light cast a red sheen over everything. A low hedge grew on all four sides around the tree, making it look as if it were in the middle of a playing field.

The identical graves lay behind the unkempt hedge. They were spaced two to three meters apart. Simple and chilling. Louise froze; she felt as if she'd stepped into a world where time stood still. She began walking slowly toward Eik, who had crouched down at the first gravestone.

"Ellen Sofie Mathilde Jensen," Eik read. "Born 1908, died 1920. Twelve years old, she was."

Louise walked down the row of graves, reading the names and dates chiseled into the gravestones. All the girls were very young when they died, none of them over sixteen. The hairs on her arms rose, and she shook her head at herself. Then she heard Dina whining eagerly, and Charlie barked. She was familiar enough with police dogs to know that he was marking territory, and she was about to ask Eik to call him when Dina also began barking. Annoyed now, she walked over. The German shepherd was digging, growling to warn Dina away.

"Eik, damn it!" She'd already pulled a dog leash out of her pocket to hold the deaf Labrador.

"What did he find?" Eik asked. He'd taken the other way around the graves.

"I don't know, but I do know that there are forty-two hundred-year-old corpses here, so if that's what he's after, there's more than enough for him." Louise grabbed Dina while Eik ordered Charlie to stay. "Is he hurt so bad that you can't take him to a graveyard without him flipping out?"

"Of course not. He was a Grade One dog; only the best reach that level." Eik sounded insulted. He was about to say more, but then he stopped. "What the hell!"

He dropped to his knees and began scraping the compact soil aside.

Louise tied Dina to a tree. "What did he find?" she yelled, running over to him.

"A body."

Charlie had dug a small trench, and now he lay beside it and looked at them attentively.

Eik's voice was dark—the warmth that she had heard before had vanished. Carefully he pushed a bit more of the dirt aside. "This is no child's hand," he said, "and it hasn't been here a hundred years."

Louise felt a chill. Eik had uncovered a pale white hand. From the swollen tissue and waxy film over the skin, she knew it was utterly impossible that it been buried since the early 1900s.

Her heart hammered as she squatted beside him. Eik scraped a bit more earth away to reveal the arm. The corpse wasn't fresh; several places showed only bone and sinew.

She looked at the gravestone. "Klara Sofie Erna Hermansen. Born 1916, died 1918."

They sat there for a moment. Louise leaned against Eik's knee as she studied the skin left on the upper arm. She was about to stand up when he grabbed her and pointed. He swiped more of the dirt away, and she saw that some of the fingers were intact. A gold ring, much too big, adorned one of them.

"Female?" he guessed. He stood and wiped his hands on his pants. "Or a teenager. Not a grown man, anyway."

"It's hard to say," Louise answered as she rose up from her knees. "It may have been lying here a long time. The clothes are almost rotted away."

Dark scraps of material were scattered around the ground, as if a sleeve had slowly deteriorated.

"My guess is five, maybe ten years," Eik said. He walked off to smoke a cigarette, while Louise found Frederik's number on her phone. "The grave is shallow."

"I don't think it's a grave," she said. She measured the distance from the body to the top of the ground. "Someone has tried to hide a body."

"Couldn't you find it?" Frederik asked when Louise called.

"We found it, all right," Louise said. She didn't know how to begin. "We found a body out here that's not from the girls' orphanage."

After several seconds Frederik asked, "What do you mean?"

"It looks like someone has been buried on top of one of the old graves."

She told him about Charlie sniffing it out. "The body is about half a meter down, far enough so the animals haven't dug it up."

"Couldn't it be an animal?"

She could hear he was shaken. "No, it's human, no doubt about that." She said the Roskilde Police would definitely want to speak with him.

"I'd better come right now," he said.

Louise heard gravel crunching; he was already on his way. "Can you make sure the police have someplace to enter the forest? And there's no reason to tell Jonas and Markus about this until tomorrow morning, let's not get them all excited tonight."

Frederik agreed, and he promised to have Tønnesen take down the chain blocking the road.

"Tell the police to drive in at the forest parking lot and

I'll meet them. But won't they want to wait until tomorrow, when they can see?"

"They'll definitely come immediately," Louise said, nodding at Eik, who was signaling to her that he'd call Mid- and West Zealand Police in Roskilde. Meanwhile she explained to Frederik that a team of technicians would come in addition to the police, even though it was already getting dark.

"They'll probably have the Emergency Management Agency put a tent over the grave, then they'll set up floodlights," Louise said, adding that of course a forensic pathologist would be there to look at the body before it was carefully dug up and taken in to be examined.

Ten minutes later Frederik trotted out of the forest. He stopped for a moment to get his bearings in the near-darkness of the summer night, then hurried over to them.

Louise tried to stop him in time, but he got close enough to see the arm sticking out of the ground.

"My God!" He stared at the ground, his hand over his mouth. He shook his head. "How could something like this happen?"

He seemed uncertain of where to go. "Who would do something like this? Hiding a body in our forest?"

He backed off a bit, still staring at the arm in the ground.

You'd be surprised at the things people can do, Louise thought, but she didn't say it. He was shaken up enough already.

"That's probably one of the things the police will ask you," she said. "Is the forest open to the public?"

Frederik nodded. Finally he tore his eyes away. "It's a private forest, and we have NO VEHICLES ALLOWED signs up, but we've just seen that some people ignore them."

Eik's phone rang. He nodded crisply at Frederik. "They'll be here soon. You'll show them the way?" He walked off to take the call.

When Frederik left, Eik came back and put his arm around Louise's shoulder. "We better take the dogs back, so they don't cause so much commotion when the police arrive."

She'd untied Dina from the tree and was now holding her leash, but it seemed as if the yellow Lab had lost interest in the corpse. Charlie still lay where Eik had left him. The big German shepherd didn't budge, even though Dina egged him on to play.

Louise shook herself. In a few minutes the evening quiet of the forest would be transformed into a crime scene, and all the relevant investigations would begin. More people would show up, and the floodlights would blaze coldly down onto the old graves of the girls. She thought about the boy hiding somewhere out there. Maybe he'd left the area, but if not, the lights might flush him out. Or frighten him to death.

20

"What the hell kind of place is this?" Nymand yelled after he'd stepped out of the car and peered down the rows of identical gravestones.

"It's a private graveyard from back when the old orphanage owned the forest," Louise explained. She led Roskilde's deputy commissioner to the body.

Nymand had headed the investigation when Frederik's young niece had been kidnapped; it was the beginning of a family tragedy. She hadn't spoken to him since, but she caught something in his eye that told her he knew about the episode at the gamekeeper's.

"It'll be half an hour or so before emergency and the techs arrive," he said. Meanwhile he wanted to know how they'd found the body.

Eik stood a few meters away, lighting a cigarette. "It was the dog; he started digging. But Charlie is experienced—he knows when to stop." Eik sounded a bit proud as he stuck the pack of cigarettes in his pocket and blew smoke out.

"In other words, he ruined the crime scene," Nymand stated sullenly. "Why the hell isn't that dog leashed?"

Louise was afraid that her partner would lock horns with Nymand. Criticizing Eik's new best friend wasn't the way to get on his good side; she'd found that out. But he merely tilted his head.

"If the dog had been on a leash, there'd be no crime scene," he said drily. "And if you walk over and look at the grave, you'll see that he only dug down to the hand. I'm the one who uncovered the arm, and we haven't touched the rest of the grave."

Nymand grunted.

"Charlie's a police dog, not an amateur," Eik continued. Louise had to look away to keep herself from smiling.

"There's probably not much left that can help us anyway," the deputy commissioner admitted. He joined his men.

Louise followed and asked if there was anything more they needed to know before she and Eik took the dogs back to the manor house.

Nymand shook his head. "But we need to talk to Frederik." He looked over at Camilla's husband, standing in the background with his hands in his pockets.

"You might get more out of talking to his manager," Louise said. "Tønnesen has been around for decades. Frederik has only lived here the last twenty years."

"It's possible we'll wait to search the area until early tomorrow," Nymand said, as if he hadn't heard her.

Louise nodded and looked toward the grave.

"But of course we'll secure the crime scene right now," he continued, "and take the remains in to Forensics when the techs finish tomorrow." He gazed around. "We probably should cordon off the area."

From whom? Louise thought. She told him that she was staying with Camilla that weekend, and she mentioned the hit-and-run and the missing boy seen in the forest.

"Frederik," Nymand called out, ignoring her. "Can we talk in the morning?"

"I can stay out here. I'd like to help if I can."

Nymand shook his head violently. Clearly he didn't want any outsiders contaminating the crime scene. "Go on. I'll call if I need you."

Louise noticed that Frederik hesitated.

"We're taking the dogs back," Eik yelled. "Drive on ahead and grab a few beers. I could sure use one, anyway."

Camilla lay sleeping on the sofa when they returned. Out in the kitchen, it was obvious that the boys had made toasted sandwiches. Sliced bread, ham, and cheese were scattered around the counter beside the big toaster oven, which smelled of melted cheese. The two boys flew down the stairs.

"Where've you been?" Markus called before he had even reached the kitchen.

Louise and Frederik glanced at each other. They had

agreed to tell the boys what had happened, but without making a big deal about it.

"Eik and Louise found a dead person out in the forest," Frederik began.

"Possibly someone who took their own life." Louise lied to make it sound less dramatic, but she could see it didn't work. "The police are there, and we really don't know much yet."

"So maybe there's a murderer in the forest?" Markus asked, his eyes wide as he looked from Eik to Louise to Frederik.

"But it is a murder, right?" Jonah said.

She spread her hands in exasperation. "Boys, it's way too early to be certain of anything. But yes, it's possible that someone hid a body out in the forest. It doesn't necessarily mean that the person was killed here."

Jonas's shoulders slumped; Markus gave the chair in front of him a push, the legs stuttering across the floor. Obviously, both of them were uneasy with what they'd heard.

"Could it have something to do with what happened to Mom?" Markus asked.

Louise quickly shook her head. "No, definitely not." She walked over and put her arm around his shoulder, stroking his hair lightly. "This probably happened years ago. Long before you moved here. And nobody can say this is where it happened."

Everyone seemed to take in what had been said.

"Can we take the big bottle of cola up with us?" Markus asked Frederik. With that, the boys' moods lifted, as if the corpse no longer had anything to do with them.

Louise smiled when they grabbed two glasses out of the cupboard and hit Frederik up for the bag of chips on the top shelf.

"Is there anything you'd like?" he asked after the boys had gone back upstairs. "You hungry?"

Louise shook her head and suggested they make a few liver pâté sandwiches. She felt a bit dizzy, so she sat down while Frederik rounded everything up.

First the session with Bitten, Thomsen threatening her, ordering her to stay away. Then Camilla being run down in the forest. And now this. Thoughts swirled in her head. After a few bites, she pushed her plate away. "I think I'll lie down," she said, even though it was only a few minutes past eleven. "Are you going back to town?" She looked at Eik.

Frederik quickly intervened. "You're welcome to stay. It might be best, if the police need both of you."

Eik needed no encouragement. "Great. I just need to find out what to do about feeding the dog. I'm not nearly as well organized as Jonas, who brought along a doggy bag for Dina."

Frederik pointed to the refrigerator. "We have steaks in there, so if Charlie isn't a vegetarian, you're welcome to give them to him."

Louise had her own bureau drawer in the guest room, with everything she needed for an unexpected visit. Camilla had arranged it—she felt obligated to do so, since she had moved out on her friend in Frederiksberg.

The only time Louise had slept with Eik had been in this guest room, the night after Camilla and Frederik's wedding. They drank tons of champagne and kissed for the first time. Louise had no idea how she had gotten up the stairs and into bed, but now she suddenly remembered every second of that night with him, the feel of his skin, the stubble on his face, his hands.

In the bathroom, the thought of his caresses aroused her. She rinsed her face off when she heard him come up the steps and walk into the guest room.

Eik had confided in her that night. He told her about the woman he had lost, about sailing with her and two friends in the Mediterranean during his vacation, then quarreling with her outside Rome. He'd left the boat and returned to Copenhagen, where he heard about the accident. Sailors had found their rented boat drifting around a small harbor. Their two friends had drowned, but his girlfriend had disappeared without a trace. No one had seen her since. It had left a black hole inside Eik, into which he sometimes fell. Once in a while it was hard to pull himself out of it.

Eik knocked on the bathroom door. "Are you okay in there?"

Louise turned off the water. "I'm coming," she said, and dried her face.

21

Louise had been awake for a while when her phone rang. She hadn't had much sleep. She felt ashamed. Eik had been very understanding when, in the middle of all the warmth and fondling, she suddenly had rolled up into a ball and begun crying. Much later, when the tears stopped, she told him the rest of the story. About the sorrow and shame she had been living with her entire life. He stroked her back as she talked about Thomsen and his gang, who'd kept their claws in Klaus even though he wanted out.

At one point in the night, she turned to him and slid her hand over his chest, down over his prominent ribs, his hip bone, his groin, but when she felt him growing and stiffening, images from the gamekeeper's barn entered her head. She turned away from him.

"Don't you think you should speak with someone about what happened?" he'd whispered.

Louise had in fact considered making an appointment with a crisis counselor; Jakobsen was his name. Homicide had been using him for several years, and she'd gone to him before. She knew Eik was right, and she decided to contact Jakobsen, but first she was going to find the boy. And also get to the bottom of what happened the night Klaus died.

She reached down to the floor and picked up her buzzing phone.

"There's an old woman standing here. She's in our way, and I can't get hold of Frederik Sachs-Smith," Nymand said without introduction. "You're going to have to get her out of here."

Louise sat up. It was almost seven thirty; she must have gotten some sleep after all. "Where are you?" Eik stirred.

"Out at the graves of the girls. You *did* find a body out here yesterday evening, presumably a woman, and now we have to fine-comb the entire area. We can't have this woman hanging around in the middle of it all."

"What do you know about the body?" Louise asked.

"We don't know a damn thing as long as this old woman prevents us from doing our job!"

"We're on our way."

Camilla sat staring out the kitchen window. Her hands held a cup of coffee, while her thoughts were out in the forest with the boy who wouldn't come home.

Besides everywhere else in her body that hurt, she had a crick in her neck because Frederik had let her sleep on the sofa all night. When he'd come in to say good morning, she quickly gulped all the pills he handed her. He told her about the corpse Eik's dog had found out by the girls' graves. She'd been very annoyed that he hadn't woken her up so she could go along, but he dismissed her by saying that no one had really known what was out there, and anyway, she'd needed sleep.

She turned when she heard Louise's footsteps on the stairs. She assumed that her friend and Eik had slept together, and she was expecting her to be radiant, but Camilla's smile disappeared when Louise walked in the room. She looked harried, with dark rings under her eyes.

"What's going on?" Camilla asked. She groaned when she stood to get another cup. "You could have woken me up. I'd like to have gone out there with you."

"Can you get hold of your manager?" Louise said. "The police are out there, and they want to inspect the site, but Elinor has planted herself on one of the old graves and refuses to move. The police want someone to take her away."

"What the hell is she doing out there?" Camilla said. "And what happened yesterday?"

Louise shrugged. "The dogs ran around, and before we knew what they were up to, Charlie had dug down and found a hand."

"Christ! What is the deal with this place? If I'd known there were hit-and-run drivers, Vikings, ghosts, and double graves, Frederik would have had to move in with me, back in the city."

"We don't know if it is a double grave," Louise said.

"We really don't know very much yet, only that there are bones that shouldn't be there."

Eik walked up behind her with a bad case of morning hair, heading for the Nespresso machine. "We have time for a cup?"

"Only if you bring it along," Louise said. She was half-way to the hall to put on her shoes.

"I'm going with you," Camilla yelled. She'd called Tønnesen, but he hadn't answered. "I'll take care of Elinor."

She looked out into the yard. Dina lay stretched out under a tree. Charlie trotted around with his nose to the ground, tail wagging. "Should we shut them in, or do you want to take them along?"

"Nymand's team will have their own dogs out there, so it's probably best that ours stay here," Louise said. She looked over at Eik.

"Sure." He called the two dogs in. "You don't let an old circus horse smell the sawdust if you're not going to let him dance."

22

Elinor looked like a tiny pawn on an enormous chessboard. She leaned on her cane, a bowed old woman standing on the grave as if someone had nailed her to it.

"Hi, Elinor," Camilla called out.

Morning dew still covered the grass in the forest meadow. The graves were ringed with dark gravel all the way around. They had probably been well cared for at one time, she thought, but now bushes had overtaken several of them. The low hedge from long ago, probably a windbreak, had grown out of shape, and long tufts of grass had sprouted up on the graves themselves. The entire area had been neglected and was fast returning to nature.

"The police need her out of the way," Louise repeated.

She walked over to join Nymand and his crime scene technicians. They had carefully dug down beside the body, and now they were pushing a plate in underneath to lift it out. The corpse and the earth around it would be taken in for examination.

Shadows from the treetops danced on the earth in front of Camilla's feet; ground mist rose from a small hollow at the edge of the forest, just beyond the old gnarled tree. She shivered in the cool morning breeze.

"The wagons are rolling on the Death Trail," the old woman mumbled.

"How is she in the way?" Camilla asked the dog handler, who stood a few meters away. "When you're focused on the graves over there."

"You have to get her to move so we can do our job," was all he said. He stared openly at her black-and-blue face.

Elinor kept mumbling. Camilla held a hand out to her, but she ignored it. Camilla lowered her hand and stepped back. The earth was dark where the old woman stood; there was no green grass. It looked as if someone had been digging around.

"Listen, goddamn it, she's not doing this just to bother you," Camilla said. She hobbled over to the policeman. "Instead of standing there looking like an old grouch, you could walk over to her and take a look. The dirt's different from the other graves."

"Yeah, maybe! Except it's hard to see as long as she's standing on it."

Camilla looked around for Nymand.

Elinor stirred. Hunched over, looking down at the ground, she turned and walked away from the grave. Camilla followed her. Now she was convinced that Elinor only wanted to point out the grave to her. Once she was sure that Camilla understood, she moved away.

Camilla hurried to follow the old lady. It wasn't just the morning chill bringing out goose bumps on her skin; she had a vague feeling that something was about to happen. Something not at all nice.

Elinor strode past two gravestones and stopped beside the third. The grave looked like all the others, the same gray, simple stone plate set slightly crooked in the ground. Camilla crouched down and was about to read when a man's voice boomed from behind and startled her.

"Got something over here!" said a tall, husky policeman. Camilla noticed that the dog handler had straightened up, now that his dog showed interest where Elinor had stood. Nymand and his men rushed over.

"What's happening?" she yelled. She put a hand on Elinor's arm. "I'm going back to see what this is all about."

But as she was about to turn, Elinor grabbed her. "The wagons are rolling on the Death Trail."

Technicians in a blue van backed up to the grave where Elinor had been standing. Two men in white coveralls carefully began scraping the earth away.

"Positive!" someone yelled.

Camilla was rushing toward them when suddenly she felt a strong hand on the back of her shoulder. "Stay here!" a policeman said.

"What's going on? And take your hand off me!" She squirmed.

"It looks like they found another body," he said, letting go of her.

"You mean, a body buried there where Elinor was?"

"It looks that way."

Camilla froze a second before whirling toward Elinor, her feet planted on the grave behind them. Their eyes met, then the old woman turned and walked toward the forest.

Camilla called her name. She wanted to run after her, but the pain in her legs and the husky policeman stopped her. "What's that old witch up to?" He stared after her.

Camilla slumped. She looked at the grave the old woman had just left. She heard the dog handler praising his dog, the dog snapping at the snack the man had tossed at him. She sensed the stillness of the forest, though everything around her was in motion. It was as if she were in the middle of a movie set where a mass grave was being uncovered right before her eyes.

"I think there's another grave here you should look at," she said, pointing.

"Nymand!" the policeman called out across the clearing.

Camilla couldn't move when the officer asked the dog handler to check the grave she'd singled out. She felt she knew what she was about to see.

Her eyes followed the policeman and his dog in slow motion. They stopped at the grave. The dog sniffed around, but it made no noise when it looked up at its handler. He said something to the officer beside Camilla; she couldn't hear what, could only see his mouth moving. She looked back down at the grave.

"Negative," the officer said.

She grabbed him before he walked away. "There *is* something. Or else she wouldn't have shown us the grave." She ignored his remark that crime scenes always attract weirdos trying to draw attention to themselves. "She was right a few minutes ago," Camilla said, pointing to the first grave, which several of the technicians huddled around. The mood was tense. They worked fast, focusing on what was being dug up while speaking in low voices.

Louise came over to her. "It's a young woman. It looks like she's been in the ground only a short time. She probably won't be difficult to identify, if we can find a missing person matching her description."

"How could this happen?" Camilla whispered. Her chest felt tight; even though she had covered many cases while on the crime desk at *Morgenavisen*, she had never gotten used to the sight of a corpse. "Why are all these bodies showing up here?"

She had to sit down. Her scalp tingled as the blood drained out of her cheeks.

Louise shook her head. She had no answer.

"You have to check the last grave Elinor showed me," Camilla said. She looked up at her friend. "The dog may not have smelled anything, but I'm sure there's something. It's obvious she wanted us to look there."

"My guess is that the entire area will be cordoned off. Nymand will call in an archaeologist with knowledge of disturbed sites, who can tell us where someone has been digging recently." Louise started to walk back to the others.

Camilla followed her. "Who could she be, that woman you just found?"

"It's hard to say. She's young, probably early twenties."

"What's she look like?"

"Thin, almost naked, long blond hair," Louise said. "A tattoo around one wrist, another one down by her hip. I couldn't see what it was."

Camilla stayed in the background as Louise approached the technician and pointed out the final grave Elinor had stood at.

"Can you see how the young woman died?" Camilla asked when Louise returned. But at that moment Nymand ordered everyone to leave.

"We don't want anyone tramping around here until we've secured the entire area," he yelled. He looked at Camilla.

Several times over the years in her work as a journalist, she'd gone through unsolved cases. She could remember several of them, but none involving the murder of a woman in the Roskilde area.

"This is going to take some time," Louise said. She put her arm around Camilla's shoulder when she began to sway. "Nymand is calling everything to a halt until an archaeologist looks at the site. He'll also look at the last grave Elinor pointed out to you. If there's been any digging there, the vegetation will probably show it."

A policeman came over and asked Camilla to leave. "We're securing the entire area," he said. He nodded toward the forest, as if he expected her to run right in there.

"We're parked over there," Camilla said. She pointed at the other side of the gnarled tree.

"Then you'll have to walk around," he said, and he began pushing her.

She'd had enough. She was freezing, her leg hurt, and

the whole scene in front of her was surreal. The last thing she wanted to hear was a young officer with a shaved head ordering her around.

"Get your hands off me! This is my forest!"

"That may be, but right now it's a crime scene. So I'm going to have to ask you to leave the area."

There were probably a thousand things she could have snapped back at him, but instead she sighed and gave up. She just wanted to go home and lie down.

"Eik and I are heading back to town," Louise said, as she followed her to the car. "We're going into the station to check the national missing person files."

23

They found her. They found her! Sune felt as if he were about to explode.

The last few days he had watched the police cars from his hiding place; he'd heard their dogs, listened to them yelling. They had dug all over, and the earth from several of the old orphanage graves lay in uneven, coal-black mounds.

He'd stood hidden among the trees as two men in white coveralls unfolded a body bag. Even at a distance, he recognized her long, blond hair when they laid her in and zipped it up. They'd carried her back to the car with the tinted windows.

Now the police were finally gone, and he scampered back across the forest floor, away from the clearing and the dug-up graves. His heart hammered, and he felt dizzy from blood rushing through his temples. He'd been right all along. Deep inside he had hoped that he'd imagined it all, that he had been scared for no reason. But he'd seen her in the light of the bonfire, lying on the ground, so still.

The moon's pale light cast ghostly shadows around Sune, but he wasn't afraid of trees or dark forests. Nothing in nature unsettled him. It was all the other things.

He stopped to catch his breath, but he whirled around when he heard limbs cracking behind him, then the sound of heavy footsteps. He hadn't been paying attention, and he was about to run when he recognized his father's voice in the darkness.

"Wait! You have to listen to me. Your mother wants to see you!"

Thoughts flew through his head. His desperate flight. Punishment, the oath ring. His legs wanted to run, but his craving to see his mother stopped them. His heart beat so loudly that it would have scared the forest birds away if they hadn't already gone to roost. Now he and his father were alone.

"Sune." His father approached him with open arms; it felt like a magnet to Sune, yet he kept his distance. His father's arms sank.

"The police came by asking about you. I had a tough time figuring out what to say. People think you've taken your life. They're talking about you."

Sune didn't know what to say, either. He wanted this to end. His father seemed completely different from the night he had hissed in Sune's ear to pull himself together; to not shame him.

"Your mother's doing badly, and she's terribly upset. Come home for her sake, and we can work everything else out. You're a grown boy now—you have responsibilities."

"I'm not coming home," he whispered, unable to control his voice.

"You have to. I can't take care of you out here."

"I can take care of myself," Sune said, more self-assured now.

"Not anymore you can't. It's too dangerous. Come home with me, and swear on the oath ring. You're born into this; there's nothing to do about it."

For a moment they stood in the clear moonlight, staring at each other. Then Sune shook his head; he realized what his father was after, and it had nothing to do with his mom.

"I'm trying to help you. You're one of us; we'll take care of you."

Sune could almost see the bonds of the Asatro his father wanted to bind him with. They tightened, cutting into him, snarling like the worm that wrapped itself around Midgård and bit its own tail. But then his father's shoulders seemed to sink again as his expression loosened. He sighed.

"Don't decide right now. Why don't I come back tomorrow? But I have to tell you that if you still say no, you're on your own. Completely. Like a child who hasn't been knee-sat."

Sune understood what that meant. A baby who hasn't been knee-sat belongs to no one. It could be abandoned to the wolves if the parents felt unable to take care of it. Sune had been knee-sat at the ceremony where he was given his name and his parents had officially accepted him. He'd been very young back then; he didn't remember. But no one had told him that the acceptance could be revoked.

"Tomorrow evening after sunset at the sacrificial oak," his father said. "I'm holding the door open for you, but if you don't come in I can't protect you any longer."

He turned and left.

24

"Have you moved your unit out of the station, or what?" Olle asked when Louise met him in the hall Monday morning.

She was about to say that they'd been in during the weekend, but instead she explained that they were assisting Roskilde; that now they had three persons to identify. He asked if it was Nymand's case, and she nodded.

"Rønholt talked about it at the morning briefing," Olle said. "He said they found three double graves and to expect that they'd need our help. We might have to contact Interpol and search their database for wanted persons."

"I wouldn't doubt it," Louise said. "Nymand is twisting arms and the pathologists are going to examine all three corpses this morning. As soon as we have the teeth, we'll start working on identification. There's more to go on with the most recent corpse; she had two tattoos and we've got the photographs. I'll gather everything up and bring it to the briefing."

She smiled at her colleague and hurried down the hall to the Rathole.

"I'm guessing you'd rather drink your own tea," Eik said when he came in five minutes later. He set a tray down on his desk and pushed a plate with two rolls over to her.

Louise was surprised by the mountain of sandwiches on his plate. Two slices of bread with cheese and four liver pâté sandwiches.

"Looks like the fresh country air gave you an appetite," she said. But when he began scraping off the pickles and aspic from the four sandwiches, she realized what was going on.

"You're not. You're not feeding him that!" She looked down at the German shepherd, who was staring up at the source of all that aroma. "He'll fart all day and drive us out of the room."

"Take it easy. I'll go over to Netto later and buy dog food," Eik promised. He set the plate down on the floor.

Louise sighed. She knew who would have to stop by the vet and pick up some decent food for Charlie. But before she could say anything more, Olle knocked on the door and stuck his head in. He eyed the dog nervously.

"Take a look at these photos." He held out a folder. "It's a twenty-four-year-old woman from Tårnby. Her sister reported her missing about three weeks ago. She has a little boy; she disappeared the night before his third birthday. And she has two tattoos."

It was Station City's case, and the young woman was

a prostitute. Presumably, it hadn't been given a high priority, Louise thought. Normally the police stalled on a missing person case anyway, as people often turned up by themselves.

"Lisa Maria Nielsen," she read out loud.

"When exactly did she disappear?" Eik asked. He brushed the crumbs off his T-shirt.

"May thirty-first or June first," she said. She cocked her head and thought a moment. "The same time as the boy."

She turned to Olle. "Can I keep this for a while? We need to be sure, of course, but thanks, Olle."

He left, and Eik asked her to read it out loud.

"Lisa Maria has a young son. He turned three on June first, and he's the reason her sister reported it at once when she didn't come home. Lisa would never willingly be gone on her son's birthday. He meant everything to her. She had invited his friends from the day care for a birthday party, with sandwiches and a birthday cake. Her sister was to have taken care of that. It was difficult for her to explain to her nephew where his mother was."

"Unfortunately, it happens in that profession," Eik mumbled. "Who's taking care of the boy?"

"Her sister. They shared one floor of a house. She has a four-year-old daughter."

For a moment she studied the photos of Lisa Maria that her sister had given the police. Louise recognized both tattoos. She called Olle.

"Get hold of the sister and make arrangements for an identification. I don't know how soon Forensics can have the body ready. Try Flemming Larsen. He was on duty this weekend; he was there when the bodies came in."

She hung up and pushed the folder over to Eik. Then she opened the green folder she'd started on Sune Frandsen and looked it over. "They've been missing within the same time period."

"But we don't know if they disappeared in the same area," Eik pointed out. He tossed the last half of his cheese sandwich down on the floor.

"Stop that, you're going to make him sick," she said. "It's true, we don't know that, but she was buried where he's hiding."

"So you're thinking, he might've seen something?" He nodded. "And that could be the reason he's hiding. He witnessed a crime and doesn't dare come home. What do you think?"

The pieces were falling into place. "He might have been the one who killed her!" Louise said. Murderer or witness to a murder. Two good reasons to go into hiding.

"It's a possibility. But he's fifteen years old. Could he do it?"

"He might've seen something that scared him out of his senses; he could have reacted like a wounded animal."

"Teenagers disappear every day," he reminded her.

She nodded. Normally the search for teenagers was intensive at first. Police dragged lakes, searched often-used routes, checked debit card usage, and if nothing showed up, later on they would check Freetown Christiania—a haven for quirky and troubled characters, who could find refuge and a place to hide from the authorities—and then youth houses. Often the latter steps would be unnecessary when hunger set in and the comforts of home became too inviting. When the smell of their own bodies became too much.

155

"The pattern just doesn't fit here," she said.

"We have to look into it," Eik conceded. He asked if it was true that the father said he was going to look for his son, now that they knew approximately where he was hiding.

Louise nodded. "He promised to call if he found him. Anyway, I'm calling Nymand. If the boy can be connected with this killing, it's his case."

Louise was put through to the deputy commissioner. She told him that they likely had identified the young woman and added that Sune Frandsen had been hiding in the forest since the day Lisa Maria disappeared.

She summed both cases up for him and gave him the number of the missing person case concerning Sune, so he could see a photo of him.

Nymand decided to instigate a search for the boy in the area. "If he's there, we'll find him. But if he has nothing to do with my case, we don't have time to run around looking for runaway teenagers for you."

"Of course," Louise said. Odd, she thought, that his ridiculous remark hadn't angered her. She must be tired.

"I'll call the father and let him know that Roskilde is organizing a search," Eik said.

Louise took a bite of the roll, but the dry bread clogged her throat. She was hungry, though. She unwrapped a block of butter, spread a thick layer onto the bread, and attacked it. By the time Eik had finished talking, she'd cleaned off her plate.

"Tell Nymand to cancel. Sune is back home."

"And that idiot didn't even call?" Exhausted or not, Louise was furious.

"He kept apologizing, said it was very emotional when the boy was reunited with his mother. They needed some time alone, and he just forgot about calling. Apparently the boy is already back at school, but that sounds really strange. I mean, he's been gone three weeks!"

"That's how it is in a small town," Louise said. She shrugged sadly. "Everything has to get 'back to normal' as soon as possible."

Eik shook his head. "You'd hope that somebody will look in on the boy, check to see how he's doing. Is that how it works there, or is it just more convenient to forget about it?"

That last remark sounded like an accusation against Louise. "He'll be checked on. By us. Before we cancel the search and close the case, we're driving over to talk to him. I want to know why he hid for three weeks in the forest. And when we're done, we'll make sure someone keeps an eye on him."

"Shouldn't we do that now?" Eik laid his palms on his desk, as if he was about to stand up.

"You mean, while he's in school?"

He nodded. "Wouldn't it be easier for him to tell us why he didn't want to go home if his parents aren't around?"

Of course, Louise thought. An adult would have to be present, but they could find a schoolteacher or perhaps an administrator.

"Let's go," she said. She was on her feet.

25

When they drove past the lake, Louise realized she hadn't been inside Hvalsø School since she'd graduated from ninth grade. School had practically been her whole life back then. It had ended so abruptly. But why should she have come back? After you graduate, there's no reason to return.

She did remember her way around. She directed Eik to park in front of the auditorium, and they walked past the bicycle sheds. It was a shortcut, plus they wouldn't have to use the main entrance. But they would have to go through the cafeteria, where curious eyes would follow them all the way to the principal's office.

The sense of being in familiar territory slowly faded when she discovered that the cafeteria wasn't there anymore. And of course she realized Mother Ellen wouldn't be selling sandwiches and candy to the older students. She actually felt a bit indignant over all the changes in her old school.

They explained to the woman in the secretary's office that they wanted to speak to Sune Frandsen, and they were sorry it had to be during classes, seeing that he had just returned to school.

The secretary looked surprised, but she recovered quickly and smiled. "I wasn't aware he was back. That's so nice to hear. He's a very sweet boy, and no one could understand why he would do such a thing. To take his own life…" She seemed upset suddenly. "No child or young person—no one at all—should be able to go so far. Oh dear. Well, if you'll have a seat, I'll bring him in a moment."

She pointed at two chairs under a wide photograph of the school. Gray cement, rust-red square windows. A long line of students stood in front of the school. Louise remembered when that picture had been taken. In fact, she was in it somewhere.

The principal came out of his office. They introduced themselves and nodded when he said that he'd been hoping this regrettable case would have a happy ending.

"Last week we held an assembly for ninth-grade classes. We talked to them about how life can be difficult and confusing; how sometimes you just want to give up."

The secretary returned, accompanied by Sune's class teacher.

"Who told you that Sune was in school?" The teacher looked back and forth at Louise and Eik. "Because he's not. His classmates haven't seen him, either. Who told you that?"

"We've just spoken with his father," Eik said. "He said that Sune had started school again."

The teacher was visibly upset. "I've talked about it several times. We should contact social services and find out what's going on in that home. But no one does anything. I've called the district, tried to convince them to visit the parents. Nothing happens. It's not so strange that things like what happened in Tønder and Mern take place—no one has the time anymore to protect the interests of children. It's all about money, passing the buck to someone else, taking on less yourself."

"Easy now, I think we should…" The principal sputtered, then recovered. "I'll call his parents and see what they have to say."

"I'm not saying this is a case of abuse or neglect," the teacher said. "But when a fifteen-year-old boy vanishes into thin air this way, something is very wrong. I've said so from the beginning, and even when he showed up on that photo, no one wanted to listen."

"We've done nothing but work on this case, ever since you pointed out that newspaper photo to the police in Holbæk," Eik said, and stood up. He was a head taller than Sune's teacher. Ordinarily this cop in black clothes and leather jacket, his longish hair combed back, didn't look threatening. But he was annoyed. "There's no certainty that the family is in any way at fault. But we suspect that Sune might have witnessed a serious crime. That could be why he's hiding. We can't really fault the family for that."

Louise watched the young schoolteacher retreat.

"Could he be in danger?" the principal asked.

"Possibly," Louise admitted. She emphasized that they very much wanted to talk to Sune. "If he does show up, please call us at once. We're going to pay a visit to his parents. Hopefully, we'll find him there."

On the way out, she glanced once more at the school photograph. Klaus had to be somewhere in it, too.

26

It took only five minutes to drive from the school to the farm where Sune's parents lived. The courtyard was deserted when Eik parked his junker Jeep Cherokee beside the big walnut tree.

He knocked a few times, then opened the door and shouted, "Hello!"

Louise followed him into the hallway. Eik shouted again, but no one answered. They waited a moment before entering the living room and calling Jane's name. Louise walked over to the bedroom door and knocked. "Jane, it's Louise—may I come in?"

She thought she heard a noise, and she opened the door a crack. Only a streak of sunlight broke through the edge of the closed curtains. "Jane," she repeated.

"Louise! Have you found him?"

Louise pulled a chair over to her old friend's bed and motioned for Eik to come in. "Jane, we're here about

Sune. My colleague spoke with Lars earlier today. He said that your son came home. We need to talk to him; we believe he might have witnessed a serious crime."

Jane's lips quivered, and she turned away. She took a deep breath then looked back at Louise, her eyes full of tears. She shook her head. "It's not true. He hasn't come home."

She reached for Louise's hand and squeezed it. "You have to find my son before they do! Help me…"

The rest of her words were drowned out in a long sniffle. Louise gave her the handkerchief that lay on her night table.

Louise stroked her hand mechanically.

"All I want now is to see Sune again before I die." Jane looked up, her eyes pleading. "They drive around looking for him at night. He's just a boy. He doesn't understand what he's up against!"

Louise held her hand as she leaned forward. "Jane, you need to tell us what's happened. Is it something we haven't heard about?"

Her old friend nodded slowly. Tears rolled down her sunken cheeks, but her voice was steady as she told them about the initiation ceremony out in the forest, the ritual everyone had been looking forward to.

"But something happened that night, and I can't get anyone to tell me what. All Lars will say is that Sune suddenly disappeared. I know my husband; I can sense that something very bad happened, and I'm afraid that they're going to harm Sune."

Anxiety flared up inside Louise. Eik brought over another chair, and she made room for him.

"Tell us what you know," he said, "and start at the beginning, so we can understand just what happened."

The sound of his calm, low voice made Louise regret that she hadn't let him sit by the head of the bed. Jane regarded him for a moment, as if considering what to say. Then she turned back to Louise.

"I'm not sure if you know anything about this, but it goes a long way back, to when we were kids. Klaus was a part of it, too."

Louise lifted an eyebrow and shook her head. "What goes a long way back?"

"Their brotherhood. They made a vow to stand together and protect each other. Just like Odin and Loke. They're blood brothers."

Louise's anxiety turned into an icy chill at this sudden mention of Klaus, along with things that Louise had never been aware of. "What are you talking about? Asatro?"

"So they mixed their blood?" Eik asked. "Is that what you mean? And made vows to each other?"

Jane nodded, her head barely leaving the pile of pillows. "You could put it that way. It's just more complicated; it's something peculiar to our group, and they take it very seriously." She paused for a moment. "Apparently more seriously than I was aware of."

"And how is your son mixed up in this?" Eik asked.

"I don't know exactly what happens during the ritual. It's only for the men. It's secret. They call it a rite of passage. A sacrifice must be made in order to gain something. They call themselves blood brothers, a term with roots in Nordic mythology. That's where our beliefs come from."

Louise could hear the fear behind her words.

"The boys are accepted into the brotherhood at their initiation ceremonies. It's different for girls, more like a confirmation without a priest. Girls confirm their belief in the Nordic gods and they're accepted among the adults. But it's special for the boys, becoming part of the inner circle. They make a vow to support each other. It's a male thing. Sune had been looking forward to it for a whole year, and that's where he was the evening he ran away."

It sounded more like an initiation into a biker club to Louise, but that's also how Thomsen and his gang seemed to think of themselves.

"Do they also vow to avenge each other?" Eik asked.

Jane's expression darkened. She nodded. "Yes, exactly. But what keeps me awake at night is the part of the oath that says, if you leave the fellowship you're an outcast. I don't know what's happened, but ever since you told us that Sune was hiding in the forest, I've feared the worst."

They sat for a while in silence. Finally Louise asked who was in the inner circle, and who would have been in the forest the evening Sune disappeared. She was afraid she knew the answer.

Jane stared straight ahead for a few moments, then spoke to Louise. "Thomsen, of course, and John Knudsen from Særløse. Do you remember him? They called him Pussy."

Louise nodded.

"And Lars Hemmingsen, he also ran around with Ole Thomsen back then, even though he lived out in Såby."

"The mason?" Louise asked. She was fairly certain he

was the man Camilla had fired during the renovation of Ingersminde; when Frederik had refused to let him work as a moonlighter to avoid paying tax, he'd begun to work slower.

"Yes. And my Lars. And René Gamst. Though he wasn't there that night, of course. I don't know if there are more. I've always just assumed it was the same group from the old days, back in school."

They hadn't mentioned the body of the young prostitute, and Louise started to ask Jane about her when Eik leaned forward.

"Why haven't you told the police about this before?" he asked.

Jane stared blankly for a moment. "I didn't dare. I didn't dare turn their anger on us, with me lying here like this."

She paused for a moment. "But what do I have to lose now?" she mumbled, as if she was talking to herself. "At any rate, nothing is more important than my son."

She was beginning to fade. Louise realized that the person in the most trouble from Jane talking to the police was Jane's husband.

"I know Sune well enough to know he'd come home if he could, that he'd want to be with me at the end. I've heard Lars get up many nights, I've seen the car lights when he backs out. Sune is out there, and I believe he's afraid."

"We found the body of a young prostitute in the forest where Sune is hiding," Eik said. "She disappeared the same night as your son, and we think he might've seen something, and now he's too frightened to come home. Do you know anything about this?"

For a moment Jane looked as if she had fallen asleep,

but then she shook her head and opened her eyes. "Did she die that night?"

"It's too early to say. But no one has seen her since she dropped her son off at her sister's, on the way to a job."

Jane hid her face in her thin hands. "The men perform a fertility ritual."

She paused, her face still hidden.

"And they…" Eik said.

"And they hire a prostitute…"

Jane's shoulders began to shake.

"They share a prostitute?" Louise said, almost shouting now. Immediately Eik laid a hand on her arm.

Jane lowered her hands from her face. "I don't know, but I think that's what happens. Lars has never talked about it. What I've heard comes from Ditte, the bricklayer's wife. Once they had an argument, and he told her that even though the prostitute was young, and a lot of the men shared her, she was a lot better than what he was getting at home, which was nothing."

"Christ," Louise whispered.

A car outside drove up to the house.

"Find Sune." Jane gripped Louise's arm. "Find him before they do."

Louise had almost reached the kitchen when the front door opened. The butcher walked in.

"Are you going to tell us what happened out in the forest, the night Sune disappeared?" she snarled. She walked up to him. "Your son isn't home."

167

"We take care of our own. We never asked you to butt in." The butcher's face was expressionless.

"You lied to us," Louise said. "That's bad enough. But you're also withholding information from the police, and I intend to press charges if you don't start cooperating."

His face hardened, but she didn't stop. "And if we find out that you or your friends are connected with the murder of the young prostitute we just dug up in the forest, I'm going after you and I'm going to put you away. For a long, long, long time. Do you understand?"

Louise knew there could be trouble if the butcher had the smarts to complain that the police had threatened him. It was a small risk to take, she thought. And worth it.

27

"We have to find that boy, and now," Louise said, back in the car with Eik. "If Sune saw Thomsen and his gang kill Lisa Maria, they're going to stop him from talking."

"What kind of a father is this butcher?" Eik said. She'd never heard him so angry before. He drove way too fast down the narrow gravel driveway; Louise put a hand on his arm to calm him down. He seemed to be channeling all his anger through the gas pedal, and he didn't slow down until he rammed his head against the roof of the car after hitting a pothole. "You just can't treat your child that way."

"You're right." Louise said. "This is how people behave when they get involved with Ole Thomsen. He and his buddies have their own rules, and unfortunately too many people get tangled up in them."

She'd never heard about the brotherhood, but she wasn't surprised. Especially after Klaus's parents telling her about the janitor and Gudrun. They covered up for each other; they always had. She couldn't care less what they called themselves, but she wasn't going to let them get away with forcing a fifteen-year-old boy into this sick form of solidarity.

"Pull over; let's wait until we know where we're going."

Before he got out of the car for a cigarette and to let Charlie run, she was calling Nymand to make sure he was organizing the search for Sune. "I believe a group of men from around Hvalsø murdered the prostitute," Louise said. She explained that the boy had likely witnessed the killing. "And I suspect that they're looking for him, because he's a witness and can testify against them. We have to protect him." When Nymand asked why she suspected all this, she told him about the initiation the night the prostitute disappeared. "If they can't be directly tied to the murder, we at least need to talk to them. They were in the area at that time."

Nymand cleared his throat. "There's nothing in the preliminary results from Forensics that points to her being killed in the forest. I'm afraid we're going to have to wait."

"Shit!" Louise tried to calm herself down, realizing she might be pushing things because she was burning to get Big Thomsen. "Okay. But for your own sake, make sure the techs have a look at the clearing behind the girls' graves. There's a bonfire site, and a big oak with a partially hollow trunk. Let's talk again when they've examined the area."

170

Louise knew how that sounded; she was telling him how to employ his personnel, when she had absolutely nothing to do with his murder investigation. But she had to take a chance.

"Eik and I are going to talk to four of the men who were there that night."

"Oh no you're not!" Nymand yelled. Louise held her phone away from her ear. "If you think these specific men could be involved in the murder, my people will talk to them."

"These specific men are involved in my investigation," she answered. "They *may* have something to do with the murder."

She knew it would be a feather in his cap if he could tell the media that the police already had carried out the first interrogations in the murder case. So she gave him the four names and said they had spoken with the boy's parents. She promised to send him the report on what Jane had told them as soon as she'd written it.

"We're very close to where two of the men live. We'll take care of them, but the last man lives out in Kirke Såby."

Camilla had told her that. Otherwise, she'd had no contact with the mason since she'd left Hvalsø.

"Put the screws to him," she said. She explained that Lars Hemmingsen had admitted to his wife that he and his friends hired a prostitute once a year for a fertility ritual in the forest. "In other words, they gang-bang her to honor Freya."

Nymand had no more to say.

171

"Turn to the right up here," she said.

"Where do we start?"

"Thomsen, in Skov Hastrup. And if it turns out he's moved in permanently with Bitten, we'll have to take a drive into the forest."

Louise was surprised to realize that she suddenly looked forward to confronting her old demons. She was ready.

"I think we should keep Jane out of this," she said when they were close to Thomsen's house. "Let's hear what they have to say about the initiation rites. This won't take long. I just want to see their reactions when we tell them we know about their brotherhood. When we're finished here, we're going to Holbæk."

She saw that Eik wanted to know more, but he just nodded.

They turned off the highway and drove down a small road with broad ditches. Thomsen's whitewashed farmhouse appeared just after a short curve, and immediately she spotted his Toyota Land Cruiser parked close to the house, beside an old black Mercedes.

They drove in and parked. Big Thomsen and a gray-haired man were walking around out by the woodpile behind the house. She recognized the old police chief, dressed in blue coveralls and holding a chain saw.

"Damn it!" she said. "His father's here. Thomsen won't tell us anything."

As if he would have anyway! she thought.

172

Before she was even out of the car, Thomsen and his father were standing shoulder-to-shoulder, their arms crossed. They watched their visitors without a word, but when Louise and Eik began walking across the gravel parking lot, Roed Thomsen stepped forward.

They did nothing Louise could characterize as threatening, but it would be hard to look more contemptuous. Despite that, she tried to sound friendly when she said they were happy to find Thomsen at home. She didn't offer her hand; she knew instinctively he would ignore it.

"We'd like to talk to you about Sune's initiation. We understand you were both there that evening. Of course, you know that the boy hasn't been seen since."

Slowly, old Roed Thomsen turned his head and looked at his son. Big Thomsen was leaning back slightly; he appeared to be looking down at Louise. "That was a private affair," he said.

"We'd like to hear what happened anyway," she said. She refused to be provoked. She looked him in the eye without blinking.

For a moment he seemed to be weighing his words, but then he shook his head. "We celebrated the boy's birthday and partied," he said. "His father brought along some good cuts from his shop, and we drank some beer."

Eik stepped forward. He was a big-city cop in a black leather jacket and just as tall as Ole Thomsen. He lit a cigarette in Thomsen's face and threw the match down on his property. The fat man in overalls struggled to maintain his contempt.

"What are these rituals actually like, to get into your brotherhood?" Eik blew smoke toward the two men.

"We know about the oath ring, and the business about pledging loyalty. And silence."

Louise could have killed Eik. He was talking too much. He needed to stop.

"But what about the test of manhood? How to prove your courage."

Now it was Eik leaning his head back, looking down at Big Thomsen, who glanced over at his father.

The old police chief laughed drily. "Boys nowadays don't have any guts. Might be that school softens them up; it's not like it was back when I grew up." He asked Eik what sort of test of manhood he was talking about.

A muscle quivered under Big Thomsen's eye, but he kept his mouth shut.

"You met out in the forest," Eik said, unruffled by the elder Thomsen. "And made a sacrifice, I'm assuming."

"How much do you really know about all this?"

Roed Thompson had taken over now. Even if Louise hadn't known the old man, she would have seen that he was used to doing the talking. He did the questioning; other people didn't question him.

"Not a whole lot," Eik answered calmly. "I messed around with stuff like that when I was a kid."

"It's not something you mess around with!" Big Thomsen snorted. He gave Eik the evil eye and stepped forward. "The Church Ministry recognized Asatro as a religion ten years ago, so don't you come here with your disrespect and mock us."

"We're not intending to disrespect anybody," Eik said. He flipped his cigarette in an arc. It landed beside the Land Cruiser's left front tire.

"Why should I stand here and tell you about something you don't even take seriously?" Big Thomsen continued, his voice full of scorn.

"Because we've found the body of a young woman who disappeared the night you had your fun in the forest. And because we're interested in what happened."

"I don't know anything about that," Big Thomsen said.

"Right now, the area is being fine-combed. Every leaf is being turned over, and you can be absolutely sure we're going to find out if there's the slightest connection between your little party and her death." Eik nodded at him to emphasize his point.

"You still have no right to come in here and accuse us, just because our beliefs come from nature, not the church," Roed Thomsen spat out at him.

His hands were in the pockets of his coveralls and his chest was puffed out—it wasn't hard to see where his son got his attitude from, Louise thought.

Eik stepped back. "We're not accusing anyone of anything," he said. "We're just asking you to describe what you do. The rituals when you make sacrifices."

"I'm going to have to ask you to leave my son's property now, or else I'll sue you for slander," the old police chief said. He waved them back to their car.

"Don't worry, I think we've got enough," Louise said, looking at Big Thomsen. "We need to get to Holbæk anyway, to talk to René. Shall I tell him hello for you?"

She enjoyed seeing the marine-blue irises of his eyes turn black with anger. They both knew he had no chance to coach René about what and what not to say.

28

W hat the hell happened back there?" Eik asked. He rolled the window down and lit another cigarette.

Louise was about to complain, but she let it go. She craved a cigarette, too. It wasn't so much what the two men had said as it was the mood. As if she and Eik had rammed into a wall.

"Welcome to Hvalsø," she said sadly, though she knew she wasn't being fair to the rest of the town. "Where the best defense is a good offense."

It had always been that way, she thought. It was protection, though it took some time to learn how to use it. Back when she was in school, after she got a horse, her father had started a dung heap on the other side of the road. Before long, a man from Lerbjerg began complaining. And he wasn't even their closest neighbor. But by that time, her father had learned how the game was played; he told the man that there were lots of things you could talk about. Like how someone had run a line from their septic tank to the district's drainage pipe, how piss and shit ran out into the nearby stream. After that, her father heard no complaints about the dung heap.

"It's really incredible," she said. She laughed as she remembered more of her father's favorite stories.

"What is?" Eik said.

"When my parents bought the farm out by Lerbjerg, there were grain fields on both sides of the road, and of course they had to be harvested. My dad had never done it before. He came from Copenhagen; he knew zero about these things, so he hired one of the neighbors who owned a combine. The neighbor did the cutting, Dad stood up on the machine and tied off sacks of grain and tossed them to the ground. After that, they were supposed to be turned regularly so the grain wouldn't rot."

"That must've been a long time ago," Eik said, even though she was sure he knew nothing about farming.

"Every time Dad went out to turn the sacks, our neighbor sat down outside his house with a cup of coffee, enjoying the sight of this big-city slicker wrestling fifty-kilo sacks of grain. Of course, the neighbor wouldn't dream of helping, but he wasn't shy about showing how entertaining it was to watch Dad sweat. That's how 'foreigners' were treated. It's probably different now, with all the young families from the city moving out here, but looking down on others has always been part of the mentality. Pussy lives right up here." Louise pointed to the church on top of the hill.

John Knudsen had taken over his parents' farm in

Særløse. He'd been in the same class as Big Thomsen, and his unfortunate school nickname had stuck with him. At least as far as Louise knew.

Eik turned off and drove along the churchyard, down a narrow gravel road—two ruts separated by tall grass that rustled against the car's undercarriage. The road ended at a ramshackle farmhouse with a big barn. The barn door was a torn green tarp. The Knudsen family farm had gone downhill, she noticed. She'd passed by here almost every day when she was a kid, to catch the school bus.

It was the complete opposite of Thomsen's farm, where everything was kept up. Almost too well—Louise suspected that he coerced Hvalsø's plumbers, carpenters, and other workmen to moonlight for him. It wasn't hard to imagine they owed him favors, which they paid back by working on his house.

Chickens ran around Pussy's farmyard, pecking between the cobblestones, while two kids poured sand out of a red plastic bucket in front of the kitchen steps.

"Park out here," Louise said. She looked around. A stocky woman in tights with a cigarette hanging from her mouth stood waiting outside on the steps. Another small child clung to her legs, trying to drag her back into the house.

Eik was already out of the car. He said hello to Knudsen's wife, who nodded and pointed toward the barn behind the house. Louise didn't recognize the woman, though it could be because of weight she'd put on from all the pregnancies.

Louise walked over and held out her hand. Now she

was sure she'd never seen the woman before. "He's over in the barn, drowning some newborn kittens," his wife said. She made it sound as if it was something he did all the time. "But he has to pick up our oldest; she goes to gymnastics. He'll be along in a minute."

A gray tabby came meowing out of the house, but Pussy's wife shoved it gently back inside with her foot before shutting the door. The young child still hung on to her.

"How many children do you have?" Eik asked. He peered over at the two in the sandbox.

"Four," she said. She laid a hand on her stomach. "There's another on the way. But not until Christmas."

Eik smiled and offered his congratulations, while Louise thought about the cigarette the woman had been smoking when they arrived. The two kids in the sandbox shouted, and one of the boys began crying. The other started packing a pile of sand that looked like a steep mountain.

"They're burying a mouse. Tjalfe wanted a real bonfire for the body, but their father won't let them start fires when he's not around."

"That's a great name," Eik said. "Are they all named after someone in Nordic mythology?"

"Would be if it was up to my husband," the woman said. She smiled broadly, two deep dimples coming into sight. "They'd be called Odin, Thor, and Loke, but I put my foot down."

Eik nodded. He said that his sister had a daughter named Sigrun.

Louise didn't even know he had a sister. In fact, she didn't know much about his childhood, except that once he'd mentioned he grew up in Hillerød and that he had moved out at seventeen.

They heard footsteps. Two kids shouted, "Dad!"

John Knudsen's hair had turned gray. It lay plastered on his head; he looked exactly like his father, who had always stood and waved at his son as the school bus drove away.

He turned his attention to his children, praising their grave mound before walking over to Louise and Eik. He recognized her at once, she noted, nodding shortly to her before shaking Eik's hand. He wasn't hostile toward them like the Thomsens had been, but he wasn't particularly friendly, either.

"You can go on back inside," he said to his wife. "I'll only be a minute."

"Good-bye," she said, smiling at them. Her dimples deepened when Eik promised they wouldn't be long.

When she closed the door behind her, Knudsen said he knew why they were there. Thomsen had called.

Louise regretted that they hadn't immediately gone over to the barn.

"I don't have anything to tell you about that evening," he said in his broad mid-Zealand accent. "What is it you want to know, anyway?"

"We just want to know what happened," Louise said. "What scared Sune so badly that he didn't dare return home?"

Pussy laughed. "Oh, that; I can tell you that! That kid gets scared when someone farts. One of the boys probably let one rip."

Louise was furious, but Eik reacted first. Knudsen

was still grinning when Eik grabbed him by the collar and slammed him against the wall. "Let's hear about the young prostitute. The one you forced out into the forest," he hissed.

"We didn't force anybody. We paid her," he gasped as Eik tightened his grip on his blue-checkered lumberjack shirt.

"And after you boys had your fun, you killed her!" Eik held him a moment longer before letting go. Knudsen's knees buckled as he struggled to catch his breath.

Louise saw his wife looking out the living room window.

"Did you kill her?" Eik asked.

Knudsen held his throat with both hands, his eyes unfocused. "We didn't kill anybody," he said, shaking his head.

"We found her body out there," Eik said.

Pussy looked down at the ground.

Louise took over. "Did you kill a young woman out in Boserup Forest?" The kids in the sandbox stared wide-eyed at them.

Pussy shook his head violently. He'd recovered enough now to pull himself together. "What are you talking about? Of course we didn't."

"Who was out there with you that night?"

His expression turned blank. "I have to drive over and pick my daughter up," he said, and started off to his car.

Louise nodded. She glanced at Eik; they'd gotten enough for now. Pussy had admitted that they'd paid Lisa Maria to go along with them to the forest, a statement he could hardly deny later—she'd recorded him on her phone.

181

29

René Gamst was leaning back with his hands in the pockets of his baggy prison pants when Louise walked in the visiting room. His hair was still wet from showering. He'd drunk some of the cola in front of him on the table.

"I've got nothing more to say to you," he said before Louise had set foot in the room. He was about to say more, but he straightened up when he saw she wasn't alone.

"We think you've got a lot to tell us," Eik said. He tossed his cigarettes on the table. "Care to smoke?"

"Who the hell are you?" René said, grabbing the pack. Then he laughed. "Now I remember! You were out there when your partner here got into that trouble I saved her from."

"That's right," Eik said, nodding. "I was out there. I

know exactly how big an asshole you are. That's why I don't really feel bad about telling you this—one of your buddies is putting it to your wife while you sit around here playing tic-tac-toe."

René glanced over at Louise. "What the fuck is he talking about?"

"You'll have to excuse my colleague," she said. "He comes from Sydhavnen; they can be hard to understand. What he's trying to tell you is, Big Thomsen has moved in with Bitten. He's taken over your wife, your king-size bed, and your child."

"What is this bullshit?" René hissed. He was about to stand up, but Eik laid a hand on his shoulder.

"You don't think it's true?" Louise said calmly. "So tell me, do you have a blue terry-cloth robe? It looks silly on a man half a meter taller and a lot wider than you."

René sank in his chair.

"You're not a player any longer, René. Call it what you will: checkmate, cuckold. I'm sure it doesn't feel nice at all."

She had imagined this moment would be sweeter, but the satisfaction of revenge faded when René stared at her for a moment before folding his hands and resting his forehead on his knuckles.

"We've just been out to see Jane. You probably don't care, but she and I used to play handball together. I'm very sorry to see how sick she is. Have you seen her recently?"

Louise let the question hang in the air. He didn't answer.

"The doctors told her she might have a week left. Maybe two if she's lucky. That's it."

"Why are you telling me this?" he asked. He gazed blankly at her, his face pale now. "Sure, I remember you two hung out together."

"Because she told us about the initiation ceremony. Her son had been looking forward to that evening. He was proud. But do you know what tortures her every single minute of every single day?"

He didn't answer. All he could do was stare.

"Do you know?" Louise shouted. She leaned over the table. "The fear that she may never see him again. Do you understand how that must feel?"

"It's one thing that your wife is spreading them for another guy," Eik said. He was sitting now, over on the cot. "But at least she's alive. Who knows, you might even get back together with her, if she'll have you."

"Jane told us about your rituals and beliefs," Louise said. "Now you'll tell us in detail what happened that evening, when Sune turned fifteen."

René looked up at her. "How am I supposed to do that? I was here. You know that, you fucking bitch!"

She saw out of the corner of her eye that Eik was about to spring up, but she managed to stop him. She slammed her fist on the table in front of René; his cola toppled over and fizzed against the reclosable cap. "I think you knew the plans down to the very last detail."

"And why should I tell you anything?"

"Because it's your very best chance to get Thomsen out of your wife's bed. And because your friends have already talked. You ought to know them well enough to figure out they're blaming you for doing all the planning, now that you're in here and unable to defend yourself."

Louise knew she had him by the balls. She'd lied without blinking, without the hint of a bad conscience. She was pounding René Gamst to the floor with every word she spoke, and now she decided to finish him off.

"You don't think Thomsen wants to see you free and back home with Bitten, do you?"

He winced in obvious pain. He clearly didn't know what to believe, but finally seemed to realize that she was probably right. He looked like a broken man. "Is he shacked up with her?"

Louise twisted the knife. "When I stopped by, he was about to take your daughter to day care. So I assume that he is."

"The son of a bitch!" Gamst flared up in fury before slumping again. He buried his face in his hands.

"We found the body of a young woman out in the forest, close to where you hold your rituals," she said, after giving him time to recover. "And we suspect there's a connection. We know your brotherhood paid the prostitute to come out to the forest that night. Which one of you contacted her?"

René didn't move.

"I've heard about the fertility ritual, and I want to know what you had planned. And I promise that if it was Thomsen who contacted the woman, he won't get away with laying the blame on you."

He lifted his head up and stared straight ahead for a moment. "He arranges everything when we bring a girl out to the forest."

He spoke into thin air without looking at them; obviously he felt uncomfortable about snitching on his friend.

185

"What do I get out of this?" he asked, in a different tone of voice.

"Like I told you, if you're lucky you'll get Thomsen out of your bed," Louise said.

He thought that over a moment. "Fine," he said, his voice hoarse. He looked earnestly at Louise. "If I tell you, do you promise he'll stay away from my family?"

"I can't promise you anything," she said without blinking, "but if we round up enough evidence, that will take care of itself."

René reached for Eik's cigarettes on the table and asked for a lighter. "We knew the butcher's son hadn't screwed a girl yet, so we all agreed he needed to be a real man, now that he was entering the brotherhood."

"And having sex with a prostitute makes you a real man?"

Suddenly she remembered an evening down at the Hvalsø Inn. It had been a Friday, disco night, and she'd stood at the bar listening to some guys talk about exactly the same thing: You're not a real man until you've been with a whore.

"Yeah," Rene said. "There has to be a first time."

Louise couldn't believe it. "So the plan was that he'd make his debut in front of his father and all of you, with everyone giving him a score. That's just beautiful."

René lowered his eyes, but he nodded.

"So what went wrong?" she asked.

"I don't know. But the ritual itself is quite an experience, and the boy's soft. Maybe he didn't like having his vein cut."

Louise thought about Jane, who'd been so proud of her son, and about his father, who claimed he was a pansy.

"After the initiation, he was supposed to get his gift," René said.

"The gift being a prostitute." Louise sighed. The big test of manhood.

"I heard that he didn't want to do it, that he ran off with his pants around his ankles."

"So your friends took over?" Eik guessed.

"I don't know what happened," he said quickly.

But Louise was all over him, literally in his face. "How did she die?" she hissed.

"I don't know! They say she ran off, too."

"After they fucked her?"

A beat went by before he nodded.

Louise considered telling him about the two other bodies the police had found, but she decided to save that for later; they might need to squeeze him again for information. "Who was out in the forest that night?"

He clenched his teeth, his jaw muscles tightening. "I don't know."

"Take a guess," Louise said, getting angry again. "Thomsen, Pussy, the mason, the butcher. Who else?"

He put on a poker face.

"Come on, who else?" Eik asked, from behind him.

"Maybe the mason's son, Roar," René said. "He was initiated last year, but his father didn't know if he could make it. He's in boarding school."

"Are there others in the inner circle?" Louise said, trying to keep her voice calm.

She couldn't read René's expression. "Klaus," he finally said. "I don't think he was able to make it that evening."

He might as well have punched her.

187

"How the hell can I know who was there when I wasn't there myself? I don't know what happened and no one's going to tell me, either. You've taken care of that!"

"You've had a visitor," she said. "I assume you two talked?"

René didn't answer.

"The oath ring," she said. "Tell me about it!"

He seemed awkward in his chair, scooting forward, shifting his feet, but then he sat up. "Passing around the oath ring means taking a vow of silence. You can never tell anyone what's happened. You may regret it, but you can't break that vow."

The dim visiting room fell silent. The last of the smoke from the stubbed-out cigarettes hung near the ceiling.

"Did you pass around the oath ring the night Klaus died?" Louise asked, her voice quiet now. René sat absolutely still except for a slight nodding of his head.

"Did he really have my blue robe on?" he asked a moment later. Louise saw the despair in his eyes again. "Bitten gave it to me on my birthday."

"Tell me what happened out in the house," she said. She raised her eyebrows at Eik and nodded to the door, signaling that he could wait outside if he liked. He shook his head.

René began crying. Tears streamed silently down his prison-pale cheeks as his shoulders shook. Louise lifted a half-full pack of tissues out of her bag and tossed it onto the table.

He blew his nose loudly, sat for a moment to catch his breath, then turned to her with red-rimmed eyes. "We were all out there," he began.

Louise felt light-headed; suddenly she wasn't sure she wanted to hear what was coming. Would she be better off knowing? Would it heal what had been ripped apart inside her, or had too much time gone by?

"You weren't there," he said, as if she'd forgotten that. "We brought the beer; it was supposed to be a housewarming. First he tried to throw us out, then someone told him he can't do that to his brothers. And we walked in."

He eyed Louise angrily. "What the hell is it with you bitches? You fucking think you can come in and totally change everything around, just because you want to play house."

Louise was about to defend herself, but she realized that in a way he was right. She hadn't liked her boyfriend's buddies. Yet the change was just as much Klaus's doing; he'd simply grown up.

"That's how it was with Bitten, too, when she moved in. At first, she didn't want me hanging out with the guys. I got that idea out of her head in no time flat."

His eyes lost focus; he seemed lost in thought. Probably because he realized that now it was Bitten hanging out with the guys. Or at least one of them.

"What happened then?" Louise whispered.

René took a deep breath and looked away. "We stacked the cases of beer out in the laundry room behind the kitchen, so we could grab one on our way back in from taking a leak. We were all standing around out there when Klaus came and gave us this bullshit about having to see somebody; he had to go. Then he changed his story, said you were coming home, that he didn't want any trouble since you'd just moved in."

189

Louise felt terrible, hearing how her boyfriend had tried to get rid of them.

"Then he talked about how his father was coming by with a drill. That's when Thomsen slapped him around and said to shut his fucking mouth and open some beer. Then Klaus got mad. Those two had been at each other's throats since Klaus said he wanted out of the brotherhood. Said he was going to talk about some of the stuff if we didn't let him go."

"What was he going to talk about?" Louise asked. "The accident the janitor had out in Såby? About what happened to Gudrun at her store?"

René looked puzzled. His eyes darted as he tried to add everything up. Then he nodded. "I think so, but I don't know. Back then I figured it was just a threat to get out of the brotherhood."

It dawned on Louise why René had suddenly begun talking. He knew he hadn't given them enough about the initiation to get his wife out of Thomsen's clutches. The story about Klaus's death, however, could work. He was going after Thomsen, and she was with him all the way.

"Klaus didn't want to be part of it anymore," he told her. "Most of us have been there at some time or other. It's just that nobody's been brave enough to leave. Not yet anyway." The final words came out under his breath.

Louise wanted to hear more, while at the same time she felt like running, vanishing from the room, like smoke being sucked under the door, blowing away in the wind, into the darkness.

"He kept telling us we had to go, and take the beer with us. And Thomsen kept slapping him. And then

Klaus lost his balance and fell over one of the cases of beer. He just lay there, but then the butcher and I got him up in a chair."

An image flashed by in Louise's head of Klaus's parents' black leather recliner, which they'd given to Klaus.

"I don't know what time it was. We were listening to music, but when we ran out of beer we decided to take off. We asked Klaus if he wanted to come along, but he didn't answer, he just sat there with his eyes closed, like he was asleep. The butcher went over and grabbed him, and he was fucking dead. We didn't know until we started shaking him, he just fell off the chair."

He paused.

"No one dies tripping over a case of beer," he said. "We couldn't know. It was an accident." Another pause. "A really shitty accident."

"Why didn't you call an ambulance?" Louise asked. "Who came up with the idea of the noose? And why did you want it to look like a suicide?"

His hands were folded in front of him as he stared down at the table and shrugged. "We didn't want to get mixed up in anything. We figured it'd be better to make it look like he did it himself."

It was as if a fog had lifted inside Louise's head. As if she were on top of a mountain on a crystal-clear winter day, frozen to the bone, watching René cry like a baby. Instantly she realized the entire group had kept a secret that could have patched her life back together. She felt split in two, one part of her dissolving, the other part rising like a black thundercloud.

She straightened up. The bastards had kept their

mouths shut about an accident that no one would have blamed them for anyway. Had they lived up to their promise to protect each other, they might even have saved his life, she thought. They could've called an ambulance instead of just getting drunker. But they didn't. They punished Klaus for choosing her instead of them. And they punished her by letting her believe that Klaus had abandoned her, that she wasn't worthy of his love.

"You said nothing, even though you knew he didn't kill himself."

"It was an accident."

"What about the janitor and Gudrun? Were they accidents—killing them?"

"We didn't kill nobody!"

"You should've said something."

"You don't break a promise."

"You just have!" she pointed out.

"It's different now." He stared at her defiantly.

"You knew that Jane's son was scared, that he didn't dare come home, but you said nothing. Not until now, now that it's in your interest to give us Thomsen. What kind of a person are you?"

She leaned forward. "You know very well what they might do. The boy is fifteen! If anything happens to Sune, I'm going to hold you personally responsible!" she shouted.

"I don't know what you expect me to do," he said.

"I expect you to tell me everything you know about Thomsen, and whatever else you and your fucking friends are hiding. I want you to tell the police everything. About Klaus and all the rest of the shit you've done."

Louise's patience was at an end. The truth needed to come out, all of it. She knew she'd gone too far, though, and cursed herself for it. You should never shout, never lose control. But it appeared that René hadn't even noticed.

"I can't give you the others. You know what would happen to me if I did?"

"Like hell you can't! You're a grown man; act like it!"

He was whining now. "You don't think I have enough going on in my life already?"

"You don't have shit going on!" Louise shouted. She felt Eik's eyes on her. "You've lost everything. Your wife. Your daughter. Your freedom. You've been caught in your own shit and your brotherhood's ridiculous vows. You're going down, no matter what. And if I were you I'd take Thomsen with me. I want to help. The only condition is, you have to promise to testify against him in court."

René sat for a while, thinking it over. Then he dried his tears, nodded slowly, and spoke in a half whisper. "I'll do it."

All at once she couldn't stand the sight of him. There wasn't enough air in the room; she felt dizzy. She turned to Eik. He stood up and called the guard. Totally drained now, she followed as he led her past the guard room and out into the twilight, away from the jail. He pulled her close and put his arms around her as she cried.

She felt his hand stroking her hair, holding her back gently. Finally Louise dried her eyes, kissed him on the cheek, and backed off half a step. "Thanks," she mumbled. "Thanks for staying in there with me."

30

Sune had a stomachache, but for once it wasn't from hunger. The thought of meeting his father at the sacrificial oak had plagued him all day long, but he still didn't know what he would say.

He began to cry. He felt all alone, and he missed his mother so much that he felt powerless to act, unable to work up the will to keep going.

The sun had disappeared, leaving the forest in the dim of the Danish summer night as he approached the oak tree. His father sat with his back against the trunk, his big hands folded around his knees. He didn't seem angry. Just sad. A terrifying thought hit Sune: His mother was dead. He walked over to his father in dread.

"Has anything happened?" he whispered. "To Mom?"

His father shook his head.

"How is she?"

"She's bad, but she's fighting. All that's keeping her alive is the hope that she'll see you again."

Sune felt a horrible sorrow, a black, leaden weight around his heart.

"The police have been by again," his father said. He sounded tired. "Will you please come home?"

Sune didn't answer. The only sound was the wind swishing through the trees.

"They found the girl," Sune finally said.

"I know. That's also why I'm asking you to come home now. You're born into this, there's nothing we can do about that."

"But…" The words nearly stuck in Sune's throat. "She was murdered! The police will figure it out!"

"That's another reason why you have to get out of here. People will think you did it."

"But I didn't!"

"People will think you did."

A deep voice spoke from behind Sune. "If you don't hold the ring and take your oath with the rest of us, you *are* the one who killed her."

Terrified, Sune whirled around and saw the gothi step out of the darkness. His father got to his feet and held him from behind to protect him.

"We can't cover for you if you're not one of us," the gothi said. He walked over to them. "We'll have to say you're responsible for what happened out here."

"But I'm telling the police what you did to her."

The gothi reached out to grab Sune. His father desperately held on to him. "Leave my son alone," he yelled. "I'll take care of this."

195

Sune saw the chunk of firewood in the gothi's hand, saw him raise it, and heard it crack against his father's head. He fell along with his father, and before he knew it he was grabbed roughly and hauled out of the clearing. "This boy belongs to the gods, whether he likes it or not."

"Stop!" his father shouted, or tried to; his voice was thick and groggy.

31

W hat was that?" Camilla asked, grabbing Frederik's arm.

He tried to figure out where the shrill screams were coming from, then he vanished into the forest. Camilla tossed away the sack they'd brought for the boy and humped after him.

Moments later, she saw that Frederik had stopped; a large figure in a dark-green hunting jacket was dragging someone—the boy! He was still screaming, and her heart constricted when she saw the terror in his face.

"What the hell's going on here?" Frederik yelled. He sprinted over and reached for the boy, but was slammed to the ground as if he'd been hit by a bear. The man began tottering; Camilla guessed that Frederik had grabbed on to his legs, but all she could see was a broad back and a leg kicking at Frederik. When the man leaned over, the boy wrestled free and ran to Camilla, hiding behind her back, as if he were safe there.

Through the trees she glimpsed Frederik, back on his feet now, but swaying. He steadied himself up against a tree, then he took off after the man, who had disappeared down the forest road.

"Frederik!" she yelled. "Stop!"

Suddenly the forest was completely still. All she heard was her own rapid breathing and the boy's quiet sobbing. His shoulders shook, and he pulled away from her as if he were embarrassed to have hidden behind her. He was skinny and shabby; his hands and clothes were filthy. Camilla reached for him.

"It's all over," she said, comforting him, but she was interrupted by more shouting. She recognized Frederik's voice. Then she heard a car door slam, an engine racing furiously. The car's tires squealed as it took off.

"My dad," the boy whispered. "I have to find my dad."

"Where is he?" Camilla asked. For a moment she was in doubt; should she follow the boy or rush over and find Frederik? She humped after the boy through the forest, past a stack of firewood and a clump of ferns. They fought their way through bushes, trampling down some wild raspberries.

"Dad!" The boy started to run. Camilla tried to keep up. They both stopped when they reached the sacrificial oak. The boy had made a small camp behind a thicket, in between some low bushes and a few logs. He'd cleared a space for a campfire, and on the ground beside it was her son's blue jacket. Apart from that the camp looked deserted.

"He's gone!" the boy wailed.

"But weren't you running away from him?" Camilla asked, and looked around. Nothing was moving.

"No, Dad came here to get me. He was trying to help me."

He fell to the ground and hid his face in his hands. His thin shoulders began shaking again. Camilla eased down beside him and put her hand on his back. "We'll find your father," she said. "I can drive you home."

He shook his head almost imperceptibly. "I can't go home," he whispered, almost in a panic. "They've turned against Dad."

"I'm sure everything will be all right now," Camilla said.

"You don't understand. They'll kill me."

"No one's going to kill a child," Camilla exclaimed. Then she thought about the bodies in the girls' graves less than half a kilometer away.

A man's voice cried out, "Hello!" The boy gave a start.

"Easy, it's my husband," Camilla said. "Over here!" she shouted.

Frederik appeared in the clearing and walked toward them. "What on earth happened?" she said, shocked at the sight of him. His clothes were covered in mud, and he was bleeding at the temple.

"He tried to run me down. I had to jump in the ditch."

"Maybe he's the one who hit me," Camilla said, her fist clenched in anger. "He's a total maniac."

They both turned to the boy.

"They won't stop until they find me," he said, crying again. "And I don't know where to go."

Camilla stood and helped him up. "Come with us. We'll find a way out of this. The police are going to be very happy to hear that you're all right."

But the boy still resisted, and for a moment she feared he would run away again.

"Dad might still be out here," he said.

"Then let's wait a while," Camilla suggested. "You could also try to call him."

She handed him her phone, but he didn't take it. His stomach was growling, and she could see that he was freezing. "Honestly, you could stand a bath." She smiled at him. "And you look like you could eat a decent meal. Sometimes things look different after a good night's sleep. Okay?"

He seemed more at ease now, but he kept peering into the forest. "I want to go with you, but you have to promise not to call anyone. I think Dad will come back for me tomorrow."

"We promise," Frederik said. He placed his hand on the boy's shoulder.

32

"If they're responsible for Klaus's death, they're going to pay for it," Louise said. She took a sip of the bitter, black morning coffee that Eik had set on the desk in front of her. "Even if it was an accident. They should have called for help instead of covering up, like they've done so many times. This has to end, now."

She'd tossed and turned all night. At one point, she had gone out into the kitchen and made a cup of chamomile tea. More than once she had regretted turning down Eik's offer to sleep at his place in Sydhavnen. He started every day with a morning swim and a shot of Gammel Dansk.

That would've helped calm her down, she thought. But she had politely declined and instead brought home takeaway to eat with Jonas. He'd been sitting in his room wearing his big earphones. He'd lost all track of time and forgotten about dinner, and suddenly he was hungry as a bear, so hungry that after eating Chicken Tikka Masala she had warmed up some soup. Then they made popcorn. And then Melvin was at the door with two cartons of Danish strawberries and half a liter of cream he'd bought on the way home from the allotment.

"I just stopped by to pick up the mail and for some clean clothes," he told them, as an excuse. Before Louise knew it, he was sitting in the living room drinking coffee and a shot of something he'd gone down to pick up.

Soon she realized that their neighbor in the flat below had missed them. Which warmed her heart. While she and Jonas sat on the sofa, with Melvin sitting across from them and Dina resting her head on his feet, some of her pain faded away. Everything seemed a bit more manageable.

Until an hour later. It had all come back the second she turned her bedside light off. Everything René Gamst had said about Klaus's final night in the house.

Eik broke into her thoughts. "I hope you're not getting these two cases mixed up." He set his cup down. "All this about Klaus is Roskilde's case, if there even is a case. You and I are still looking for a boy who ran away from home."

She wasn't sure, but he sounded a bit jealous. Louise studied him for a moment. She was in love. She'd ac-knowledged it sometime that night. It was his awkward charm, the personality that behind his scrubby leather jacket was mild, full of warmth and empathy. He was both darkness and light. He'd gotten inside her in a way that made her long for him whenever he wasn't there.

Klaus was no longer the great love of her life. He was missed, and he was a sorrow she'd never moved on from.

And now she knew it was all because of a gang of boys who even as adults had never revealed the truth. It angered her, and she had to do something about that anger before it devoured her. She couldn't care less if she was mixing things up; her gut ached at the thought that these blood brothers were forcing a fifteen-year-old boy to become part of their sick brotherhood.

"The two cases are connected." She looked over at Eik. "Can't you see it? They're all covering each other's ass, and if we ever hope to break through we have to gather every possible shred of evidence against them. We also need to take a good look at the cases concerning Gudrun and the janitor, now that René is willing to testify against the others."

Eik still looked dubious.

"Before I came in, I spoke with Klaus's parents," she said, ignoring his skepticism. "Nymand is trying to get authorization to dig up his coffin and have Forensics examine him. There was no autopsy back then because of the suicide note, but if he died of the injuries from the fall, there's a good chance we can prove he was dead before they hung him up. That would support René's statement and make him more credible."

That morning, Nymand had told her he'd interrogated René Gamst the evening before.

"They're preparing warrants, but before they arrest anyone for the murder of Lisa Maria Nielsen, he wants to have compelling evidence against the entire group, so they don't end up detaining only one of them. He wants to make a case against all of them."

Louise agreed 100 percent with Nymand. The case

resembled the latest instance of honor killing, in which a family picked someone to carry out the deed—a seventeen-year-old son, whom they reasoned would receive a mild sentence. It had sent a message when the entire family received sentences of various lengths for murder and attempted murder. But the case had required massive preparation. Nymand had set into motion similar preparations, and it involved her and Eik.

Her partner shook his head. He didn't say anything at first, though it wasn't difficult for Louise to see what he was thinking.

It finally came out. "You don't *know* if the cases are connected. You don't *know* if they killed the prostitute, or if the boy ran away because of them!"

"No," Louise admitted. "I don't know that, but I have a strong suspicion. And if I'm wrong, it'll be my ass. I'll deal with that if it happens."

"Take my advice." He rested his elbows on his desk. "Be careful. Don't be unprofessional just because you're emotionally involved. I made that mistake back when Sofie disappeared. All I got out of it was that no one took my case seriously."

Louise didn't like knowing the name of Eik's former lover. Up until now, she had only been a vague presence in Louise's mind.

"I was so focused on what happened to her," he said, "that I ignored the drowning of the two others in the boat. And when people suggested she might have had something to do with their deaths, I had blinders on; I refused to take it seriously. I just knew that she'd drowned at sea with them that night."

"But strictly speaking, you can't be sure that she's not out there somewhere, right?" Louise ignored a call from Camilla.

Eik shook his head. "I never heard from her, even though she knew my phone number and where I lived."

He was trying to stay calm, Louise noticed, but his eyes weren't playing along. She cleared her throat and nodded. "I can see what you're saying. And I'm grateful that you're spelling it out for me. But this isn't just about Klaus. You're also right that we don't know what's happened to the boy. But we know that the same men who had a hand in Klaus's death, who probably have killed a young prostitute, whose methods we now have a good picture of—these men won't stop at anything to stay out of prison. And I can't let that happen. Lisa Maria was a single mother to a three-year-old boy. Thomsen paid her to show up in the forest, and a month later we dig her body up in the same forest. If I can't bring them to justice for that, I might just as well hand in my badge."

"That's Roskilde's case. Not ours. Weren't they the ones who investigated the death of your old boyfriend?"

"But there was no investigation! Thomsen and his gang got away with making everyone believe it was a suicide."

"But it's still within their jurisdiction."

"Exactly. That's why Nymand gets to dig him up. It's Roskilde's case, from start to finish. But if we're going to get these men, I have to help them. The only reason René will play along is because I can put the screws to him. Anyway, Nymand doesn't know anything about these old cases. Why should he? He wasn't even at Roskilde back then. Everything has to be considered; the old cases have to be opened again. When I've gathered all the evidence I can, it all goes over to his desk."

Eik considered this for a moment. Then he nodded, first thoughtfully, then more decisively. "I'm with you. Of course we can't let those assholes get away with murdering a single mother. By the way, have we heard anything about the two others they dug up out there?"

Louise shook her head. "Not yet."

Her phone began blinking again, and she answered. "Camilla, I'll call you back in just a bit." She was about to hang up, when she realized that something was very wrong.

"You have to come." Her friend was crying. "I've already called Roskilde Police, but they told me the boy is your case. Someone's taken him and declared war on us."

33

"That's all she said?" Eik asked as they neared St. Hans Psychiatric Hospital.

All the way to Roskilde, Louise had been trying desperately to call Camilla back, but her phone was busy.

"Did she say why Sune went home with them?"

Louise shook her head. "She said it would be easier to explain when we got there. But she was scared. All I know is, somebody broke in while they were asleep and took the boy."

"He could have left of his own free will," Eik said. He'd already said that, several times.

"He could have. It's the most obvious explanation, but somebody did break in. Apparently, there's no doubt about that. I just don't understand the bit about the declaration of war, or how they got the boy to go with them."

She spotted the two stone pillars marking the entrance

of Ingersminde. Charlie perked up in the back of the car when Eik pulled into the long driveway and floored it. The car slid to a halt in front of the broad stone stairs, and before he'd killed the engine Camilla had stepped outside. She stood in her pajamas, pale as a sheet. She waved them in. "There's something you have to see," she said, and immediately she hurried into the large hall.

The house was quiet. A jacket had been tossed on the floor; Frederik's rubber boots stood beside the door to the kitchen. Through the kitchen windows looking out on the enormous lawn, Louise noticed Frederik and the manager by the path that led into the forest, the start of the old Death Trail.

Camilla turned to make sure they were behind her, then she walked out into the small hallway behind the kitchen and opened the outside door. She stepped aside and let them by.

A post had been stuck into the ground. On top of it was a large, black horse's head.

Louise froze. Eik bumped into her from behind, and she stepped on his foot. He grabbed her shoulders to steady her. The horse's head had been cut off far down the neck; its mane lay draped over the post like a veil. Black, dead eyes stared at them. A few big blowflies buzzed around the corners of the eyes and the bloody bottom of the neck.

"What in hell is this?" She pushed at Eik to get away from it.

"Frederik calls it a nithing pole," Camilla said. She sounded feeble. She led Louise back into the kitchen while Eik walked over the lawn to join Frederik and

Tønnesen. "It's part of the old Nordic religion. It means that someone has cast a spell on us."

"I've never heard of anything like this," Louise said. Her legs were still shaky.

"He says it's like when the Viking ships sailed in with a dragon head carved into the stem. It was considered an act of aggression."

Camilla sat down and pulled a chair over for her bad leg. "God knows where they got the head. Everyone around here has horses. I hope it's not one from close by. The whole area will be screaming!"

Louise walked over to the Nespresso machine and asked what Camilla wanted.

"Strong, big, with milk." Camilla leaned over. "I started crying, I was so scared." She breathed deeply for a moment before straightening up. Louise handed her the coffee.

"First thing in the morning," Camilla said, "I open the door and step outside. We eat breakfast on the terrace when the weather's good." She looked up at Louise. "I didn't see it until I was standing right in front of it."

Louise watched through the window as Eik let Charlie out of the car. He ran across the lawn, his snout to the grass. "How long have you been hiding the boy, and why didn't you tell us? You knew we were looking for him!"

"We weren't hiding him." Camilla held the coffee mug with both hands and stared down into the foam.

"You do realize, don't you, that a young woman has in all probability been murdered in your forest. Sune might be an important witness, but instead of calling the police and saying you found the boy, you do nothing. Until you let our witness disappear again." Louise's hands were shaking with fury, but she knew she had to get hold of herself, to focus. "How long have you been hiding him from the police?"

Now it was Camilla's turn to explode. She slammed the mug down, splashing coffee onto the table. "I haven't been hiding him, goddamn it. Not from the police. Something terrible happened yesterday evening, and we took care of him. The only person we hid him from was the idiot dragging him over to a car."

She shook her head and closed her eyes for a moment. Then she explained that she and Frederik had been taking some supplies out to him.

"We heard screams, and we saw a man dragging him on the ground. We did what anyone would have done; we brought him back to safety."

"What anyone would have done is to call the police," Louise said.

"Damn it, Louise! We wanted to, but he wouldn't have come with us if we did. Besides, he needed somewhere safe, a meal, and a shower."

"Did he speak with his father out in the forest?"

Camilla's explanation had eased her somewhat. And she had to admit that she probably would have done the same thing. The well-being of the boy came first, of course it did.

Camilla nodded. "I don't know how long they spoke; we didn't get there until Sune started screaming, and Frederik ran over to him. Then I followed him to his camp, but his father had disappeared."

Before Louise could ask about the man who had

abducted Sune, Camilla shoved a scrap of paper across the table. "This is the man's license plate number. You can check it out. It was a black four-wheel-drive, Frederik said."

She paused for a moment. "Sune was shaking like a leaf when he ran over to me. He was so scared. This may be just another case for you, but that boy screamed like it was life or death. And he was in shock."

Louise nodded. She read the license plate and was immediately stunned; she recognized the ST in front of the numbers. That those two letters and her friend's description pointed to Thomsen's four-wheel-drive didn't surprise her. But knowing that he was a step in front of them made her skin crawl.

"How much did Sune tell you?" The three men and the dog were walking across the lawn now, back to the house.

Camilla shook her head. "Nothing. Only that now *they* were after his father, too, because he tried to protect Sune. He looked terrible, and he had no place to go. That's why Frederik told him he could stay with us. But he wasn't in any shape to answer questions; he needed to sleep before we tried to find out anything more. He was sleeping like a rock in the guest room beside yours when I went to bed."

"Would you have heard if the boy got up and tiptoed out during the night?"

"No, I doubt we would have. But the kitchen door was broken into from the outside. And he could have just unlocked the door and walked out."

Louise thought for a second. "You're sure his father was protecting him against the other man?"

"I didn't see it, but that's what he said. I only saw the man who hit Frederik before he drove off. Actually, I only saw him from behind. But like I say, the boy was totally shaken up and very afraid for his father. He said that his father had tried to stop the man who'd taken him."

"And you saw the man?"

"I told you, only his back. It wasn't light enough to see a whole lot. Mostly, I saw a shadow walking away." Camilla rubbed her forehead with her fingers. "I don't know what shocked the boy most, seeing his father get hit or the argument between the two men."

"He might've been surprised that his father was defending him," Louise suggested. "He might have felt he didn't need to hide anymore, knowing that his father would fight for him."

Camilla frowned. "Why in the world would anyone put their child in a situation like this?" she mumbled.

The men walked in. "No doubt about it," Frederik said, "they used the old trail to get up here." He set coffee mugs on the table. "The grass has been trampled, and it looks like there's been a struggle."

Louise glanced at Eik. "Let's go. We need to find the butcher, and I have a feeling we need to find him fast."

34

The butcher's white van was parked in the middle of the lot, as if it had been abandoned in haste. Otherwise the farmhouse looked dark and deserted.

Louise was apprehensive, less about the quiet than about her uncertainty—about not knowing what awaited her. She had the unmistakable sense that something was slipping away.

Eik slammed the car door behind her. As she walked up to the door, she flashed on an image of Jane's pleading expression. She hoped with all her heart that the family was finally together. Hoped that Sune had been taken to his parents, and right now he was sitting beside his mother's bed. But she couldn't forget the horse's head. The threat and the skirmish out in the forest pointed in a different direction, toward some sort of a showdown.

Louise knocked, and after a moment she tried the

door. It was open. She listened for sounds from the house, then stepped inside. The kitchen was empty, as was the living room, but the door to Jane's bedroom stood open a crack. Louise looked around. A phone and a wallet lay on the dining room table. A pair of slippers had been kicked off over by the sofa; a wrinkled blanket hung over its arm and down to the floor.

"Hello," she cried out. She walked to the door. "Anybody here?"

She stopped. She thought she heard a sound, cloth or some material being rubbed, but no one answered. Then she heard someone breathing in heavily and sniffling.

Louise pushed the door open. The butcher sat hunched over in a chair beside the empty bed. His forearms rested on his thighs, and his hands hung down. His face was pale and streaked with tears, his eyes red and shiny. *Here is a man falling to pieces*, Louise thought. The bed was made, the comforter's cover smooth, the pillows fluffed up.

Suddenly she had difficulty breathing, as if air wasn't reaching her lungs. Fragments of sentences, images from school, long-forgotten memories swarmed inside her head. She and Jane exploring Hammershus during a camping trip to Bornholm. Summers with swimming lessons in Uggerløse's outdoor pool, where she reached her hundred- and thousand-meter levels. The school bus had picked them up beside Skolesøen every morning, and when school was out they went to the grill and ate French fries.

She laid a hand on the butcher's shoulder. He didn't say a word, but his eyes followed her movements. Now he sat up and looked over at the doorway where Eik was standing. His mouth trembled, but he pressed his lips together and formed what ended up as a grimace.

Louise pointed to the bed and raised her eyebrows.

The butcher shook his head. "Jane is at her parents. She's left me."

A dying woman doesn't leave her husband, Louise thought. Her anxiety returned.

"Did you tell her that you ran away yesterday instead of staying and helping your son?" Eik asked.

The butcher lowered his head. "I didn't run away," he said softly. Not as an excuse. More to inform them. "I followed the people, who rescued Sune, up to their manor. I watched them take him inside. I don't expect you to understand, but believe me, my son is safer there than with me."

He buried his face in his hands, his thick fingers seeming to hold his desperation. "They can't do this to me." His voice was hoarse. "To him. He's just a boy. I don't know where to take him so they can't find him. I don't know how to protect him."

He whispered the last words. Then he sat up. "I have to go get him; we have to get away from here. There's just so much. What'll I do with the shop? And what about Jane? I'm not sure she's strong enough to be moved again. She didn't have the strength to even speak to me last night when I called."

Eik walked over to the bed and sat beside Louise. She would have given the butcher a few more minutes, but Eik took over. "Unfortunately it's too late."

His voice was neutral, no hint of accusation or blame. At first it seemed as if the butcher hadn't understood what he said, but then he looked angrily at Eik.

"What do you mean, too late?" he sneered. "If you're going to sic social services on us, go right ahead. But I'll be damned if you're going to stop me from trying to protect my boy!"

"Sune's not at the manor anymore," Eik said. He explained that someone had broken into the house during the night. "This morning he was gone."

The butcher's arms fell; he stared silently at Eik, as if trying to understand what had been said.

"They stuck a post in the ground with a horse's head on top, just outside their door," Louise said. "What should we make of that?"

The butcher's face twisted and strained. Desperation, Louise thought. That's what it looked like. Genuine desperation and fear.

"They'll kill him," he whispered. "The nithing pole means that they're turning against the people who were hiding Sune. And they'll sacrifice Sune to the gods as punishment for breaking out of the brotherhood."

"You don't kill somebody for leaving a group of friends," Louise said. Then Klaus came to mind.

"This is no group of friends," he said. "I thought you of all people had that figured out. This is hell. No one gets out."

35

He could be anywhere. The possibilities seemed endless to Louise as she sat in Eik's car, watching the fields around Skov Hastrup slip by. There were so many places you could easily hide a fifteen-year-old boy. Empty Boy Scout cabins. All the barns in the area. Haylofts, sheds out in the forest. A search would be immensely difficult if Thomsen had decided to stow the boy away.

After they had handed the butcher over to a few of Nymand's men so he could help find Sune, Louise thought the gnawing in her stomach came from knowing there was little time. It had started when she heard of Sune's disappearance from Camilla and Frederik's house. But now, as Eik turned onto Kvandrupvej and headed for Big Thomsen's farm, she realized the source of her dread was the thought of what these men might put the boy through. The butcher was absolutely right. If anyone knew how far they would go to stop whoever was in their way, she did.

"Come on, come on, damn it," she barked as Eik took a curve and Thomsen's farm came into sight. Instead he slowed down.

"Have they called in?" he asked.

Louise clenched her teeth and shook her head. Nymand had sent his men out to the mason in Såby and Pussy's farm in Særløse, which was less than a kilometer from her and Eik. The plan was that when they were close to their destinations they would text Nymand, who then would ensure that the searches took place simultaneously.

Louise had just texted him that they were ready. She stared at her phone's display, waiting for *Go*.

She gave Eik points for not saying anything about her pushing him, when all they could do was sit and wait. She glanced at him. His longish dark hair was combed back. He had thrown his leather jacket in the backseat of the car, and now she noticed he was wearing a white T-shirt, not black. He always wore black T-shirts.

When they had first met, he admitted to her that he dressed in black solely because he hated shopping. He bought clothes in stacks. Ten black T-shirts, five pairs of black Levi's, same model. Black socks. He didn't wear underwear, he told her. He picked up that habit during a long journey in India.

Now she noticed that the T-shirt wasn't the only thing different. The two thin yellow and green strings he usually wore around his wrist were gone, as was his shark's tooth necklace. She'd never asked him about these things;

she had the impression that he'd been wearing them since his girlfriend disappeared.

She wanted to lay her hand on his arm, to feel his sinewy muscles, the warmth of his body.

"Do you really think they might kill the boy?"

Louise straightened up. Was it possible? She thought about it for a while, then nodded. "I'm afraid so. To save their own asses. I'm afraid they'll do almost anything to avoid a murder charge. If they have any brains at all, they'll know that's exactly what they're facing if Sune talks. And if things start falling apart for them, who knows what else will come to light."

"But killing a boy?"

"That's not how they see it. He's not a boy to them. In their world, he's an adult who broke a vow of silence."

"In their world?"

"Maybe that's not how things work in the city," she said, annoyed at him now. "But out here, people stick together. I think that's how it is in most small communities. You stick together, and from what I've seen, it's plain that Thomsen and his gang have taken this type of solidarity to extremes. The butcher said it. It's not a question of friendship now, it's like a street gang or sect no one can get out of. That's why I think it's all the same to them if someone's fifteen or thirty."

That feeling in her stomach, that anxiety, was anger now. "Back when we had parties in school, friends took care of each other. If someone was getting beat up, friends stepped in. Those were the rules, and I think everyone was okay with that, with what friends were expected to do."

Eik grunted, but he didn't comment. She wasn't sure what he thought about all this.

"It's not very politically correct," she said, "but I can't say I wouldn't do the same. If I were out with Camilla, and somebody jumped her, I'd get involved."

"That'd be something to see," he mumbled.

Louise ignored him. Instead she leaned over, and she was about to comment on his T-shirt when her phone rang. "Let's go," Nymand said.

Eik floored it. Fields and corrals flew by, but all Louise saw was the image of Big Thomsen, Sune's tormentor, who had resorted to violence to nab him. She was more than ready to get in his face about that.

The farmhouse's white gable came into view. Thomsen's Toyota Land Cruiser was parked at the end of one wing, its tailgate open.

"Showtime," Eik said, and he drove in.

Their plan was that if Thomsen didn't come out, Louise would take the back door, Eik would stay out front. If he wasn't home, they would have to contact a neighbor to witness the search. But none of this was necessary; Big Thomsen walked out the minute Eik drove up.

He didn't seem thrilled to see them, but neither did he act as if he'd been expecting them. He looked like his normal self, laid-back, his hands in the pockets of his blue work pants. He clearly meant to appear standoffish, but for whatever reason it didn't work on Louise, who walked up to him and said they would like his permission to search his property.

Eik spoke up from behind her. "We have a warrant, of c—"

"Stop!" Louise shouted, as Thomsen lifted his phone to his ear. "No calls. You're going back inside with my colleague, and you two can have a chat while I look around."

"This is not all right, you going around harassing citizens this way all the time. What is it you think I've done?"

She wanted to tell him there were plenty of reasons why they'd returned. She wanted to yell it in his face. She couldn't stop thinking of Sune, and of the three-year-old boy without a mother to care for him. But she contented herself with giving him a dirty look.

"We're not saying you've done anything," Eik said as he herded him toward the house. "But we know you were out in Boserup Forest last night, dragging a fifteen-year-old boy to your car. We also know you had a scrap with the boy's father, but Sune managed to get away. We want to know where the boy is."

"I wasn't out in any forest last night. And how the hell should I know where the boy is?" Thomsen sounded amused. "And I haven't 'had a scrap' with anyone. Either you fight or you don't fight."

"You argued with the boy's father out in the forest," Eik stated.

"I don't know what you're talking about. But in case you don't know, the boy's mother is very sick, and don't you suppose she'd like to see her son before she kicks the bucket?"

Louise's fists were clenched; she was two seconds away from jumping all over Big Thomsen, but Eik held his hand up to stop her. For a moment she quivered in anger, but then she turned on her heel and strode over to the barn wing of the farmhouse.

"That boy needs a whipping, the way he's making his mother suffer..."

That's all Louise heard before entering the darkness of the barn. Long ago, animals had probably been kept in there, pigs or cattle, maybe chickens. The ceilings were low, and tall bricked-up steps divided the three rooms. It smelled dusty and sour from the moldy walls. Only the middle room looked to be in use.

She walked over to the discarded furniture and junk piled up on the floor. Against the wall stood a packing box filled with porcelain and an old trunk, its lid missing.

But there was no sign of the boy, not there or in the two other empty rooms, their windowpanes too gray from dirt and cobwebs for the sunshine outside to penetrate.

Eik and Big Thomsen were gone when she walked outside, and the door to the middle wing where Thomsen lived was closed. She hurried over to another wing. Its inner walls had been torn down, and it smelled like dried grass and motor oil: a garden tractor big enough for a city park dominated the middle of the room. A sheet of plywood covered with black outlines of various tools hung on the end wall. Hammers, saws, squares. For a moment she was impressed with the level of organization, in contrast with the mess Thomsen had made at Bitten's house.

Outside, she looked at the gables for a way to get

up into the lofts of the two wings. She spotted a black wooden hatch door on the one gable, flush with the wall, its latch covered with as many cobwebs as the windows below. It hadn't been opened for ages.

She walked over to the middle-wing residence. Through the window, she noticed Thomsen gesturing at Eik, as if he was emphasizing a point. Coats and rain-coats hung on one wall of the hall; shelving covered the other side. On the wall beside the door was a small faucet with a short hose attached, hanging over a drain. Her parents had something similar, a place to rinse footwear. She wiped off her rubber boots and walked into the living room, where Big Thomsen was yelling.

"I slept with my girlfriend last night. Can't you get that through your head? I was there all night—just ask her!"

Eik nodded calmly as Louise began a systematic search of the house. A large, black leather corner sofa had been pushed into the nook beside the porch door. Pictures hung on the walls, and on the buffet sat a large glass plate. A very expensive plate, Louise thought. This was no bachelor pad; she'd expected to see a billiard table or a dartboard. The kitchen had a large refrigerator with a freezer compartment below, an ice cube dispenser above. She checked the bedroom with attached bath, the two guest rooms on the other side of the hall. Still no boy. And the bedspreads were smooth, everything appeared to be in its place, with no sign of anyone having been there recently.

Louise peeked into Thomsen's bedroom. A framed photo of his parents stood on a chest of drawers. His father was as she remembered him, back when he was police chief of Roskilde. They'd called his mother Mrs. Police Chief. Louise knew her as the woman behind the counter at the bank, long before Unibank became Nordea.

Strange how these small flashes of memory popped up, she thought, as she looked at a photo of Ole Thomsen as a schoolboy. Broad face, thick hair, with happy eyes and a light smile. His arm was around a young girl. Louise had forgotten that he'd been good looking back then.

Right after they'd moved to Lerbjerg, when she started at Hvalsø School, he was one of the boys she watched during recesses. She couldn't remember when his charm had disappeared, when whatever he was now had taken over.

"Fine, we'll all go see her," she heard Eik say from the living room. Someone began walking. "Stop right there," Eik shouted. "Hand over your phone. No calls until we've spoken with Bitten Gamst."

Louise stood out in the hall and waited while they put their shoes on. Then she glanced into his office behind the kitchen.

"I'll take a look in the attic," she told Eik as they were about to walk out. Stairs in the laundry room led up to a whitewashed trapdoor in the ceiling. She pushed it open and found a light switch on the floor beside the chimney.

Several packing boxes and a Christmas tree-holder were stacked up close to the door. She stepped inside, the attic floor sagging a bit from her weight. Dust swirled; dark shadows lined the walls. Things, stored and forgotten. There was no sound, no sign of life. Louise shone her flashlight in the corners. Nothing.

Eik had started the car outside; she heard the diesel purring. She shut off the light, lowered the trapdoor onto her head, and crawled down the steps.

She glanced around the living room one last time before walking out and getting into the backseat. She sensed Thomsen looking at her in the side mirror. Their eyes met for a moment, then she jerked her head away, leaving him to stare at her profile.

36

They drove over the hill outside Særløse. Louise gazed at John Knudsen's dilapidated farm. Two unmarked police cars were parked on the road, and several people were milling around the farm.

He could be there, she thought. They could have hidden Sune in the big barn where Pussy had drowned the newborn kittens.

No one spoke in the car, but she saw from Big Thomsen's expression in the side mirror that he was thinking. He must have realized by now that he wasn't the only one the police were interested in. Apparently that relieved him; he slumped down in his seat up front and stared straight ahead.

She called Nymand and reported in a few short words that they had finished their search. Negative, she said. They were headed for the address where Thomsen claimed he'd spent the night.

"Have the others reported in?" she asked. He told her that the team searching the mason's house in Såby had finished. No sign of the boy there, either.

"At first he claimed he knew nothing about Sune Frandsen. He'd never heard of a nithing pole and had no idea where Ingersminde was," Nymand said.

Liar, Louise thought. The mason had worked a long time at Camilla's manor. She'd hired his company to do the renovation.

The team searching Pussy's farm hadn't reported back yet.

Louise looked away as they drove past the gamekeeper's house and into the forest. She hadn't been there since the night she was attacked, but she knew that the house had been empty since Bodil Parkov had moved out.

She smiled to herself at how Eik confidently took the road past Avnsø to get to Bitten's house. The first time they were in the forest together, she'd had the impression that he'd never been that far away from Sydhavnen. And now, he was driving around as if he'd lived there his entire life.

Bitten's forest ranger house came into sight, and Louise noticed someone outside. From the boyish form and the short hair, she thought it must be Sune walking around, though she'd only seen his picture. Then she realized the figure in tight jeans and long-sleeved T-shirt was Bitten.

"What the hell!" Thomsen straightened up in his seat as they neared the house. All his things lay piled up in the middle of the courtyard. Bitten had gone back inside, and now an armful of clothes came flying out the door.

Thomsen shoved the car door open. "What in hell are you doing, you crazy bitch?"

Bitten whirled around; she hadn't heard them drive in. She stood with her hands on her hips, her expression telling the world that she wasn't backing down.

Louise and Eik were on Thomsen's heels as he strode across the courtyard; several of the tall, broken hollyhocks outside the door drooped close to the cobblestones. Bitten meant business, it seemed.

"You can take your fucking shit and go to hell," Bitten snapped when Thomsen started shouting at her again.

René's frail wife had also managed to drag his big chair out to the courtyard. It lay on its side, the large flat-screen TV on top of it. Thomsen's face turned red when he saw it. He stepped up to Bitten, and before Louise and Eik could stop him he punched her in the face.

"You're going to regret this," he said, hunched over now as Eik twisted his arm from behind and pulled him back.

Bitten didn't answer. She held her hand to her cheek as blood began to flow from her nose onto the back of her hand. But she looked defiantly at Thomsen.

"You are the biggest asshole to ever walk on two legs," she said. "I never want to see you again."

"What happened?" Louise asked as Eik steered Big Thomsen back to the car, threatening him with charges of battery.

"René refused to see me when I visited him today." Bitten's voice was nearly unrecognizable from bitterness.

"Asshole there apparently delivered a message to him, told him I wanted a divorce, that I'd hired a lawyer, the papers were already written up. I've never said I wanted a divorce, and then when I tried to use my debit card, it was blocked. I went to the bank, and they told me that René's salary, which usually goes into our joint account, hadn't come in. And I thought I was helping René by being friendly to Thomsen while he was in jail."

Bitten wiped her hand on her jeans, a smear of blood appearing on her thigh. Her nose was still bleeding, and Louise suggested they go inside so she could put ice on it.

"All the while he's been saying he'd help me and my daughter—that everything would be all right. He'd keep René on the payroll so we wouldn't suffer." In the kitchen, Louise wrapped a washcloth around ice and held it to Bitten's nose. She continued to explain how she'd been used, how she felt like she'd walked into a trap.

"He's here all the time. The deal was that he would come only when my daughter was asleep or not home, and now he insists on taking her to school in the morning and being part of the family. He's taken over everything. Today he was sleeping in bed when I came home from the jail. Do you know what he said when I asked why he was destroying my family?"

Bitten's face was contorted with rage. "He said he would crush René, just because he could! Like he was talking about swatting a fly!"

She threw the washcloth down and dried her cheek on her sleeve. "He said that nobody got away with stabbing him in the back."

"Stabbing him in the back?" Louise said.

"He'd heard that René told you about the rituals out in the forest, and the woman, too, the boy's gift."

Louise was stunned. "Just how did he know about that?"

Bitten looked away. Finally she answered, "He shoots skeet with an officer who helped question René."

Enraged, Louise grabbed her phone to call Nymand. Bitten rested her forehead on her hand and shook her head, as if she had no idea what to do. "So while I'm being told all this, the bastard is in my bed, snoring!"

Louise stuck her phone back in her pocket and put her arm around René's wife. "Did he spend the night with you?"

Bitten nodded. "He came around eight, emptied the refrigerator, and plopped down in front of the TV. He didn't even say good night when he came to bed, and he was still asleep when I left to visit René."

"And you're sure he was here all night."

Bitten frowned at her. "When a man snores like he does, you know he's in the house."

Louise's phone rang. Camilla's name popped up on the display. She excused herself and answered. "Hi."

"I found Sune," her friend whispered.

37

Camilla had been sitting in their yard, under a parasol, when Elinor suddenly appeared on the terrace and held out her hand. She'd smiled and said hello; she was getting used to the old woman showing up out of nowhere. But Elinor walked off, still beckoning at Camilla, who then got the message.

They went down the forest path silently. The old woman's cane crackled each time she planted it on the ground, but she kept a pace that Camilla, her leg still hurting, struggled to match.

She was apprehensive when they neared the sacrificial oak in the silent, mysterious forest. Elinor stopped and pointed, and her expression made Camilla even more anxious. She gathered her nerve and looked, then she covered her mouth in shock when she recognized the dark blue jacket and the lifeless body leaning up against the tree.

Sune's head hung on his chest, his hair covering his eyes. What froze Camilla, however, was the sight of his right forearm covered in dark blood. She dreaded doing it, but she had to kneel down and press her finger against his throat, check for a pulse. She closed her eyes and concentrated.

When she stood up, she was shaking so badly that she could barely pull her phone out of her pocket. She crouched down and punched in the emergency number. Time seemed to stand still; she feared she'd gotten there too late. She surprised herself by describing precisely the location in the forest, and after she asked that the information be given to Deputy Commissioner Nymand, the dispatcher told her the ambulance was on its way.

"I think he's breathing. It's hard for me to tell," Camilla said hesitantly, unsure whether the dispatcher was listening. Then she called Louise, but later she could hardly remember what she'd said; all her attention was on the boy, checking for signs of life. Fingers moving, chest rising. But he simply wasn't moving.

Slowly, she realized what had happened. The blood came from his right elbow, and his vein had been cut. There was no doubt about the symbolism—Sune had been placed under the tree as a sacrifice to the gods.

Desperately, she watched Elinor walk around in small circles over by the bonfire site. Her lips were moving, but no sound came out.

From her stint on the crime desk of a newspaper, Camilla knew that a person with a main artery cut had very little time. She pulled herself together and ripped off her blouse, tearing it into rags.

"It's going to be all right," she mumbled. She began speaking to him in a calm voice, as much for her sake as his. She lay him on the ground and lifted his legs, rested them on the tree trunk so the blood would run down to his head, and bound strips of cloth around Sune's upper arm. The ambulance wailed in the distance. Her mind was racing; heart massage, artificial respiration— would she be doing more harm than good? She grabbed a small stick, stuck it in between the windings of cloth, and twisted the stick to tighten the tourniquet.

38

They left Bitten's house immediately after Camilla's call. When Thomsen had demanded to know what was going on, they told him to shut up.

Eik dumped Big Thomsen off at the roundabout near Særløse. Louise ignored his bitching about not being driven all the way home. She knew they were going to hear about it.

Thomsen pounded his fist on the hood. "You'll find your way home," Eik said from his open window. Before the big man could answer, Eik put the car in gear and floored it, gravel rocketing off the car's undercarriage. Louise watched in the side mirror as Thomsen stood yelling. Nymand called.

"The father is on his way in. The boy is in emergency, he's in critical condition."

The first thing she noticed when they walked into the hospital was the butcher, hunched over in a chair, crying. Louise stopped. Eik put his hand on her back. "I'll find Nymand. Go on over to him." He approached a receptionist in a white coat who had just come out of her glassed-in office.

Louise studied the butcher for a moment. When they'd left him earlier in the day at his home, he'd looked like a man about to fall apart. Now it had happened.

"Hi," she said quietly. She sat down beside him. "Have you heard anything?"

He shook his head and breathed in deeply. They sat for a while in the turmoil of the emergency room. A child screamed in the waiting room, and a nurse rushed off.

"Come inside," a low voice said. Louise looked up into the face of a black woman. "You shouldn't have to sit out here. You can use the lounge; no one will have time for a break the next few hours anyway."

Her badge identified her as a head physician. Louise felt a pang of shame over being surprised that she spoke fluent Danish.

"When can I see him?" the butcher asked, unaware of anything except that this person could tell him something about his son.

"We'll join him in a moment," the doctor said. She put a hand on his shoulder and led him to a chair at the long table. "But there's something I have to tell you first."

The butcher froze.

"I've come down from the oncology ward. Your wife was admitted early this morning, and it was decided at our morning conference that she should receive terminal care."

The butcher, obviously confused, looked first at her, then at Louise. "What does that mean?"

"That means that we've stopped her treatment. But we need your permission to remove nutrition support and stop providing her with fluids. We'll continue with medication for pain."

Again he looked at Louise, who felt tears welling up. She held his hand. "It means that Jane is about to die, Lars." She pressed her lips together and blinked until her eyes cleared. "You're her nearest relative; they need your permission. If they keep giving her fluids and nutrition, her death will only be delayed, and it could be a long process." She looked over at the doctor, who was sitting at his other side.

"Unfortunately, there's no more we can do for your wife," she explained. "She's entered the final phase, and right now she's semiconscious. She sleeps most of the time. We're making sure she's in no pain. We can't say exactly how long it will be. It might happen today, or it might take several days, maybe a week. Of course this is more difficult, now that your son has been admitted."

The butcher had begun shaking his head, mechanically, from side to side. Louise could see he was unaware of what he was doing. She caught herself pressing her hands against her stomach.

"But Sune?" he whispered. "What about him?"

"Your son is on the way to intensive care. He's lost a lot of blood. His pulse is rapid, but very weak. He was very close to bleeding to death. We're giving him fluids and oxygen while we prepare a blood transfusion."

"Is he going to make it?" he whispered without looking at her.

"It's too early to say," the doctor answered. "He was in bad shape before he received treatment."

Louise couldn't handle it any longer. Tears ran down her cheeks as she stood up. "We've arranged for your wife to be taken down to his room, so they can be together," was the last thing she heard before walking out.

At six thirty the butcher walked into the ICU's family room, which the duty nurse had given them permission to use. Louise and Eik had been driving back to Copenhagen when Nymand called and said that the boy's father had asked to speak with them.

He was pale when he sat down across from them, his eyes dark and red-rimmed. He seemed to be staring through them. "Right now the doctors think there's a chance he'll survive." He folded his hands on the table, as if he needed support. "But Jane won't. They pushed her bed up against Sune so she can reach his hand. I don't know how much she understands, but she knows he's there. She spoke his name."

At first his crying was silent, then he began sobbing from deep within. He shook his head and stood up, walked over to the sink in the corner of the room, grabbed a paper towel, and blew his nose. He stood for a moment with his back to them before throwing the paper in the trash and returning to the table.

"I'm sorry," he mumbled. He breathed very deeply,

as if to compose himself. "I told you that Big Thomsen's gang isn't your normal group of friends," he said to Louise. "It's like some sect that none of us can get out of. I want you to know I always respected Klaus, a lot, because he tried. After what's happened today, I'll never forgive myself for not having the same courage."

Louise felt empty inside. What good was courage when you died because of it?

"I want to tell you how it started."

She felt Eik's arm around her shoulder, and she leaned back, tense now. She thought she'd heard the whole story.

"Do you remember Eline? Thomsen's little sister?"

Louise tried to think: Thomsen had a sister? Then she remembered her, a pale, thin girl who had been in her little brother's class. She had also been in a photo on Thomsen's dresser. She nodded slowly; the girl had been sick, though she couldn't recall what it was.

"It's a really sad story," the butcher continued, looking down at his hands. "When you're young, being around sickness and death can overwhelm you."

His expression and, in particular, the way he talked about Eline told Louise that something had affected him deeply.

He looked up. "I don't know, maybe I'm just trying to justify what happened."

"What was wrong with her?" Eik asked. He'd stuck a match in his mouth, a substitute for a cigarette.

He ignored the question. "I've thought about it a thousand times. Back then, none of us understood the consequences. You can't, not when you're just teenagers. We thought we could save her. It turned out we couldn't."

238

He was practically talking to himself now, Louise thought. He straightened up. "Thomsen had taken his sister up in this tree house he'd built. He wanted to show her the view. That was in 1983, when she was eight years old. A limb broke, she fell down on the left side of her back, but she kept on playing, she felt okay. After dinner that night she started complaining about pain. She got worse as the night went on, and they ended up taking her to the emergency room. The doctors told them she was bleeding internally, that she had ruptured her spleen."

The butcher paused for a moment. "She had to have a blood transfusion, it was a matter of life or death," he said, quieter now. "And that's how she contracted HIV. The blood hadn't been treated. Five years later she had AIDS."

"But that doesn't make it anyone's fault that she died," Louise said. "The girl suffered from a serious illness."

The butcher shook his head. "Eline didn't die from AIDS. Thomsen killed her. She's one of the girls you found in the old graveyard."

39

The butcher's words hung in the air, but before Louise actually grasped what he'd said, he averted his eyes and continued. "She'd reached the point where the doctors thought she didn't have long to live. A month, maybe two. At the end she was really sick; she just lay in her room and felt like hell. But she made a fight of it. It was strange for all of us who knew her; she'd been a real ball of fire. And there she was, wasting away from all that AIDS shit." He looked up at Louise. "You know Roed Thomsen. He couldn't handle his daughter having AIDS. Nobody talked about it. It was like they were ashamed, but it sure as hell wasn't her fault."

Louise knew exactly what he was talking about. Some people had panicked. They'd thought you could get the disease by kissing or drinking out of the same glass. It wasn't hard to imagine that this locally well-known

Hvalsø family had gone into denial about what the poor girl suffered from.

"You may not believe Thomsen can be sensitive, but he was just totally wiped out by all this. He was the one who'd taken her up in the tree. He adored his little sister; he'd have done anything to make her well. I can't remember exactly when he called us all together. His folks were over on Fyn or in Jutland, visiting friends, staying overnight. Eline had asked him to drive her out to the sacrificial oak, so we could call upon the gods to take care of her. In a lot of ways it was really tough, but we didn't think so much about it back then. The important thing was to support Eline, or maybe to feel we meant something to her."

Louise leaned forward. "What gave her the idea?"

"Thomsen's grandmother grew up at the old girls' orphanage. Eline heard the stories about the girls about to die being taken out to the tree, to make sure the gods were ready to receive them. The stories made an impression on her. She wanted the same for herself."

"I wonder, is it because of his grandmother's childhood that Thomsen is Asatro, and did he pressure the rest of you to join?"

"He didn't pressure nobody," the butcher said, irritated at the question. "You become an Asatro because it gives meaning to your life, being one with nature. For Scandinavians it's the most obvious faith there is."

His aggressive outburst told Louise that he was used to defending himself. "All right. But how did it begin?"

"Like I said, his grandmother grew up with the faith at the orphanage. The director was a gothi. That's what we call our priest. A lot from the old Nordic myths takes place right here in Lejre and Roskilde. It's a part of the region's history, and now we've made it a part of our lives."

Louise nodded. She thought about Sune, only fifteen years old, yet these men had tried to force him into their brotherhood. The poor kid. The more his father talked about it, the more it sounded like a sect, however much they made it out to be a faith.

The butcher shifted in his chair. "I've never told this to anyone, but I guess there's no reason not to anymore." He looked first at Eik, then at Louise. "You know anything at all about the sacrificial oak in Boserup Forest?"

He looked surprised when they both nodded. "Anyway, it was a full moon the night we drove Eline into the forest. It was a coincidence, it wasn't like it was something Thomsen could control. But it made the mood special. She wasn't strong enough to walk, so we carried her. There was a lot more undergrowth back then. We hadn't cleared off our bonfire area, either. Eline thought the moonlight looked like silver that fell from the sky. We put blankets out on the ground and built a small campfire."

Louise couldn't make herself ask if Klaus had been there.

"So she just sat there with her back against the tree, in the campfire's light, wrapped up in her white comforter. We sat in a circle around her and called upon the gods."

His voice was gentler now. It sounded a few shades darker, as if the memory was fresh enough for him to remember the mood.

"Something very special happens when you're in harmony with nature. When you stand in a circle with the heat from the campfire, the light of the moon, the stillness

242

of the forest, you can feel the force of the gods. You feel their presence, spiritually and physically. You get the very strong feeling you're not alone. It's very peaceful."

He looked at them hesitantly, as if he'd just exposed himself and was waiting to see how they'd react.

"I know, you're right," Eik said. "I've been at a winter solstice celebration. It's a really special feeling."

Louise looked at him but chose to not say anything.

"None of us had discovered it yet," the butcher said. "Not until we opened up the circle to give Eline some cola to drink, and to sit for a while and enjoy it while the fire burned down."

"Discovered what?" Louise said.

"That she was bleeding."

He rubbed his nose and had difficulty continuing. "She'd brought along a pocketknife. She'd cut herself around her elbow—deep cuts—the blood was streaming down on the ground."

Louise felt a chill; she remembered what Camilla had told her about Sune.

"Thomsen flipped out, he tried to stop the bleeding. He tried to bind her arm, but she kept taking it off, and at last he left her alone."

Louise could almost sense how it must have felt that night in the forest.

"I don't know what she and Thomsen talked about, and I never worked up the courage to ask."

"And she died?" Eik asked.

The butcher shook his head. "Yes and no. She didn't die right off. She died later at home that night." For several moments they took in what they had just heard.

Then he leaned over with his forearms resting on his thighs, his hands together.

"How did Thomsen explain this to his parents?" Louise asked. She could almost hear the old police chief's voice as the butcher told them what happened.

"His father wouldn't listen when he said it was Eline's doing, or that we couldn't prevent it. He didn't believe Thomsen had tried to stop the bleeding, either. He never accused us of killing her, but we knew he blamed his son for her death."

He bit his lip. "In a way it was his fault, of course. Our fault. We should never have taken her out to the forest when she was dying."

He spoke quietly after a long pause. "Eline chose to take her own life, and we helped her."

Eik broke the difficult silence that followed. "But I don't understand how she ended up in one of the old graves of the girls."

The butcher squirmed. Louise could hardly stand to look at him. He was allowing them access to what lay deepest inside, down where it was truly gruesome. "The police chief didn't want it to be said that his little girl had committed suicide. As if he hadn't been able to take care of her, or hadn't loved her enough."

"Why is this something no one talks about?" Louise said. "Why don't I know anything about this story?"

"Because no one wanted it to come out. She was reported missing, and that was that. The police chief took care of it somehow; I don't know how. No one dared to ask. Everyone was scared of getting on the wrong side of Roed Thomsen."

"And then he buried her out in the forest?" Louise said.

He shook his head. "*We* buried her. He kept out of it. I mean, think of what it would have looked like if he'd somehow been involved with his own daughter's death?"

"And then...?" Eik said.

"And then we passed the oath ring around. We'd all been Asatro for quite a while, but this was when we formed a brotherhood and took an oath of silence. Klaus did, too."

He looked at Louise, but immediately she realized she didn't want to know more.

"We promised each other to never say anything about it, and we swore to be each other's brothers, no matter what."

Suddenly he seemed drained; in despair. "I've failed Sune. I've never been strong enough to break free of what went on back then. I've been a shitty father. The brotherhood with Thomsen and the others has always been more important than my family, and it's my fault anyway that they punished him. I should never have pushed him into it."

It's a little late for that, Louise thought.

He was clearly tired now. His forehead furrowed.

"You do know you'll have to tell Roskilde Police what you've told us, don't you?" Louise said.

He'd nodded even before Louise had finished speaking. Apparently he'd already realized that, which was a relief to Louise.

"Of course. I know I've kept my mouth shut way too long. That's over with."

40

Camilla poured herself a large gin and tonic in a beer glass. She sat on the terrace and looked out over the fjord at Ring Island, at the ducks rocking in the lazy waters. Her body still tingled with some exhaustion she couldn't shake.

Frederik startled her when he yelled from the kitchen. She hadn't heard him come home; she hadn't even noticed that the wind was chilly now, that she had goose bumps on her bare arms.

She'd called him when she got home from the forest, after the ambulance had left with Sune. He still had a board meeting and a telephone conference with the American office, but she had been okay with that. She needed some time alone.

Jonas and Markus had gone into Roskilde to "hang out," as they put it. She'd lacked the energy to determine how likely it was that beer and cigarettes were part of the plan. Or if they were just sitting innocently in the city park, listening to music.

Her thoughts had been with Sune after Louise had called. The latest report was that his condition had stabilized. She'd found him in time.

She caught herself feeling useless. Even though she didn't know Sune, and she couldn't help at the hospital, she felt close to him. Suddenly everything seemed empty.

"What the hell happened to the tree?"

Camilla turned, and she jumped up when she saw Frederik's face. "The tree?"

"Someone disfigured the warden tree. They must have used a chain saw." He was already on his way back to the courtyard.

She emptied her glass; the alcohol burned all the way down. She followed him through the kitchen and out to the front steps, where she stopped abruptly.

Large patches of white wood showed where the tree trunk had been ripped into. On the ground under the tree lay piles of wood shavings, like hair on the floor of a beauty salon. When she touched the exposed wood, it felt damp.

The defacing began half a meter above the ground. Camilla's first impression was that it looked like graffiti on a newly painted wall. It enraged her. Slowly, she approached the tree while Frederik walked around it with his phone to his ear. Tønnesen, Camilla guessed.

Why hadn't she heard it? Camilla counted twelve separate areas where the trunk had been damaged. That must have taken time. Then she thought about Sune.

"They were here while the boy was dying," she said, shocked at the notion that someone was cutting here while she and Elinor were calling the ambulance. She'd returned directly from the forest without coming around front.

"Tønnesen is on his way," Frederik said. "I want that tree taken down. I'm not going to let them think they can scare us this way."

"Do you think that's wise?" She hadn't realized it before, but the old superstition in fact made Camilla nervous.

Frederik backed off and craned his neck, looking up at the treetops. He shrugged. "At least it will show people that we won't be threatened." From the way he spoke, she knew he'd already decided.

"Who knows we have a warden tree?" she asked. She noticed one mark on the trunk that seemed different from the others.

"Probably everyone around here who believes in that sort of thing, who takes an interest in the old mythology," he said.

She wanted him to look at something, and he joined her. "Has this always been here?" she asked, though the question was unnecessary—the exposed wood was fresh.

Frederik ran his finger around the carved circle, inside of which was a cross with small marks on the ends. "I think it's a rune."

Camilla took a picture with her phone. She assumed she could Google runes. At that moment, the manager drove into the courtyard and jumped out of his car.

"What the heck happened here?" he said, though

Frederik had already told him everything. It was obvious what had happened.

Camilla walked back to the house in a daze. A week ago she would have thought role-playing and Viking markets if someone had mentioned Asatro. It would never have occurred to her that some people actually practiced it, truly believed in it.

Confused, she sat down in the kitchen. What were they trying to say? She didn't understand why someone had turned against them. But she agreed with Frederik: The tree had to come down. They couldn't let anyone intimidate them this way.

41

Pizza, cola, and French fries covered the table, like a cliché about how the police ate when they were working feverishly. They sat inside the Roskilde Police Station, Louise with half a pepperoni pizza in front of her. She felt as if she was mooching, because she and Eik had done their job: They'd found the boy and reunited him with his family. But there were a few details to take care of.

Every time Louise saw the image in her head of Jane lying in bed, holding her son's hand, she swallowed. She'd thought she had control of her emotions; she shook her head at the memory of all the sessions with Homicide's psychologist to learn how to separate her emotions from her work. At the same time, she could hear Sune's voice. Homicide's leader had always maintained that people without empathy could never be good investigators. They didn't belong in his division.

Louise blinked quickly a few times when Nymand said that one of the two bodies found along with Lisa Maria had just been identified. "We haven't notified next of kin yet," he said, with a look that said the following information was extremely confidential.

"The body is that of a young woman, Anette Mikkelsen. She disappeared in 2005, shortly after her twenty-third birthday. She worked as a prostitute." He paused and glanced around the group of policemen.

"I know the identity of the last one," Louise said, quickly wiping her fingers on a napkin. "Her name is Eline Thomsen. She was the daughter of your former police chief." Nymand turned to her, surprised. "The girl was thirteen years old when she died in 1988. Her brother and his friends buried her out there, but her father forced them to do it."

Nymand lifted his eyebrows in disbelief. "And where did you come up with that insane allegation?"

She ignored the look he gave her. "It's not an allegation. I have a witness who described what happened. He helped bury her."

"I think we should keep Roed Thomsen out of this. His son might be a bad apple, but there's no reason to bring accusations against a man well respected in the community for many, many years."

"If you don't believe me, I suggest you investigate what happened to the daughter when she disappeared in 1988. My guess is you'll find she was reported missing and no one has seen her since."

Nymand shook his head at her and changed the subject. "I've also spoken to your forensic pathologist, Flemming Larsen. He's finished with the examination of the body we dug up at Hvalsø Cemetery."

Her pathologist? Louise thought. It was quiet in the room. She saw from the looks on several faces that no one knew what he was talking about. Apparently they hadn't heard there was another body involved.

She nodded without replying.

"They found the old report from the inquest." He turned to the others in the room. "It took place in the house where the deceased was cut down from a rope in the hall." He explained that it concerned a twenty-one-year-old man who had been part of Ole Thomsen's gang. He tactfully left out Louise's connection.

"The report states that the deceased was found with his legs slightly bent. There was lividity in the hands, feet, and lower legs, which is consistent with hanging."

Nymand looked at Louise. "During the autopsy, Larsen found he'd sustained a hard blow to the back of his head." Now he read from the paper in front of him. "The lines of fracture issue from the middle of the back of the head in several directions, and some evidence still exists of a subdural hematoma."

He looked up again at Louise. "Do you know about the suicide note found in the house?"

Every eye in the room was glued on her. She wanted to duck her head, but she just nodded.

I'm sorry. That's all the note said. He hadn't even signed it, or addressed it to her. When she was told about it, she had asked not to see it.

Nymand stuffed the papers back into the plastic dossier file. "We're going to investigate this. We'll have an analysis made of the handwriting. I assume you still have something bearing his signature?"

Louise nodded again. She thought about her small suitcase up in the attic, filled with pictures and letters from her past. Some of them came from Klaus.

The meeting continued with a list of what had been seized at Pussy's farm. Illegal agricultural products, poisons, Polish soda pop, vacuum-packed meat in a large freezer in the barn. At the mason's, they had confiscated large piles of cash and some receipts that the people at the Economic Crimes Unit would entertain themselves with for some time. Double-entry bookkeeping, black-market money, value-added tax fraud. None of this surprised Louise.

Nymand didn't mention Gudrun or the janitor from Såby. She knew that a few of his people already had spoken with René Gamst, who was still prepared to testify against Ole Thomsen. She suggested that they also speak with Lars Frandsen.

"He can also tell you about Gudrun and the janitor. And about Roed Thomsen's daughter."

The meeting continued. They were planning to arrest Big Thomsen and his gang that very evening. Presumably the men would be interrogated immediately, though it was possible they would be stashed in cells until the next morning. But Louise had no doubt they at least would be shaken that evening to see what fell out. It was still unclear if others were seriously involved in the gang.

"Should we take off?" Eik whispered in her ear.

She pushed her chair back to stand up. She glanced around at the personnel who were about to begin what would be a long, arduous shift. For a moment she envied them, but she knew she couldn't be part of this, no matter what. Her focus wouldn't be on the young prostitute or Sune. Or on Klaus, Eline, the janitor, or Gudrun. For her it would be a personal vendetta against Big Thomsen. She felt relieved to know that despite everything, she was professional enough to realize this.

"Good luck," she said. She followed Eik out into the hall.

On the way to the car, she reached over and pulled a cigarette out of the inside pocket of his leather jacket. Without a word, he handed her his lighter.

42

Cars were parked everywhere. She heard Eik mumbling each time he thought he'd spotted an empty parking space, but when he got close there was always a tiny car tucked in between two behemoths.

Many years had passed since Louise had been in the city park to hear music, but now it all came back to her. How she had sat with friends on the slope, drinking beer. She would meet someone up at the ice cream store, and after sitting down on the grass they would keep looking around to find others they knew. Mostly she had looked for Klaus. That was before they became a couple.

"Did the boys say where to pick them up?" Eik asked.

Louise noticed they were in a taxi lane. "You can't park here!"

"I can't park anywhere else, either, so I'm parking here."

Louise tried to call Jonas again. She sighed in irritation when again he didn't answer, but then Eik saw them walking up the gravel path, surrounded by laughing girls with long, flowing hair.

They were so big now! Fifteen years old, almost sixteen. For a moment she just sat and stared, as if it had happened while she wasn't looking. Markus did the talking; he was making everyone laugh. When he turned to say something, Louise suddenly noticed that Jonas was holding hands with one of the pretty girls. His long, dark hair was combed off his forehead. No more hiding behind a curtain, it seemed. His big smile transformed his face.

A warm feeling spread inside Louise, and she sat a moment longer and enjoyed it before opening the car door and calling to them.

The two big teenage boys took their time hugging all the girls good-bye. Seconds later, on the way to the car, they were already talking, laughing about something Louise couldn't hear.

Louise missed that life. At least in a way. She could have been the girl getting the hug, and the moment the boy turned away he would move on to the next thing in his life. While she might spend the next several days turning over in her mind what the hug meant.

She missed those days, yet she was glad they were over. But it was good for Jonas; it had been a long time since he'd seemed so happy. Now there was something carefree in his expression. Louise felt at peace. Maybe he hadn't been scarred for life after all, from all the traumatic experiences he'd gone through. She asked them if they'd eaten, though it was past ten now.

Jonas didn't have to be in school until late the next morning, so they decided to stay at Camilla's and drive back early. Melvin was keeping Dina; there was nothing pressing they had to return home for.

"What the hell?" Markus shouted from the backseat as they drove up the long driveway to Ingersminde. Eik slowed down and they all leaned forward.

At the entrance to the courtyard, a gigantic log lay blocking the road. Several men in helmets walked around carrying ropes. The boys jumped out and ran toward the house.

"Watch out!" Louise yelled after them.

Eik backed up and parked off to the side. A chain saw buzzed, and male voices rose up from the din. Several cars lined the driveway. The air smelled of wood, of a sawmill. Something felt terribly wrong about all this activity, so close to nightfall.

"They cut down the warden tree," Jonas yelled when they reached the courtyard. "Frederik decided to do it. He's standing over there. They're cutting up the trunk to haul it away."

He sounded like a reporter broadcasting live from some important event.

Louise took Eik's hand and followed him to the tree, where the men were shouting instructions at each other. For a second they eyed the enormous trunk of the oak, which stuck several meters in the air. The lowest limbs were to their right, everything else blurred out in the twilight.

Camilla was in the living room with her laptop when Eik and Louise entered the house.

"Get in here and look!" she called out when she heard them.

She explained about the warden tree being vandalized and Frederik's decision to fell it, to demonstrate that he wouldn't be intimidated by threats. She handed them her phone and showed them the photo of what had been carved into the tree trunk.

"I think it's this rune," she said. She turned the laptop around so they could see the screen.

Louise enlarged the photo on the phone and studied the circle and cross with the small markings. Eik leaned over her shoulder. "Ragnarok," he said, after a single glance. "The rune symbolizes Ragnarok. Someone's trying to tell you something."

"Yeah, and you know what?" Camilla snapped. "This someone needs to shut up and get the hell out of our lives. They think they can walk right on our property, try to scare us with all their Asa shit, but we're not going to stand for it. That poor boy almost died out in our forest. And the graves of the girls, what the hell is going on?"

She turned to Louise. "Did you find out if it's all connected?"

"It seems to be." She told Camilla that Thomsen and his gang were to be arrested that evening. "It's probably already done. Which means Nymand and his people have twenty-four hours to collect enough evidence to present to a judge. Hopefully they'll be remanded into custody."

Right now she wasn't concerned with that case. It was out of her hands. Sune had survived, and he was reunited with his parents. She had informed Rønholt that she was taking the next day off, and when she'd had time to distance herself from all this, she was sure the investigation into Klaus's death by Roskilde Police would give her peace of mind.

She was free of the guilt she'd been carrying around for years. Knowing Big Thomsen and the others would be brought to justice for all they had done over the years gave her a sense of satisfaction. Her work did make a difference.

She stood and asked if it was okay to grab a beer in the refrigerator. She wanted to sit on the terrace and look out over the fjord. Let the day settle inside her. She dragged Eik along with her.

43

For a moment she didn't know where she was. She didn't know how long she'd slept, only that she'd been far away, deep into a dream. She and Eik had talked for a long time in bed the night before, then she'd pulled him over on top of her, and when he'd asked her solemnly if she was sure, she'd pressed her lips against his neck and nodded.

Now, returning to the surface, she heard shouting and a piercing, wailing sound. Eik was shaking her, throwing her clothes on the bed.

"Get up, it's a fire!" he yelled.

The door to the room burst open. Thick smoke rolled in as Frederik, holding his T-shirt against his mouth, signaled for them to get out—*now!* Through the noise of roaring flames, she heard Camilla scream.

"Jonas!" Louise yelled. "Are the boys out?"

Eik pulled his pants up as he ran out. Camilla screamed again, and Louise only took time to grab her T-shirt before she was out the door. She saw her friend through the smoke, leaning over something at the end of the hall, just outside their bedroom.

Louise ran over to her. Flames from the stairs shot up the heavy curtains covering the tall windows in the hall.

"I can't get her up!" Camilla sobbed. "This shitty fucking leg!"

Elinor lay on the floor. Her long braid had almost burned off, and her skin was singed. Quickly Louise knelt down, and with Camilla's help she lifted the old woman up in the fireman's carry her father had used when little Louise was too tired to go to bed herself.

Frederik returned. His face was black and he was coughing so terribly he could hardly stand straight as he dragged Camilla along. A fire extinguisher droned from below, but the fire there on the second floor had taken hold of the carpet.

Louise pinned Elinor's thin body to her shoulder with both arms. She screamed with all her might as she ran to the stairs and blindly flung herself down through the flames, trying to keep her balance, taking every other step until she stumbled and fell near the bottom. She felt a tug from behind, as if hidden forces were sucking her away from the fire.

Everything seemed quiet now. Then she realized she was inside herself, in a silent film playing in slow motion. Elinor lay on the ground. Tønnesen leaned over her, and slowly Louise understood that he must have pulled them out of the house. Camilla stood hugging Marcus, who was in his undershorts.

Jonas!

"Where's Jonas?" she screamed. She was instantly on her feet, the silent film having vanished. The skin on her leg stung; her hair stank. "Where's Jonas?" she screamed again. "Is he out here?" She ignored the gravel under her bare feet.

"Eik and Frederik went in after him." Camilla hugged her son tightly while staring up at his bedroom on the second floor.

There came a deafening blast; one of the tall windows on the second floor had exploded, and flames shot out of the hole and climbed up the outer wall, as if they were trying to reach the roof.

Louise's throat was raw as she screamed again for Jonas. "Is there anywhere else they can get down if they can't use the stairway?"

Relief overwhelmed her when Camilla pointed at the gable and said there was a fire ladder on the end of the house.

Another window exploded, flames reaching out greedily. The heat and smoke stung Louise's eyes. Her heart was pounding, her voice raspy and broken as she asked Markus, "Was Jonas in the room when you ran out?"

"I didn't see him. I don't know—I thought he'd already gone down." His voice was weak—his words blew away with the black smoke from the house.

"Ragnarok," Camilla whispered hoarsely while stroking her son's bare arms.

Tønnesen sprayed the flames inside. He might as well have been pissing on a bonfire.

Louise ran back to the house. She screamed her son's name again into the thick smoke. A thunderous crash on the second floor drowned out her scream. For a moment she considered running up into the smoke-filled darkness; the fire hadn't spread to the first floor yet; it was rising up to the peak of the roof. But she knew she'd never come down again.

Her thoughts were interrupted when a third window shattered right above her, showering glass all over the courtyard. She jumped back then ran around to the gable at the other end of the house, close to Markus's bedroom. She heard shouting, and when she rounded the corner she saw Eik and Frederik climbing down the fire ladder. Without Jonas.

Sirens sounded like distant howling in a fog.

"Where is he?" she yelled as the two men neared the ground. She grabbed Eik before he stepped off. His hair and eyebrows were singed on his left side. He was black with soot, and the blisters on his arm had already broken.

"He wasn't there," he said, gasping for breath.

Frederik tumbled to the ground beside him and curled up. He had burns all over his chest, all the way down his stomach.

"Where is he?" Desperately, Louise shook Eik, as if she could make him say something to stop her panic. "Did you look everywhere? In the bathroom?"

She tried not to yell with him standing right beside her. Her blood was pounding in her veins as her muscles began to cramp.

Behind her, enormous fire engines flew toward the courtyard, but they couldn't get close to the house because of the warden tree blocking the driveway. Louise wanted to run over to them and yell that her son was still in there somewhere, but her feet refused to do anything other than stutter nervously around.

She watched the thunderous flames raging, as if all hell had broken loose. Suddenly her shoulder stung where she'd been burned; Eik had grabbed her and was pulling her to him.

"Jonas isn't in there," he said, his voice wheezy and strained. He stuck something hard into the palm of her hand. "This was on his bed."

She looked down at a polished oblong stone, with an arrow pointing up carved into it.

Eik seemed to have suddenly thought of something, because he began running to his car. Louise saw Charlie barking like crazy in the back.

Her hearing again seemed distorted. The big German shepherd's mouth opened and closed soundlessly, the barking drowned out in the roaring fire and ambulance sirens.

Louise's body was all pain, yet she didn't feel it; not really. Eik let Charlie out, and they started toward her. She walked over the grass to meet them.

Elinor had already been packed into a blanket and fastened onto a stretcher, but it wasn't until they lifted the old lady into the ambulance that Louise noticed the blanket also covered her face.

She watched them push the stretcher into the ambulance.

Camilla still held Markus; it was as if they'd both gone into shock in the midst of everything. A lieutenant wearing a helmet tried to lead her away from the courtyard, but she wouldn't budge. She faced the fire and watched the great manor burn down. Tønnesen stood at the front steps holding his fire extinguisher.

A stretcher was placed on the ground beside Frederik. He stared straight up in the air. Finally Camilla roused herself, and she reached her husband before they lifted him onto the stretcher. Paramedics began treating his burns as they carried him to the ambulance. He had sustained the most serious injuries, having fought to get everyone out. But he was conscious, Louise noticed, as he reached out for Camilla.

The stench in the courtyard was overwhelming. Flames engulfed the peak of the roof as the glazed roof tiles exploded.

Eik joined Louise. Charlie whimpered and rubbed against his leg. "I should've known something was wrong," he said quietly. He explained that during the night, Charlie had been barking so loudly that he'd taken him out and locked him in the car before he woke the whole house up. "I should have trusted him," he added, nearly whispering now.

"What is this?" Louise asked. She showed him the stone. He held her wrist, as if he thought the stone was too heavy for her.

"It's the rune for the war god, Tyr," Eik said. "He was ruthless. Merciless. I think someone abducted Jonas and left this for you."

44

Louise shrieked, screaming at the forest until every-thing turned black. Eik put his arm around her.

"The bastards. The fucking goddamn bastards!"

She felt no pain, not in her leg, not on her shoulder. She snapped viciously when a doctor in some weird blazing-yellow spacesuit asked her to follow so they could have a look at her injuries. "I'm not going anywhere except out to find my boy."

She suddenly remembered that she'd left her phone beside the bed. "May I borrow your phone?" she said, civil now as she trotted after the doctor. Then she saw Ny-mand, walking toward her like a zombie. He'd maybe slept an hour, or possibly not at all, she noticed, before she was in his face.

"What in the hell were you thinking? Why did you let them go?" She pointed toward the house and was about to say a lot more about what Thomsen and his gang had done now. But instead she shook her head.

"They have Jonas."

Nymand stared as if he didn't quite recognize her. She realized she was only wearing a T-shirt and panties, and she gratefully accepted one of the ambulance's white blankets.

He closed his eyes a moment, seemingly to take in what had happened. "If you're referring to the three persons you yourself assisted in having arrested last night, they're still in Roskilde Jail. None of them has been released."

Louise felt as if the earth were crumbling under her. "Jonas is gone," she repeated. The lump in her throat stopped her from saying more.

Eik told Nymand about the empty bed and the stone that lay on the comforter.

"We need to get an overview of what's happened out here," Nymand said. He asked them to accompany him to the manager's house; the ambulance had driven Frederik away, and Camilla and Markus were walking over there with two officers. Tønnesen still held his fire extinguisher, staring up at the black smoke disappearing into the sky.

"Does anyone have an idea of when the fire started?" Nymand asked.

"Jonas," Louise said, not the least bit interested in theories about where or when the fire started. "We have to find Jonas. They took him in place of Sune!"

"The rescue personnel are still looking for him inside," Nymand said, placing a hand on her arm, a gesture obviously meant to comfort her. "Ole Thomsen and his friends are in jail, so they couldn't have taken him."

He spoke to her as if she were a small child, which made Louise so angry that she almost hit him.

"Were there any witnesses to the fire breaking out?" Nymand continued, looking around at them.

They were in Tønnesen's kitchen. Camilla sat on the bench along the wall, wrapped in the same type of white blanket that Louise had been given.

"Elinor came to warn us," Camilla said, staring into space. "She wanted to save us. She's the guardian angel of the place, talk to her."

Louise looked down at the table.

"Elinor Jensen died half an hour ago," said the officer sitting across from Camilla. He looked over at Nymand.

Markus cried quietly, his eyes closed and his head leaning back against the wall. One side of his face flickered a bit and the corner of his mouth trembled, as if he were trapped in a horrible nightmare.

"I got up about three thirty to shut my dog in the car," Eik said. He'd taken a toothpick from Tønnesen's table, and it flipped up and down in his mouth as he spoke. "He was barking, and I didn't want him to wake everyone up."

He was bare from the waist up but still wearing his jeans. He leaned awkwardly across the table, as if he couldn't find the words to explain something. "That must've been when Elinor came upstairs. But there was no sign of smoke, and I didn't see or hear anyone upstairs or out in the courtyard. I assumed it was some animal or a bird at the window that set him off, it was so quiet."

His face was contorted with remorse. He shook his head and ran his fingers through his wispy hair, then stood up, walked to the sink, and threw his toothpick in the trash underneath. Louise noticed a cut on his back, shallow but long, as if he had unknowingly scraped it.

"So who took Jonas?" Louise leaned against the refrigerator. She was getting cold. Adrenaline kept her body alert, though her muscles trembled, her head thudded, and her eyeballs hurt. She felt dizzy.

"We don't know that he's been abducted," Nymand said. "We can hope he's not in the house. There were gasoline cans on the first floor; there's no doubt it's arson. It also explains the explosive manner in which the fire spread. But we can't be one hundred percent sure of anything, and as I said, they're still looking for him inside."

Louise covered her mouth and whispered through her soot-blackened fingers. "You don't understand!"

Nymand was about to say something, but Louise stopped him. "You don't understand. Someone has started a war! They have Jonas, and every minute we sit here gives them that much more of a head start."

Louise noticed Markus staring at her emptily, as if he weren't really there. Her words, however, made him wince. *He's about to go into shock*, she thought. She walked over to him. "No one blames you for not hearing anything." She put her arm around his shoulders. They seemed so frail, even though he'd grown taller than her. "It will never be your fault that they took him."

It stung Camilla when Louise implied that her son possibly could have prevented it, could have intervened, stopped someone from coming into the room under cover of night and abducted Jonas. Louise could see it in her friend's eyes. But this was a cold-blooded act, well planned and with one objective, and even if Markus had gotten in the way, he could never have stopped them. And if he had, he might not have been sitting there on the bench, leaning his head on Louise's shoulder.

"There was nothing you could have done," she whispered into his hair. She squeezed his shoulder as he huddled against her.

Camilla began telling Nymand about the warden tree. "It's said that your house will burn down if the tree is felled. And that happened this evening. Louise is right, someone has started a war against us. They carved a symbol for Ragnarok into the tree, and now Eik says that they left behind the rune for the Nordic god of war."

"*Three* persons," Louise exclaimed. She'd suddenly recalled what the deputy commissioner had said out in the courtyard. "What about the butcher? Didn't you bring him in, too? He was there the night the prostitute was killed, and he's been in the brotherhood right from the start. He's part of it, even if they've turned against him!"

"We questioned Lars Frandsen after you talked to him. He's agreed to make a full confession. But we didn't bring him in. He's still at the hospital. Damn it, Louise! His wife is dying. He's not the one who was out here tonight. They brought a bed into the room for him. He has the right to be with his family—you have to respect that."

"He doesn't have the right to shit before we know where Jonas is!" Louise said. She jumped up and followed Eik, who was already out the door.

45

"I have a weekend bag with a change of clothing in the car. Take my jogging pants—you can tighten the waist." Eik shut Charlie in the back of the car while Louise walked to the front steps. The fire squad's lieutenant stopped her.

"I just need to get our shoes," she explained. "They're right inside."

Quickly, she grabbed her own shoes and Eik's pair of size forty-sixes, plus two pairs that she guessed belonged to Camilla and Markus.

It already smelled like a sodden, burned-out house. Water flowed across the dark gray marble floor in the hall, and soot ran down the walls visible above the stairs.

She felt empty inside when she returned to the car. Empty, yet seething with the knowledge that her past was boomeranging back on Jonas. She couldn't handle her pain, her anxiety, the thought of his joyous smile as he'd walked with the girl and held her hand. What forces had been unleashed, who had taken him? She tried to reason it all out.

Perhaps abducting Jonas was an act of war against her, in retaliation for the arrests. Rape, murder, attempted murder: There were reasons enough to go to extremes to avoid these charges. But those who would be charged were already in jail. It made no sense.

Maybe they had taken Jonas as revenge for Camilla and Frederik helping Sune. But why Jonas and not Markus?

Could Bitten be involved? She was definitely capable of reactions wilder than anyone would suspect—Louise had seen that when she kicked Thomsen out of her life. But such a frail woman couldn't carry a fifteen-year-old boy down a flight of stairs, certainly not without anyone hearing her; nor was she capable of setting fire to a house as successfully as had been done. And it wasn't Louise who had arrested her husband, though his friends had tried to make it look that way.

"Can we come along?" Camilla said, interrupting her thoughts.

Behind her, Nymand objected to their leaving just when he had ordered them to stay.

Camilla put her arm around Markus, who still looked beaten up. "I want to be with Frederik. I won't have my husband alone in the hospital while his childhood home burns down."

"You two come with us," Nymand said, pointing at Camilla and Louise. He had already gestured for one of his people to join them, a younger officer with a high forehead and muscles that strained at his shirt. Then he asked Eik if he could take Markus along in his car. "I need to know everything about Jonas," he said to Louise. "Description, height..."

Louise was wearing Eik's much-too-long jogging pants. She loosened the shoelaces on her sneakers to relieve her injured feet, then with Camilla walked past the felled tree to Nymand's car down the driveway. Only a few tanker trucks remained now, in addition to a vehicle with a crane in back that was dragging the enormous tree off the driveway.

"He has dark hair," Louise said. "A hundred eighty centimeters tall, normal build. He's missing the little toe on his right foot..."

The words stuck in her throat, and she began to tremble. Camilla put her arm around her shoulder and took over. "He's got dark eyes, prominent cheekbones. If you have Internet access on your phone, I can show you his photo on Facebook."

"Does he have a phone?" Nymand asked.

"It won't help much to track it if he left it in the bedroom."

"Why didn't we hear him yelling?" Louise asked. "He would do that. He would yell if someone tried to drag him away."

They'd reached the end of the driveway. She looked out the window as they drove past the gatekeeper's house and Kattingeværket, the old factory complex beside the lake. She answered herself. "Either he went along of his own free will, or else he was drugged."

Louise didn't even glance at the nurse trying to stop her from entering Sune's room in intensive care. Eik and Nymand were right behind, and she turned to the deputy commissioner just before walking in. "I hope for your sake that Lars Frandsen is in there. Otherwise you're responsible if anything happens to Jonas."

Nymand reached out to put a hand on her arm, but Louise turned to open the door. She reminded herself that Jane and Sune were also inside.

The nurse caught up to them. "You can't go in." She tried to stand in the way, but Louise elbowed past her into the dim room. The curtain swished from the door being opened, and the butcher's shoulder moved. He'd heard them.

He sat hunched over beside Jane's bed. The air in the room seemed to stand still, even though the window was open. Sune lay over by the wall, staring at them with small, tired eyes.

Louise raised her hand to stop the others behind her. The nurse retreated when Eik explained that Louise was a close friend of Jane Frandsen.

Used to be, Louise thought. The door closed. "When did it happen?" she whispered.

"An hour ago." He put his hand on the blanket. "I'm thankful that we were here. Her folks have stepped out for a minute."

The nurse brought them coffee. Louise closed her eyes and thought about Jane. Young and full of life. It had been long ago, but they'd been a big part of each other's lives. Silently she said farewell to her friend, waxy-pale now, her head on the white pillow, her eyes closed and lips slightly parted.

She couldn't play rough; not here, not now. She still felt the rage, but the room was so quiet and peaceful. And besides, Sune lay there staring dismally at his mother.

"Excuse me. I'm sorry to interrupt, just when you've lost your wife." She knelt down beside his chair. "My son Jonas has disappeared. He's Sune's age, and he disappeared last night. Lars, did you have anything to do with it?"

"Disappeared, how?" The butcher's voice was monotone, weak. But his eyes flickered a bit when he turned to Louise.

"Who took my son? Thomsen and the others were arrested yesterday. René is in jail in Holbæk, and you've been here. Who has him?"

The butcher grimaced. Not from anger, Louise thought. It looked more like fear, as if something was out of control. She leaned back, frightened herself now.

"Last night, I tried to get hold of my father. I called him shortly before Jane died, but he didn't pick up." His shoulders sank, he looked spent. "I tried later, too, on my phone and also a phone here at the hospital, but he still didn't answer."

Louise realized that they were talking as if Jane weren't beside them, as if Jane's son weren't staring at them. But they had no time to find a more private place, if what she feared was true. And she could see that the butcher understood.

"Talk to Roed Thomsen. If anyone's after your boy, he's the one who's set it in motion."

"Thomsen's father?" She leaned forward to be sure that she'd heard right.

"He's our gothi. If my father has been involved in anything last night, the gothi ordered him to do it. There's never been a weak link in our fathers' generation."

46

An hour later, along with Nymand and the extra personnel assigned to him, they drove into the courtyard of Roed Thomsen's beautiful country manor in
Nørre Hvalsø. It faced open fields that stretched all the
way to Såby. Tall beech trees surrounded the main house,
and the grass had been cut in rows straight as an arrow,
the edges trimmed perfectly.

"Is there a Mrs. Roed Thompson?" Eik asked, before
they got out of the car.

He'd been quiet most of the way from Roskilde.
Louise had sat with eyes closed, grateful that he hadn't
tried to break through her anxiety, which at the moment
made breathing very difficult.

"There used to be a Mrs. Police Chief," she answered.
"But I don't know if she's still alive. After she quit working at the bank, you mostly saw her at the kiosk, buying

aquavit. Asking to have it wrapped as a present. Now I understand why she preferred life to be blurred."

Two officers stood by the front door as two more went around the house. Nymand knocked on the door and shouted, "Police!" He shook the doorknob a few times, as if he didn't believe it was locked.

Louise and Eik were approaching the wing used as a barn when they heard a commotion from behind the house. Immediately she took off, with Eik on her heels.

She rounded the corner. A large, gaudy fountain spouted water up in the air. The two policemen stood beside a well-trimmed hedge, gazing at something on the ground between them.

Louise ran across the huge lawn. The men pulled a large tarp to the side and stumbled back at the sight of what lay under it. Eik passed Louise when she slowed down. She dragged herself the final few meters, and he tried to stop her.

"You don't need to see this," he said with a gentleness she had no need for. The men quickly replaced the tarp, but she jerked free, grabbed the green covering, and threw it aside. On the ground below lay a headless horse. Dark brown, a black mane, white markings above the hooves and on the chest.

She jumped back. Not so much from the sight of the dead horse, whose head she had seen stuck on the post at Camilla's, but from relief that she wasn't staring at the body of a boy.

"Do you recognize this?" Nymand asked as he walked across the lawn carrying a black T-shirt. He unfolded it and held it up with the logo facing her. A round face with a happy smile and big ears. She'd given it to Jonas. The American DJ deadmau5 had become his idol after he'd begun writing and sampling music, which he uploaded to YouTube.

For a moment everything stood still. Including her heart, Louise feared for a moment. But then her rage exploded from a place inside her she'd never felt before. Her fingertips turned cold, but the colors around her suddenly grew brighter, as if her senses were no longer deadened from anxiety.

If anyone had hurt one hair on Jonas's head, they were as good as dead. She would kill them.

47

Markus was asleep on a chair by the window. The nurse had given Frederik pain medication, which made him drowsy. Camilla sat beside his bed. Adrenaline still coursed through her veins, her body on constant alert. She couldn't fight off the image of the flames and Elinor's frail, lifeless body lying in the courtyard.

She jumped at the sound of a voice from the doorway. "Excuse me," said the nurse who had been keeping an eye on Frederik. "You have a call. The phone is in the office."

Camilla got to her feet. She was chilly now. She had on the T-shirt she'd slept in, along with a dark-blue cardigan they'd dug up for her in the lost-and-found bin that patients regularly added to.

A redheaded nurse in the office pointed to the phone on the desk. Camilla picked it up. At first she didn't recognize Louise's voice; it sounded so bleak. "Who is this?"

she asked, anxious at first, until she realized that whoever had taken Jonas and set fire to the house couldn't know where she was. "Louise?"

"It's about Jonas," her friend said. "Go down to intensive care. Sune is in room six. Get hold of the butcher. You saved his son, now it's time for him to return the favor."

"Who took him?" she whispered. She looked at the nurse still standing in the doorway. "Where are you?"

"At Thomsen's father's house. The body of the dead horse is here. They're not even trying to hide the fact they're threatening you."

"Unbelievable!" Camilla said, amazed and angered at the ruthlessness they were up against. "Tell me what to do."

"We need to know places where they might have hidden him. He's been here, now he's gone of course."

Camilla nodded and thought for a moment. "Could they have taken him out to the sacrificial oak? Has anyone been out there?"

"That's the first place Nymand checked. No one there. Not at the girls' graves, either. Find out if there are other places connected to their religion. Areas with a special meaning for their rituals."

"Got it. You want to know everything."

"Yes."

The door to intensive care swooshed as it closed behind Camilla. She hurried down the hall, passing rooms 2, 4, 6. She knocked gently before pushing the door open and stepping in. The room was empty. There were no beds or people inside, only two night tables pushed up against the wall.

"Yes?" Camilla turned to find a nurse wearing an open white coat looking at her.

"Lars Frandsen and Sune," she stammered. "I'm a friend of the family. We've just recently been in touch."

The nurse sized her up. Camilla remembered that she still stank from the smoke. She must look like something the cat dragged in. Which might have been the reason why the nurse took her elbow and led her down the hall. She probably looked like she'd dropped everything to rush to the hospital.

"My condolences," the nurse said. She led her to a door in the same hall. "They're in here."

Uneasy now, Camilla knocked. Four pale, red-eyed faces turned to her. "Excuse me," she said, before anyone could speak. "Lars, I need to talk to you."

He stared at her as if he were about to refuse, but then he stood up. An elderly woman clutching a white handkerchief in her hands was sobbing. Sune sat beside her, pale and unfocused, but when he looked up he recognized her. His expression changed, and he seemed about to say something when Camilla hurried out into the hall with his father.

"Where have they taken Jonas?" she asked after she'd introduced herself.

The butcher's face went blank. "My wife just died!"

"I know, and I'm very sorry, but this is a matter of life and death."

"I don't know what you're talking about." He turned around to walk back into the room, but she grabbed him.

"I'm the one who found your son!" She was in his face now. "Tell me where they could've taken Jonas."

She shook him. She was so angry that she didn't even think about how strong he was. "Our house is burning down. Goddamn it, we could all have died. And now Louise's son has disappeared."

She kept shaking him. "Where could they have taken him? Come on, talk to me!"

Suddenly he seemed very interested. "Who burned your house down?"

"Good question, because I have no fucking idea!" Camilla let go of him and backed off a bit, her arms falling to her sides. "Someone started it while we were asleep. The only person who might have seen something is Elinor, the old lady who found Sune and dragged me out in the forest. But she died of smoke inhalation."

Now, having said the words, she made the connection: Elinor was dead because she had tried to warn them. That the wagons were again rolling on the Death Trail, that someone in the summer night had snuck up to the manor house. And it saddened her.

They must've come in from the forest, she thought. They had surveillance cameras along the driveway. If they had been activated during the night, Tønnesen would have been aware of it.

"What do they want? What have we done? This has to stop; these are children they're hurting."

Her voice faded at the end, along with her anger. But she had to make him cooperate.

The butcher lowered his eyes for a moment before again meeting hers. "They've turned on you because you helped my son. You should never have done that. You interfered in something that should have been taken care of within the brotherhood."

"What the hell are you talking about? You know how frightened that boy was when we were out in the forest with him. Of course we had to help!"

She grabbed his arm. "You of all people know what they're capable of. Tell me what they might do with Louise's son; you owe me."

He looked at her as if she'd just slapped him. "Blood vengeance. When one of us has been wronged, there has to be revenge."

"Why him? Why Jonas?"

"Your friend was the one who had him arrested yesterday. Bitten told me when she called to ask about Jane. In a way, she was asking for it."

"What the hell is it with you? Ingersminde has burned down, Jonas been kidnapped—are you all crazy or what?" One moment he was Sune's father, a man who'd just lost his wife, and the next he was part of Thomsen's brotherhood, for whom revenge was normal, as it had been back in the times of the Asatro. "This has to stop, and you have to help me. There's no one else I can turn to."

Silence. A cart farther down the hall clattered against something, a door closed.

"I'm sorry," he said, shaking his head. "I don't know what to say."

Camilla breathed in deeply several times, until she had composed herself completely. "Tell me where you think they might have taken Jonas," she implored. "They found

284

his T-shirt at Ole Thomsen's father's place, but he wasn't there. Where can he be? Think about it. Think about Sune being sacrificed, almost bleeding to death. You owe them nothing! For God's sake, they wanted to kill your son!"

The butcher made a fist, pressed it against his mouth, then closed his eyes, as if he were forcing his mind to play along. "They could have taken him to Avn Lake or to Blood Springs. Maybe to the hillside at Gyldenløvshøj?"

Camilla pressed him. "Which is most likely? Are there rituals connected with these places?"

"Hell's Cauldron," he mumbled, looking away from her now. "That's another place we make sacrifices to the gods. But it's best known for human sacrifices. Back in the days of the Asatro the farmers met every ninth year, and according to myth they sacrificed ninety-nine men, ninety-nine horses, ninety-nine dogs, and ninety-nine hawks. The sacrifices were made to the goddess of death, Hel, Loke's daughter. She reigns over the kingdom of death."

His voice sounded mechanical; he was going to pieces right before her eyes. He leaned against the wall and sank to the floor.

Camilla froze up inside. "Human sacrifices," she repeated. She shook her head. "Can I borrow your phone?"

48

Not here, either!" Louise shouted. She hopped off the attic ladder. They had searched the wings of the house, barns, and the enormous attic over the country manor. Police were combing the main residence, and two dog patrols had arrived, but Louise was certain that Jonas was nowhere around.

He had been there. His pajamas had been found piled up on the kitchen floor. Again, there had been no attempt to hide anything. Pajamas, T-shirt, not even the white plastic bottle of animal tranquilizer. Cotton, nylon rope, and rags lay on the kitchen counter, and the blood on the kitchen floor had coagulated, though when she touched it her finger showed a slight stain. Had an hour gone by, an hour and a half?

She heard the police dogs returning from the fields behind them, being led to the other side of the main residence.

She stared into space. It was as if the world had

stopped, in the same way she had begun shutting down inside. Her temples throbbed, her scalp tingled. She put her hands on her knees and let her head hang loose with her eyes closed, waiting for the blood to reach her brain. She knew she wouldn't get one step closer to Jonas without getting herself under control.

Someone put a hand on her arm just as she was about to straighten up. She stared into Eik's solemn face, and suddenly all the strength she'd tried to muster disappeared, replaced by tears.

"Hell's Cauldron, where is it?" He led her away as he explained that he'd just heard from Camilla. He carried Jonas's striped pajama bottoms.

Louise went blank. What was he talking about? Then her brain slowly began working. "It's close to Ravnsholte." *Why does he want to know?* she wondered.

He pushed her gently. "Let's go. I've already told Nymand."

Louise trotted to the car. Ravnsholte was in the forest on the other side of Hvalsø, where her parents lived.

Charlie whined in the back of the car, his snout against the window, ears pointing forward. He was following the other dogs so intently that he didn't turn when Louise and Eik got into the car.

"That's enough," Eik said, as he made his way among the growing number of police cars.

"Hell's Cauldron," he repeated, when they'd reached the highway. "Can you find it?"

"Drive through Hvalsø and out to Lerbjerg," she said as she tried to remember how to get there. "I can find it if we enter the forest where I used to ride."

Her mind was in turmoil as they drove the six kilometers from Nørre Hvalsø to where she grew up. She couldn't shake the image of Jonas. She imagined him being woken up in the dark, drugged, and pulled from his bed.

She tried to sort everything out. The old police chief had taken Jonas to punish her; that much she knew. Now, however, she was beginning to understand how he had misused his position to protect his son and his son's friends.

She thought about the janitor from Såby. About Gudrun, Klaus, and the young prostitute. Each time he covered up for them, he was actually saving his own ass. They had something on *him*.

Roed Thomsen was a weak man who had been unable to deal with his own sick daughter. Instead he'd let everything get out of hand when she died. And since then he had done all he could to maintain the facade.

"The old police chief has always known what's gone on," she said, giving voice to her thoughts. "But he never stepped in because he was afraid of being found out. Everyone's got something on everyone else, and that makes them deadly."

"Roed Thomsen was their gothi," Eik said a moment later. "Asatro was his way of ensuring he wouldn't be alone if someone turned against him."

"And the worst thing is, they're convinced their beliefs give them the right to do what they're doing," Louise said.

They reached the forest and drove past the parking lot and down the hill, where she told him to turn right. "I'm not sure we can drive all the way in."

She straightened up when they passed the Snipe House and saw Verner Post standing by his woodpile. "Stop!"

She waved. The old man had always lived there. Several of his upper teeth were missing, and the ones left were stained from the ever-present wad of tobacco he kept inside his upper lip. He'd been born in the Snipe House and had taken possession of both it and his job in Bistrup Forest from his father, who had been killed when a tree kicked out wrong. Louise knew this only because Verner Post had helped his father several times when a tree needed felling.

"We're going to Hell's Cauldron. How close can we get there by car?" She felt strangely calm. She didn't really believe Jonas was there; she was sure she'd have sensed his fear or the men's anger if they were so close.

She stiffened, however, when she saw the expression on the old man's face. "I just sent another car in there. Why's everybody all of a sudden interested in the old sacrificial grounds?"

"Sacrificial grounds? Who did you send in?" Her nerves exploded. She felt like grabbing on to him, but she held herself back. Roed Thomsen wouldn't need directions; he had to know the forest at least as well as she did.

"The butcher, the young one. He looked like he just seen a ghost. He ought to know the way, often as they come out here. We always have to clean up their mess. But he was all in a tizzy."

He moved the chaw of tobacco around with his lower lip.

"Was there anyone else in the car with him?" Eik said.

Verner Post shook his head. "He's the only one I saw." He turned his head and spat.

"Stop!" Louise pointed at the trees, and Eik parked the car. There were no other vehicles around, and the forest was quiet. Sweat broke out on Louise's forehead as she headed for the hillside farther along in the forest.

Eik held the striped pajamas and let Charlie out of the back. He followed after Louise. She stopped regularly to listen. "We're wasting our time," she said when Eik caught up to her.

Charlie raced around with his nose to the ground. He didn't seem especially interested in the pajamas Eik kept showing him.

"They're not here," Louise kept saying. "We'd be hearing something."

Eik turned to her and grabbed her shoulders, forced her to look at him. "Stop it!" he said as if he were trying to talk sense into a child. "If we're going to find Jonas, you have to start acting like a policewoman instead of a mother."

He grabbed her hand and pulled her to the top of the hillside, not letting go until they were looking down into Hell's Cauldron, which was covered with the final crop of autumn's fallen leaves. She remembered the hollow as being deeper. Probably because she had been smaller back then, she thought.

Relief or anxiety, she wasn't sure which, rushed through her body when she saw that Jonas wasn't there.

49

When they pulled up to his gate again, Verner Post was raking the narrow strip of gravel that led to his lopsided old forest house. He stopped and leaned on his rake.

Louise got out of the car. "Are there any other places than Hell's Cauldron that the Asatro might associate with the old myths of sacrifices?"

"We're not talking about myths here; it happened," he said. "They found human bones in there."

"Are there any other stories about similar places out here?"

He pushed out his lower lip and frowned under his cap. "You're thinking of King Valdemar Atterdag, riding on Valdemar's Road in the moonlight with his escort?" He spat again.

"No," Eik said, "we're thinking more along the lines

of the sacrificial oak in Boserup Forest. Places connected to human sacrifices, brotherhoods, rituals of vengeance."

"Far as I know, the only human sacrifices around here were in Hell's Cauldron. That's what they say anyway."

Louise's relief was short-lived. "But there were funeral pyres in the lake in the Black Bog. That goes back to the Vikings; they sacrificed a slave when an important man was buried. Other than that, human sacrifices were a part of war and bad blood, when they had their rituals of revenge."

Louise stopped listening, but she did catch that Eik asked directions to the Black Bog.

She knew precisely where it was. Back when she'd first started riding in the forest, her father had warned her about the bottomless bog. He also told her about a giant pike that had never been caught. He had her believing he'd seen it. No one knew how long it had been swimming around in the black water, but according to legend the ashes from funeral pyres had made it immortal. In the old days, many farmers in the area had their ashes spread in the Black Bog so the pike wouldn't come out of the water and pull its victims back in.

They spotted them when they reached the top of the hill. Louise leaned up against a motley birch trunk, trying to make sense of the scene on the banks of the coal-black forest lake.

Six men stood in a circle, and behind them the butcher

sat slumped over, watching the older men. She recognized his father, the old butcher; the owner of the sawmill; Roed Thomsen; John Knudsen's father, who had owned the farm in Særløse; and the mason's father, who also had been a mason until he turned the business over to his son. She wasn't sure, but she thought she recognized a gray-haired, broad-shouldered man whose daughter had been two or three years behind her in school. In the middle of their circle lay Jonas.

He was blindfolded and naked, save for his undershorts, his hands and feet bound, his mouth taped shut. Blood had been smeared all over his upper body. They had tied him to something that from a distance looked like a narrow raft of logs, or a bier of long branches lashed together. Louise couldn't tear her eyes away from his body twitching, like an exhausted animal trying to escape a trap.

The men ignored him, not even bothering to look when he gathered his strength and strained again to free himself.

Louise was freezing, yet sweating, too. She heard Eik step back toward the road and quietly call in for backup. He gave them the coordinates.

Roed Thomsen wore a long cape. He stood with outstretched arms, his somber voice droning as if he were reciting a mass. She watched as something passed from hand to hand—the oath ring, she was sure of it. Each man's lips moved when he received the ring, but she couldn't hear their words. They looked serious and tense, yet at the same time expectant. Like athletes before a game.

Eik returned and stood behind her. She felt the warmth of his body, smelled salt and smoke.

Thomsen's hands fell, and the men stepped back, revealing two large, gray metal gasoline cans. It felt as though a giant had grabbed her throat and was choking her as Thomsen turned to the butcher and motioned him over. But he didn't move. This time Louise heard every word as Lars's father roared at him.

"You get over here now and be a man—stop shaming us." He waved an angry finger at his son, whose eyes were glued to the ground. Finally his father walked to him and shouted, "You're no longer my son! You broke the circle when your miserable little kid ran away and shamed our entire family. You couldn't live up to your responsibility to the brotherhood. From this day on I not only have no grandson, I have no son."

He seemed to stoop as he turned away and walked back to the others, who all nodded in approval. As if the old butcher had done what a man should when someone breaches their trust.

The butcher still didn't move. He didn't even look up when Roed Thomsen jerked him to his feet.

Louise opened her mouth when the old butcher strode over to the two cans of gasoline. Every eye was on the butcher and Roed Thomsen when he unscrewed the lid from one can. She screamed as he poured gasoline over Jonas, then screamed again when spasms wracked her son's body.

Her holster bounced against her chest as she barreled down the slope. Eik followed, commanding Charlie to stay at his side. "Stop!" she shrieked.

The men beside the lake froze and stared at Louise and Eik. The butcher's father still held the gasoline can, his eyes full of hatred. Roed Thomsen let go of the butcher and shook his arm, as if he were brushing lint off his coat.

"What in hell is going on here?" Louise yelled. She reached Jonas and stood between him and the men, who now stood shoulder-to-shoulder, staring at her.

"You can thank us that your son's still alive," the old police chief said. "If we hadn't gotten here in time, these two would have pushed him out onto the lake like a living torch."

Roed Thomsen nodded toward the butcher and his father. Then he folded his arms on his chest, leaned back, and sneered.

Eik began cutting the ropes that bound Jonas. The boy's upper body gleamed from the gasoline, his skin already red in several places. Eik led Jonas to safety and ordered Charlie to stay with him.

"Shut up!" Louise shouted. "Shut your fucking mouth! Thank you? We stood up on the hill and watched; we know what you did."

Eik screamed, and they all turned at the same moment a gasoline can thunked down on the ground, followed by the click of a lighter and a whoosh. Before anyone could react, the old butcher had set fire to himself. Flames shot up around his stocky body in a bluish-yellow gleam. He shook violently but made no sound.

Eik and the butcher ran over to him. Everyone else stood motionless and watched the old man topple to the ground. His son tried to put out the fire with his canvas jacket while Eik rolled him down to the lake.

Louise hurried over to Jonas and held him. She took off her jacket and put it around his shoulders. Her eyes watered from the gasoline fumes. Charlie stood guard with raised hackles, waiting for a signal from Eik.

"It was him," Jonas whispered, his eyes on the old butcher. "I didn't hear him come into the room. I don't think I woke up until I was in the car, and then I was already tied up. I was so dizzy, I had to throw up."

She heard sirens, and moments later Nymand and several policeman came running down the steep slope; luckily they had been close when Eik called for them.

Roed Thomsen stepped away from the other men, who silently watched their old friend burn up right before their eyes. He walked over to Louise and Jonas, and though she squeezed her son's shoulder, she wasn't afraid of the old police chief. All her fear had disappeared now that she could feel her son's heartbeat.

Some of the officers ran over to the butcher's father, whose body lay still at the edge of the lake. Eik had doused the old man with water, but now he crouched down, staring out across the water.

"What in hell happened here?" Nymand yelled behind her. He was gasping as he joined them.

Roed Thomsen spoke up. "I want you to know that we'll all give witness statements in connection with these tragic events that have taken place. The same goes of course for your investigation of the murder of a young prostitute, which we just heard about."

Nymand suddenly seemed small beside the old police

chief. He looked at the man lying on the ground, then at the butcher, who cried silently. Then at Jonas, then at the raft he had been tied to. And finally, visibly shaken, he eyed Roed Thomsen.

"The young prosti*tutes*, plural," Louise said. He ignored her.

"What happened?" Nymand asked Louise. She still held Jonas. Gasoline dripped from his hair.

"The boy is still alive because of us," Thomsen said. He tried to put his hand on Jonas's shoulder, but Louise slapped it away. "We saved him from these madmen." He nodded at the butcher and his father.

"You didn't save anyone," Louise snarled. She stepped in front of him. "You may have gotten away with letting your own daughter disappear. But you're not touching my son."

The old police chief glanced at her. Out of the corner of her eye she saw Eik walk behind her, and somehow she knew, she sensed him putting his arm around Jonas.

"I have no idea what you're babbling about." He turned to Nymand, who had caught his breath and regained his color. "By the way, it's in your best interests to release my son and his friends. You lack evidence, and it could end up in court. You'd be better off working with him on this. He can tell you what happened out in the forest the night that young woman lost her life."

"You won't get away with trying to blame the butcher and his father, not this time," Louise said coldly, looking him right in the eye. "For two generations, you've terrorized the people around here, threatened them into silence. And all the time you've known exactly what was going on, but you did nothing. You were scared shitless that people would see you as the weak man you are. You make me sick."

She turned to Nymand. "Lars Frandsen is willing to make a statement about what happened when Roed Thomsen's daughter disappeared. He was present the night she took her life, and there are more witnesses to her father covering up her death by turning it into a missing person case. He can also tell you about the vows of silence taken to conceal other crimes.

"We won't be needing your son's statement," she told the former police chief. "This is the end of all the years of cover-ups. Even though you all have something on each other, this time you can't stop the truth from coming out. René Gamst and Lars Frandsen are talking."

"I don't think you want everything to come out," he said under his breath, so low that she could barely hear him. "Your boyfriend helped kill my daughter. And I'll wager that everyone will say he's the one who decided to bury Eline out in the forest, because he knew they could be charged with murder."

He stepped closer to her, but Louise looked up into his fleshy face without budging. "You stupid bastard. That's just one more attempt to blame someone who can't defend himself. Anyone who breaks out of your sick circle becomes the scapegoat. And now you try to shut me up with threats."

She shook her head at him scornfully. "You were the oldest. You're the one who should've stopped it all. But you didn't. You let it go on, because it worked out perfectly for you to have something on your son and his friends. That way they could never talk about how you abused your position, all your cover-ups. But it's over now."

She turned to Jonas and Eik. Before climbing back up the hillside, she stopped in front of Nymand. "Call if you need me."

50

The tones from the organ and the first hymn they'd sung died out, leaving the tiny chapel silent. Lissy's chair clattered when she stood up and walked to the coffin, holding a folded sheet of paper.

Louise squeezed Eik's hand and glanced at Jonas, who sat on her other side.

They had both offered without a moment's hesitation to accompany her to the memorial ceremony Klaus's parents wanted to hold, immediately after the police had released his remains. At first she had said no; she had to go by herself. But as they packed Eik's clothes and toilet bag—he was going to stay with her while Camilla, Frederik, and Markus borrowed his small apartment in Sydhavnen—it somehow began to feel right for them to be with her. Eik, and Jonas, too.

"You shouldn't do this alone," he'd said, when she told

him that she hadn't attended the service back when Klaus was buried.

Lissy began speaking. She told of the many years of doubt that had finally ended. About the peace in her soul, long overdue.

Her words echoed in the upper reaches of the chapel. Ernst sat on the other side of the coffin, together with his daughter and son-in-law and their little Jonathan. Several of Klaus's aunts and uncles she'd never met sat alongside them. And that was it.

"It will be a small, private ceremony," Lissy had said when she called. "A farewell."

Lunch would be served afterward at their home on Skovvej, but Louise had politely declined.

For her, it all ended right here.

EPILOGUE

W e have to bring his bike," Louise reminded Eik as he walked onto the sidewalk with two huge IKEA bags filled with linens and towels. Jonas was leaving for boarding school; they were packing the car with all his stuff.

"We can strap it to the roof," Eik said, energetically, heading back toward the basement door to pick it up.

Louise heard Jonas rumbling down the stairs inside. Leaning against Eik's massive monstrosity of a vehicle, she closed her eyes and exhaled. The past month had flown away. After the kidnapping and the shocking experience in the woods, she'd feared that Jonas had been damaged to an extent that could lead to a trauma. But she'd been wrong. What became clear from the very first interview with the crisis psychologist was that what really mattered to her son was that she and Eik had reached him in time. Before everything went really wrong. Jonas found great comfort in the fact that they had found him; that was what he focused on. Fortunately, he didn't fully understand how close he had been to actually being killed.

It was Jonas who had asked if he could go to boarding school with Markus. Louise had seen it as a healthy sign that he had the courage to embark on new challenges and new environments despite what he'd been through, so she immediately approved, agreeing that it was a good idea. Even if it meant that he'd be away for so long.

After Ingersminde burned down, Camilla and Frederik had accepted the offer to stay in Eik's tiny and cramped one-bedroom apartment in Sydhavnen while they tried to figure out their future. They'd lost everything in the fire; the only belongings they had left were the clothes they were wearing when Frederik was rushed to the hospital.

Markus had found the school in Odsherred all by himself, and Louise couldn't quite figure out whether it was because he couldn't handle having to live in such close quarters with his mother and Frederik in the small apartment, or if it was an urge to put everything that had transpired behind him. But over the summer holidays both boys were excited and looking forward eagerly to everything new that lay ahead. Which made Louise feel comfortable about her own decision to let Jonas go. Luckily the school had room for both of them. They'd already met with the other students in the group they were assigned to at the school, which helped to alleviate that uncertainty and nervousness that accompanied embarking upon something new.

"I forgot my sneakers," Jonas said, throwing his big weekend bag on the pavement and turning around to run back up to the fourth floor. "What about your toiletries?" Louise shouted after him. Eik leaned the bike against the car and walked over; he wrapped his arms around her.

"Are you okay?" he whispered, pulling her close.

"Yes," she muttered. "But he'll be gone for a whole year. It's going to be so empty here not having him home."

"He'll visit every weekend," Eik reassured. "And truthfully, empty is not exactly what it will be. It sounds like you've forgotten that I've moved in. And, of course, there's Dina and Charlie."

Louise knew that the students didn't go home over the first weekend; it would be two weeks until she'd get to see Jonas again. She pushed herself gently out of Eik's arms and smiled at him. "If there is one thing I cannot forget, it's your leather jacket lying around everywhere. Not to mention that your dog eats ten kilograms of dry food every week."

Just then Dina, whose smarts and expert sense of smell likely combined to get her safely out of the fire, and Charlie, with their tails wagging, came running playfully out of the front door, with Jonas right behind them. "C'mon, let's go," Jonas said as Eik finished attaching his bike to the roof of the car. Louise noticed the expectant tone in her son's voice.

Three hours later they were heading back to Copenhagen. Jonas had immediately connected with a few of the other boys who would be living in his dorm section. He was so caught up, Louise had noticed, that he had to squeeze in a quick good-bye with his mother and Eik.

The landscape expanded and contracted. Forests were replaced by grassy open areas and gentle hilly terrain; the fields looked ready for harvesting. In the backseat both dogs were snoring, as if in harmony. Of course, Louise would miss having Jonas around, but seeing him with the other kids at school was amazing and heartwarming. It was so clear he was looking toward his future, and excited about embarking upon his next chapter. She was genuinely happy for him, but not completely certain she was equally ready to see him move on and away from her. It was only natural, though; she'd have to adjust.

Feeling drowsy, Louise leaned her head sleepily against the passenger window, closing her eyes. She had never really *lived* with a man. But now circumstances had overtaken Eik's life—he had turned over his own apartment to Camilla and Frederik in their time of need. It had all happened as if by chance. But for Louise, embracing the possibilities and floating with the stream, though a bit scary, just felt right. *Yes*, she thought, she was ready for this. Something had finally fallen into place inside her.

Louise opened her eyes and looked at Eik as he drove, humming and focused. She was no longer alone.

ACKNOWLEDGMENTS

The Killing Forest is fiction. I grew up just outside Hvalsø; I love the area, and so it has been a joy to return to these familiar surroundings. I have, however, taken the liberty of both creating and relocating settings to fit my story. Ingersminde, for example, doesn't exist, the graves of the girls were inspired by a visit to Jægerspris Castle, and the sacrificial oak is located in another part of Zealand.

My story is based partly on old legends and tales, but most of it is a product of my imagination; in turn, neither the characters nor their names are based on actual people. Any likeness is therefore coincidental, though I have to admit that the stories about Louise Rick's father bear a striking resemblance to my own father's experiences as a non-native, big-city Copenhagen slicker.

Once again, many people have been generous with their time and energy in helping me research the book. A special thanks goes out to Jim Lyngvild, who taught me about Asatro. He answered many questions and showed a willingness to help, even though some of the characters in the book who share his beliefs are extremists. I have so enjoyed brushing up on my knowledge of Norse mythology and the old legends and myths.

I very much appreciate the fine people who attended my speech in Hvalsø and ended up sharing several fantastical legends and myths. Hell's Cauldron and the great pike would never have been part of the book without you all.

A special thanks also to pathologist Steen Holger Hansen and to Bo Greibe, a former dog handler at the Danish police.

Thanks to my Danish editor, Lisbeth Møller-Madsen, to my Danish publisher, People'sPress, and to my Scandinavian agent, Trine Busch, for her wholehearted support of me and Louise Rick.

Thanks to my American editor, Mitch Hoffman, to Caitlin Mulrooney-Lyski, and to the whole team at Grand Central Publishing. You're amazing.

Thanks to Benee Knauer, for being my book godmother, and to the fantastic people at Victoria Sanders & Associates: Victoria Sanders, Bernadette Baker-Baughman, Chris Kepner, and Tony Gabriel. It is a great pleasure to be working with you all!

All my love and appreciation goes out to my wonderful son, Adam. You are my very best.

—*Sara Blædel*

ABOUT THE AUTHOR

Sara Blaedel's interest in story writing, and especially crime fiction, was nurtured from a young age, long before Scandinavian crime fiction took the world by storm. Today she is Denmark's "Queen of Crime," and her series featuring police detective Louise Rick is adored the world over.

As the daughter of a renowned Danish journalist and an actress whose career has included roles in theater, radio, TV, and movies, Sara grew up surrounded by a constant flow of professional writers and performers visiting the Blaedel home. Despite a struggle with dyslexia, books gave Sara a world in which to escape when her introverted nature demanded an exit from the hustle and bustle of life.

Sara tried a number of careers, from a restaurant apprenticeship to graphic design, before she started a publishing company called Sara B, where she published Danish translations of American crime fiction.

Publishing ultimately led Sara to journalism, and she

covered a wide range of stories, from criminal trials to the premiere of *Star Wars: Episode I*. It was during this time—and while skiing in Norway—that Sara started brewing the ideas for her first novel. In 2004, Louise and Camilla were introduced in *Grønt Støv* (*Green Dust*), and Sara won the Danish Academy for Crime Fiction's debut prize.

Today Sara lives north of Copenhagen with her family. She has always loved animals; she still enjoys horseback riding and shares her home with her cat and golden retriever. When she isn't busy committing brutal murders on the page, she is an ambassador with Save the Children and serves on the jury of a documentary film competition.